The
Sunlit Pool
of the
Finished Image

David Hill

Stairwell Books //

Published by Stairwell Books
161 Lowther Street
York, YO31 7LZ

www.stairwellbooks.co.uk
@stairwellbooks

Cover design Oliver Hurst

ISBN: 978-1-913432-90-4
p6

The Sunlit Pool of the Finished Image

A Work of Art-History Fiction

"We start with the masterpiece and work backwards through the discarded ideas and near-misses; but for him the discarded ideas began as excitements, and he saw only at the very end what we take for granted at the beginning. For us the conclusion was inevitable; not for him...
"The painter isn't carried fluently downstream towards the sunlit pool of that finished image, but is trying to hold a course in an open sea of contrary tides."

A History of the World In 10 ½ Chapters by Julian Barnes.

Book One: The Painting

Chapter 1

Gustave Courbet pulled the cover off me with a flourish. There, staring directly at me, stood Constance and Khalil Bey. He had a huge grin on his face and was rubbing his hands furiously. Constance, well, she just looked dryly at me. I will never forget the shock of that first encounter: her face was my face, we were one and the same. Is that how she felt as well? How many times have I returned to that room, how many hours have I spent meditating on that moment of connection? It was the closest we ever got to each other and so, in a way, the closest I ever came to knowing myself. I scan it in my mind for something I may have missed, a clue, a flicker: the key. But I can never find it. There was a vacant coldness in her glance, a nothingness. She looked neither surprised nor shocked nor pleased. She just stood there stock-still; her eyes were empty. For that brief moment she seemed to be more inanimate than me.

Unlike my hair that was spread out in luscious curls, hers was neatly scraped down from a white centre parting and fastened in a tight bun at the back of her head. My one visible eye looked up as if the eyeball was straining to jump out from its socket. My nostrils were cavernous openings that dominated the picture, my reddened lips were parted and all the muscles on my face and neck were taut, accentuated, protruding, as if the skin (including the rather unseemly double chin) was struggling to hold my skeletal structure in check. Constance's face was nothing like this: it was controlled, tight. Her long nasal bone ran straight through the centre of her face, drawing one's gaze to her slightly downcast eyes and her remarkably perfect eyebrows. Her white skin was perfumed and supple, soft and powdered. And yet it was the same face! The same but so different. She was ephemeral, I was guttural. My one eye looked up towards the heavens like the Virgin Mary receiving the holy spirit: but instead of sacral perfection, with me it was all dirty, all pleasure and pain, desire and shame. Hers glazed with emotionlessness. This was my face and that was hers. I understood quickly that they were not alike at all. Hers was made by God, mine was a sick shadow filtered through the perverted mind of Gustave Courbet. It was *his* view of her face that I had, not the real thing. It was a failure. I knew then that she would never let me keep it. She would take my face away from me and I would spend the rest of my life searching my memory to get it back, to get her back.

I overheard a conversation many years later about an Amazonian tribe called the Kayapo. They flatly refuse to allow themselves to be photographed. An anthropologist and a medic were discussing it in front of where I was hanging. The medic had just returned from a work trip to Brazil and was telling his friend about his experiences. He was told that *akaron kaba* means to *take one's photo* but also means *to steal one's soul*. I latched on to that idea and have never let it go. What links a person with their portrait? I suppose in many ways I am the perfect person to ask about this. I am a painted version, an artistic interpretation of Constance, a distorted representation of her actual self, instigated through the arrogant human belief that it is possible for them to be depicted in paint in a fashion deeper than mere surface. Humans view this as a threat, an abomination, a curse. But as a painting, as her portrait, I see it the other way around. Am I not something more tangible and real than Constance ever was? Especially now that she no longer exists. Does it therefore not follow that her soul resides in me somehow? Am I indebted to her or she to me and how does that responsibility settle between us? As an old friend of mine once said; every debt needs paying, every single one. Somehow.

What I remember vividly from the small amount of time that we spent together on that first day was not some kind of spiritual connection but rather the distance between us; the sense of otherness that she represented for me. I had no idea what she was thinking or feeling during the moments when we were together. I was not her; I was neither in her or part of her. The things I knew from before my production I have learnt from conversation that I have overheard since, either from humans or other objects. (Yes, humans, we objects do communicate with each other, just not in a pitch that you understand; did you think you were the only ones? How vain!) In those brief moments Constance and I spent together, there was no process of osmosis by which her memories and sensations were transmitted to me, no Constance-data download. There was simply a divergence of two similar images, a balance that shifted first one way and then another, like a river that splits in two.

At the time we met she was carrying thirty-four years of life experience more than I was. I was therefore a representation of an aspect of her, a pale shadow. Now, however, I am more than double the age that she was when she died. How can it be that all my experiences, many more than she ever had, could have no impact on what I am today? Back then I was a new-born baby but now I am over one hundred and fifty years old, and she is dead. Is she not merely a representation of me? What is she now: a few photographs, some official documents, some reviews, a series of letters, a portrait by Jules-Émile Saintin that is today listed as lost, a few poems and a bunch of stories? Does she even have a voice? I needed to hear her voice, I needed to discover her lost story. Would she tell me about her career as a ballerina, her childhood, her hopes and dreams: would anyone care for this forgotten woman but me? This sounds arrogant, but is it not the case that the only reason anyone would even listen to her story now would be to gain a deeper understanding of me? Is that not what I am searching for as well?

"Well? What did I tell you?" Courbet waved his hand at me as he spoke, "Is it not something, is it not magnificent, eh? You thought *Venus*

5

and Psyche was something. You thought *The Sleepers* was good. But that was just foreplay and the aftermath of the event. This is reality right here. This is the event. The depiction of sex on a canvas. The ecstasy of the present, eh, Khalil, what do you think? You must admit. This is special." Courbet danced around me like I was a maypole. He was exerting himself, his huge waistline bouncing up and down. Khalil looked at him with a bemused expression, the way one would gaze upon an exuberant dog. Constance just sighed and crossed the room to stare out of the window, without so much as a glance back towards me.

"Excellent, Gustave," Khalil said. "Of course, excellent. I must say, this exceeds even what I could expect. The flesh tone, the delicacy of the hair - it is so real, so wonderfully, um, well, modern, I guess."

"But the head," Courbet exclaimed. "It is my best ever, I think." Constance did not even turn around.

"Yes, um, the head. Really good, but, um actually…So, Gustave, Constance and I have been talking and obviously she is worried about her reputation so..." Courbet shot Constance a glaring look.

"What, what! I don't understand. This is what you asked for. I have painted what you ask. A picture of a woman who has just been taken. I have captured the very moment the man, us, the viewer, has pulled out. We are part of this painting. All of us. Can't you see? It is a masterpiece. I have called it *L'Origine du Monde*, get it? *The Origin of the World*. It is all there. That is where life comes from, from the vagina. From there and from here," Courbet pointed to my hole and then started tapping both sides of his head with his paint-stained fingers. "From here, Khalil, from me, from my hands. I am the artist. I bring forth the origin of the world. *L'Origine c'est moi!*"

Khalil lowered his eyes sheepishly as Constance grunted, "For crying out loud, Khalil! How much longer do we have to listen to this?"

"What did you say?!" Courbet screamed across the room. "You are just a fucking whore!"

"Ok, Gustave. Ok, Constance. Look, let's calm down." Khalil positioned himself in front of Courbet with his small body blocking the path to Constance. I imagined the obese painter rolling through him, flattening him. "I agree it is a masterpiece, of course it is, Gustave. I didn't say anything else. How could I? It's just...it's just."

"Oh, come on, Khalil get on with it," Constance barked, still with her back to the room. She seemed to be growing physically, dominating the whole space.

"Ok, thank you Constance. You are not helping. Look, Gustave, what I actually asked for was the sex of a woman, of Constance. My lucky charm. And that is what you have done, it's great. However, if you want to be technical about it, I never ordered the head."

"Never ordered the head!!!!"

"No, in fact I didn't. Just to be technical. So, in a way the head is surplus to requirements."

"What are you saying?" Courbet shouted, dumbfounded. "You can't have a portrait without a head!"

"Of course you can, Gustave, it's a picture. It is simply a question of perspective. I am not asking you to do any more work. You have done more than necessary. In fact, I am happy to pay an extra 10% over the agreed fee. There, I can't be fairer than that. It is just a question of shortening the canvas a little, look," Khalil came right up to me so I could feel his breath, like an executioner and with his pinkie finger he drew an imaginary horizontal line across the canvas, through the line of my neck. "There, you see. It works perfectly. Just a small reduction in the canvas size and we are all good."

Courbet was turning crimson with rage. Khalil stepped back and busied himself with lighting a Turkish cigarette, so he didn't have to look the artist in the eye. He dropped his box of matches with a curse and bent over to pick them up from the paint splattered floorboards. Constance still had not moved from the window. It wasn't even clear she was breathing. I held my breath as one does before a beheading. The artist looked at the little man bent over in front of him and then back at me: did he see pleading in my one eye? He seemed to be bubbling over with exasperation, on the verge of explosion.

7

And then suddenly, like a kettle that has rattled, popped, squealed and spluttered furiously as it reaches boiling point and then starts to subside when taken off the heat, he deflated; became silent, still, almost shrunken within the overbearing mass of his body and returned to his normal pallor. Khalil lifted himself up and finally lit his cigarette. When Courbet eventually spoke, it was in a low menacing voice.

"No. No. I won't cut it." Khalil opened his mouth to respond but before he had the opportunity to say anything Constance had spun around and answered for him:

"Very well. No matter. Khalil, let's pay him and go. I am famished. I am dying for lunch. We can sort this later."

Courbet froze at the realisation of what was happening; he looked back and forth between them and then sighed. Constance had already reached the door and swept out of the room. Khalil settled the fee plus 10% and Courbet arranged to have me sent around to Khalil's luxury apartments in Rue Taitbout that very afternoon. Khalil encouragingly slapped him on the shoulder as he left.

"There you go, that's it, excellent stuff. Good man. A real masterpiece. Great work. Congratulations." He backed out of the room, leaving a trail of empty compliments in his wake as he passed the other canvases. "Oh," he said, "I love that one as well. Nice deer, love a deer. Where is that one headed...... the Salon, eh?.....I will have to see if I can outbid the Académie for it, eh? Lovely work. Good on you.

"Whisper it, but in my opinion, you are greater than Delacroix, there, I don't mind saying it. Better than Ingres too and you know I have dealt with them both. Good on you, good man."

I could hear that Constance was already halfway down the stairs. Courbet glanced at me with a strange tremble in his eye. We both knew that I didn't belong to him anymore, that it was out of his hands. For a massive man, he looked so powerless. Then, with a heavy sigh, he reached for the hammer and a bag of nails. I looked at the crates stacked up in the corner. They looked like coffins to me.

*

Who am I? How does one describe the process of coming into being? I guess for you it would be like trying to describe those months you spent in the womb. Could you really hear the Mozart your parents played to you? How did your mother's voice sound through the amniotic fluid?

For me, there were weeks that felt like eternities when layers were added to layers, as I was drawn up in sections, emerging from non-existence. There were sounds and flashes of lights; words maybe, a low voice bubbling along through the void like a stream meandering through the underworld. This was Courbet's voice. There were other voices of course, higher in pitch or lower but nothing as consistently present as his. They say that humans who fall into a coma can still hear the voices of their loved ones talking to them, can still sense their presence and feel the touch on the skin of their hands. Is that what it is like before one is completed? Could I feel with each passing day the paint piling up on the canvas, forming me into what I am now? Maybe so, but if I did know about it back then, it was not consciously, it only comes together now, retrospectively, as I build up my memories to fashion it into some kind of sense. I couldn't feel myself as I was being painted, even as I was close to being finished. My memories (if that is what they are) of those weeks are freshly made each time I think back: hallucinogenic reconstructions of memories that must have been. I can stand back now and see myself being painted, like I am witnessing it in a dream. It can't be a memory.

Maybe you and I are the same. For you it was like being submerged in the fluid of the womb, for me it would be like the feeling of being submerged in a dirty lake. Sounds exist but they are muffled and unclear. It would hurt to open your eyes, they would sting. Even when you do manage to get them open visibility is terrible, you can't even see a metre in front of you, just a senseless mass of sludgy browns and grey. You can't smell anything, you feel bunged up, constricted. Your sense of touch has malfunctioned, is muted, so the only sensations you register are of temperature and pressure as if touch is not something you are doing, something you control; but something the world is imposing on you. It is a claustrophobic and terrifying sensation, as if you are being crushed by a tremendous and relentless weight. And then light emerges in a blur and it is her, not clearly visible, just the outline of her. A form that is clearly distinct from you, but you feel deeply and profoundly *is* you. One and the same.

How does one know anything? You humans have ears and eyes, skin, a nose and a tongue. I remember a dinner at Lacan's house one hundred years after my birth where a zoologist held forth on the different senses that other species have. He delighted in telling Jacques and Sylvie how bats use echolocation to find their way around, how the platypus can detect the electrical pulses of their prey through the water and how some snakes can find and attack their prey in total darkness through the heat signatures they give up. Do I have to have eyes to see and a human brain to think?

Years later, hanging in room 20 after the museum had closed, lines of people came in and spread yoga mats in front of us. They sat down in lines, with their legs crossed, and breathed purposefully, then they stretched; up and down, side to side, on their feet and on their hands and some even balanced on their heads. At the end the lights were all turned off. The people lay on their backs with their eyes closed while the teacher talked, in a soft, almost whispering voice, of the five aggregates. She spoke of how everything in the world and in time is connected through physical form, feeling, mental function, perception and consciousness. Together we are all united: everything that came before and everything that is now. She talked about how one cannot have a table without all the things that make up the non-table world: the skill of the carpenter and all the humans that came before him, the metal of the nails, the wood, the sun and rain that allowed the forest to grow. Without all this there would have been no table.

This is all true but there is even more: consciousness is not just in humans, it is in the trees, the iron ore, the wind and the snow. We are all connected and it is within us. We objects suck up information through our materials. For paintings that means the pigment of our canvases, communicating through movements of the air that are imperceptible to humans and felt with a depth that most humans never comprehend. Humans feel that only they have knowledge, but their lives are brief and their insight is shallow, like a stone skimming on the water. The tree, whose wood now surrounds me as a frame, knows more deeply than any human person. That type of knowledge seeps through its rings and stays forever in the world, just as every molecule that has ever existed, exists still, circulating around and around. The cotton that was crushed to make my canvas is part of me now and its history is my history. You humans fetishize your genealogies, but you are toddlers compared to the trees and the plants. There is wisdom that nestles all around you humans, you just don't have the senses to perceive it.

When I was finished, I awoke in the darkness. There was a cloth draped over me to hide me from the room, a claustrophobic sensation that panicked me at first, so complete was the absence of light. How I have changed! I have had so much opportunity to get used to it over the years, that I much prefer the darkness now. That has been my fate: to be at once hidden away, concealed, condemned, problematic and in the same life to be looked upon, stared at, analysed, consumed. Two extremes and no equilibrium. On one hand I am one of the most famous paintings in the world, reproduced ad infinitum and on the other one of the greatest mysteries of art history. For decades no one knew who the model was that I was painted from. Who am I? What is my story? How did I come to be?

*

I was on an easel in the drawing room. Constance sat with her back to me as she said that she couldn't look at me whilst breakfasting. Apparently, I put her off her eggs. Khalil was having a green drapery fitted in his dressing room with a twisted rope that would pull the curtain back smoothly to reveal me hanging on the wall behind. I had spent the week at the framers being fitted for a gold gilded, curved, oak frame. The framer was due after breakfast to finish the job and hang me. That night was to be my first public outing, my unveiling.

It had been around a week since I had left Courbet's and Khalil had twice visited the artist's studio but had met with a frosty reception each time. He had tried to place a new commission to smooth the water, but Courbet claimed to be too busy as he had to finish his Salon pieces. Over the breakfast table Khalil complained to Constance about the artist's rudeness that seemed to really bother him, whilst Constance couldn't help but look bored.

"So, I am going to have a supper here this evening, my dear," Khalil tentatively started a new conversation after an extended pause.

"Hmm."

"I bumped into Nadar, the photographer and would you guess who is up from Croisset for a weekend? None other than Flaubert, you know that writer chap. You must have read *Salamnbô*, super stuff. One can barely believe it was the same man who got into such a pickle about the Bovary thing. I am sure you have not read it, not a novel for sensitive souls like you. All a bit of a mess of a book, if you ask me, couldn't make head nor tail of it.

"Anyway, Nadar was chatting with Maxime du Camp and they are all free, so I said they should come round to mine for a bite to eat. They are all pals with Champfleury and Nadar is bringing some young lawyer chap from down south, Gambetta, I think he said his name was, so... well and, yes, so, Courbet agreed to come as well."

"Courbet, eh? I hope you are not going to show them that thing." She nodded her head back in my direction. "For your eyes only Khalil, that was the deal, right?"

"Yes. Right, well. I wonder if we can talk about that..."

"Nothing to talk about," Constance snapped. "My position has not changed. Unless you can convince everyone that it isn't me then no chance. You could try and tell them that it is Jo Hiffernan, Whistler's girlfriend, who sat for all of Courbet's other smutty paintings but seeing as she is the most famous redhead in all of Paris, I think the hair might give you away."

"Yes, well, I was thinking about that. I mean, it is such a great piece of painting, you know, shame not to show it about."

"Ha! Don't make me laugh. You want to show it off to underline your artistic sensibilities, do you? Not sure it does much for your moral ones."

"Now now..."

"It was agreed at the start, Khalil, no ifs, no buts. I did what you asked of me and I have your word. Are you a man of your word?"

"Of course, I am, but it is not my fault if you are recognisable."

"Not mine either."

"Well, then."

Constance sliced the top of her soft-boiled egg with her sterling silver breakfast knife. The yolk ran down the side of the egg onto the cup. She paused and stared. The thick yellowness stained the gleaming silver surface. I saw her run the blade of the knife across the tip of her index finger, leaving a sticky yellow smudge. Thoughtfully, she rubbed her dirty finger on her napkin as the yolk continued to run. Khalil looked gloomily at his coffee and reached for a cigarette.

"My dearest," Constance said, laying the dirtied napkin on the table. "It so pains me to see you unhappy. I know you want to show off your new toy to all your friends. I totally understand but it will do neither of us any good to become the subject of vile Parisian gossip. Can you imagine what they will say about me? I mean, look at it, it is a painting of me having an orgasm with my private parts front and centre. Do you really think this can be shown to anyone? How can you even think this is art? We both know what this is and what it will mean. It will make our relationship, so, well, difficult. Now you don't want that, do you?" She turned around. "You, boy," she said to the liveried servant by the door, "get me a steak knife. You see Khalil, I have a compromise solution here. Something I think will work for us both."

All of a sudden, she spun around and we came face to face for the last time. She was brandishing a sharp knife and, grabbing me by the top of my head, she thrust it into my neck without saying a word, sawing back and forth in a controlled straight line until the canvas was in two pieces. She held up the top of the picture, as if pulling me up by my hair. Khalil's eyes opened wide, but he did not say anything. He just stared at the decapitation that was taking place. It was her. She was my executioner. She took my face.

She held my head out in front of her like Judith holding the bloody head of Holofernes, like David triumphantly displaying Goliath, like Salome with the head of St John the Baptist on a platter. Constance serenely walked over to Khalil who was sitting stock-still like some dumb mannequin. She calmly bent over, pulled the smoking cigarette out of his mouth, and kissed him tenderly, right in front of my face, as if the three of us were sharing one last kiss, all together. As she straightened up, they both looked over at me, or to put it more precisely, what was left of me: a cut off pair of legs, a hairy vulva, a fleshy tummy, one exposed breast and a sliver of white bed sheet.

"There, you see, Khalil, you wanted a painting of your 'lucky charm.' There it is. I think it is winking at you." Before Khalil realised what she was going to do she had raised the cigarette. She held it up to the dangling piece of canvas on which my head was painted. There was flaming agony as she pressed the burning cigarette into me. The smoke started to rise, and the fire caught. The flames licked up my pulsating neck. My eye gazed heavenward as if I could not bear to look at the advancing fire. Try to picture those paintings of Savonarola, of Joan of Arc. When you think about of all those bonfires of all those vanities throughout history, you assume that the people being burnt at the stake are looking up to meet the eyes of God. Not so, let me tell you. You look up because you are too scared to look down at the fire! And then it catches your eyeballs, the liquid boils inside and your eyes burst like swollen boils with an audible pop.

Constance handed the flaming canvas to the servant along with the steak knife and sat back down to her egg.

"Funny that," she said with a faint smile, "I guess in a way I am the *L'Origine du monde.*" And the tension broke as Khalil laughed, first nervously and then whole heartedly, banging the table with his hand.

14

"Yes, yes, very good dear, very clever. Yes indeed, indeed you are."

"Khalil, darling," Constance said dryly, "you'll need to change the frame. It's too big."

*

That was the last time I ever saw Constance. There we parted, her to live and die. Me to be hidden and be seen, to search for her through the years. That is how it began for me and how it has continued ever since. One hundred and fifty-seven years and counting, until a day in a new millennium when a talk would be given in front of me, when it would all become clear again.

After dinner Khalil drew the curtain back and there I hung on the wall in my new cut down frame, my private parts on show for the delectation of all those men. The shock on their faces showed first, an instinctual reaction that could not be hidden. No one was more shocked than Courbet himself, but Leon Gambetta collected himself quickest, as the young are wont to do and despite only having one functioning eye to look with, he almost immediately launched into such effusive praise over me that Courbet couldn't help beaming with pride. It has since become a famous description: "We finally ran out of enthusiastic comments...This lasted for ten minutes...Courbet never had enough of it." Khalil diplomatically (what else?) placed himself behind the artist gently patting his back and vociferously rubbing his ego.

Aside from him, the evening became nothing more than a room of fat white men drooling animalistically over a painting of a woman's private parts, outdoing each other to think of grandiose artistic phrases to describe the brushwork, the perspective, the flesh-tones. It was then, under the power of their eyes and lubricated with their words that I turned from porn to art. Maxime Du Camp joined in with the rest of them, just as positive. It was only years later, after the Commune debacle, that he turned against Courbet and reimagined the truth of that evening. He wrote that he hated the me from the start (not true!), that he mocked Courbet for his "inconceivable forgetfulness in neglecting to represent the feet, the legs, the thighs, the stomach, the hips, the chest,

15

the hands, the arms, the shoulders, the neck and the head." By the time that lie came out in 1889 Courbet was ruined, exiled, destroyed and dead so I expect this criticism would have been the least of his worries, but in his defence, he did not neglect these body parts. Maxime du Camp was wrong; it was not Courbet's mistake then, just as it is not a sign of his genius now. It was Constance that did it. Her and her alone. If there is a great artist in this story it is Constance Quéniaux, not Gustave Courbet.

*

The world turns and fortunes rise and fall. Especially when you bet big and there were no bigger gamblers than Khalil. Like everything beneath the sun, it is all just a matter of time. Every debt needs paying, every single one. Somehow. Khalil would often pull the green curtain back and stare at me. The apartments were silent. Sometimes I would hear the footsteps of servants creaking the floorboards, but they were always muffled as if everyone knew the silence of the space had to be maintained.

Khalil would pull out his member and stroke it until his face contorted and he bent over himself, as if suffering from abdominal pain. He would breathe heavily and on hot summer days he would sweat. At first, he did it in front of *The Sleepers* and once in front of the Ingres as well, but he always returned to me and soon he did it only with me. One time he wanted the curtain open while he lay with Constance, but she strongly refused. What was I to him in these private, silent moments that we spent together alone? What was the function of my creation, my *raison d' être*? Was I a substitute for Constance? How could I be? She was available to him whenever he needed. Was I some addition to his pleasure with her? But how could this be if we were never consumed together? Was I something that brought her closer to him in his imagination, like a conduit to her being, a surrogate for her? Or was I a distraction, a paradox wherein the specific leads to the general? He called me his 'lucky charm' but was I Constance's vagina or was I the every-vagina?

Sometimes when he was doing it his eyes would glaze over and although fixed ceaselessly upon me, he seemed like he was fading away, far away, a great distance that I would never be able to cross. He, who in one way, looked at me the most, in another way probably looked at me the least of all. Was I a way for him to escape from looking at all, was I a road to a place beyond this world, a place where nothing existed; not the apartment, not the servants, not Constance, not even me? If that was the case, the spell never lasted long and soon his vision returned to me and his eyes brightened, like cataracts had magically fallen from them. He would draw himself upright, blow me a kiss, with a thick, white liquid dripping from his hand and he would draw back the curtain. After that first public display he showed me to fewer and fewer people. I quickly became for his eyes only.

I was behind that green veil for barely a year and a half. During that time Saintin's portrait of Constance was accepted and praised at the 1867 Salon. I wonder how that made Courbet feel. That autumn he had asked Khalil for the loan of his paintings for the private exhibition he was setting up and Khalil was happy to hand them over for a few months but, of course, Constance refused to let me go with the rest of them and I stayed where I was. Khalil never saw the other pictures Courbet borrowed ever again. They went straight to the auctioneers. Khalil's bankruptcy was declared at the end of 1867 and in January 1868 the sale of his art collection at the Hôtel Drouot took three whole days of heavy auctioning. The bet that finally bankrupted him was rumoured to be twelve hundred thousand francs; some say it was more. One big number is as good as another when you can't pay. His racehorses went, the stables, the apartments, the Ingres and the Delacroixes, the Courbets (four of them), over a hundred canvases in all. But not me. I did not exist. I was locked into a crate and settled in the dark.

Khalil left for Vienna and then Constantinople, calling for the freedom of Egypt from the Ottoman Empire. And then he went on to die. I would have to wait for over one hundred years to find out what happened to Constance. A whole century wasted, my mind running through speculations looking for an answer that was unavailable to me.

*

There were shifts and sounds, bangs and long periods of silence. Things were placed on top of me and sometimes I was placed on top of things. Very occasionally a pair of male eyes looked upon me hungrily. One time the lid of my crate was pulled back and a male tongue guiltily shot out and licked me whilst a group of men sniggered in the shadows. On the whole, though, there was nothing but quiet and I calmly settled into it, accepted it, allowing the molecules in my paint to breathe. One day I was roughly taken out, stripped from my frame, and hidden within a small cabinet with a locked lid. If you opened the box from the top it looked like nothing but an empty wooden box. But inside there was a false bottom. There was a catch on the inside that detached the base of the box allowing the bottom to slide out. They slid out the base and I fitted perfectly into the space. I guess it had been designed specifically to hide me. Then they slid the box back over me so that I was hidden. It closed with a click. I had become a forgotten part of an innocuous-looking cabinet with a dirty secret hidden inside.

The door of the box was inlaid with a painting. It was a hastily painted picture of a Chateau set up on a hill. This was Courbet's *Chateau of Blonay*. The main tower thrusts phallically into the cloudy sky, all greys and whites, flashes of blue. It takes up over half of the picture. On the horizon line there is water, a lake perhaps, or a sea. It extends out into our imagination. In the foreground the dirty snow is punctuated with shrubs and clumps of grass. A line of dark, bare, trees run across the front of the image and on the right is a small cottage shrouded in shadow and yet struck with a yellow flash of light: the seen and the hidden. The real Chateau is still there. She is nearly nine hundred years old. One can only imagine the things she must have seen. She sits on top of a hill, raised up in the limbo lands between the basin of Lac Léman in Switzerland and the Alps that rise up and extend into Italy. There is no water behind the castle anymore. Was there a moat in 1875 when

18

Courbet was staying nearby in Vevey? The painting claims there was, although, between you and me, she proved herself an untrustworthy companion. That was when he painted it. By then he was drunk, obese, ruined, bankrupt and in exile. He would never see France again. He was a sad broken man painting sad broken pictures.

She was a mediocre landscape, knocked-out in an afternoon between drinking sessions. I didn't listen to the grandiose stories of that painting and her claims of his genius. She was obsessed by him; I think she was infatuated. Despite her insistence of his greatness, I know she was painted in the final days, when Courbet was already a spent force. What was he even able to see? In his beer-addled state of decrepitude did the lakes and the mountains merge, did the geography shift and flex? Do you humans think the view is a realistic portrayal of the castle in 1875 just because Courbet painted it like that? I AM COURBET! How do you know? Maybe he was so fat he couldn't drag himself up the incline. Or maybe no horse was strong enough to take the weight. Maybe he worked off a photograph, a postcard and changed the geography for artistic reasons. Or maybe he simply made a mistake. The *Chateau* said over and over that this was his masterpiece and one day she would be recognised. She told me that this is what Switzerland was like, branch for branch and rock for rock. What do I know? I have never been to Switzerland, but I would hear about it again and again throughout my life; from Courbet to Hatvany, so many of the men closest to me ended up there. When I was younger, I once laboured under the impression that Switzerland is where humans go when they are ready to die.

Hôtel Drouot also hosted Courbet's bankruptcy auction when his inevitable fall came, just a few weeks shy of the anniversary of Khalil's. Things just come together like that. The picture of the *Chateau of Blonay* somehow made it back to Paris from Switzerland but wasn't deemed good enough to make the auction, much to its consternation. It got passed around the antique stores of the south bank until it was installed on the front of my cabinet. Together we lay in a storeroom in Paris, two unwanted and worthless pieces of canvas waiting in the darkness for time to pass.

*

When you wake from a deep sleep, I mean a really deep sleep, there is a moment where you are between consciousnesses. Your eyes are still closed and elements of the dream you were dreaming are still playing vividly at the front of your mind. You are walking in the dream, still talking in the dream, the set of it; the buildings, the furniture, the space, is still there and real to you. The people or animals with whom you were interacting are still real. Most importantly, the strong feelings, whether they are of love or anxiety, are still all encompassing. The atmosphere of the dream, its emotional weight is still valid. It flows through you like your breath. At the same time, however, some sounds start infiltrating from the outside world, the world outside the dream, outside you. They start to blend into the stage-set of your dream world, the world where you feel reality exists. This meeting of two realities is jarring. It is this that produces the spiked feeling that this may in fact be a dream. It is something that you had not previously considered. You start wondering, as you feel the fear of the dream-situation, trying to hold the love or lust you were just experiencing, whether it is all a trick. The dream tries to hold onto you and you also try to re-establish the non-questioning trust in the dream, but once trust has gone it can never be fully restored. The doubt in your consciousness cannot let go. All of a sudden, the people in your dream start to fade into transparency, their actions and words drift away from you, like Eurydice being dragged down to the underworld the moment Orpheus glances back. The stage-set of the dream starts to break up, floors begin to fall away, walls collapse, tables and chairs disintegrate as you touch them. In your mind you are in both states, both conscious and subconscious and for a moment you can't totally commit to either. In humans, as far as I can tell, this liminal state only lasts for seconds as one finally wakes. I wonder if it lasts longer in animals who hibernate. The duration of their sleep is longer, will therefore the process of their waking not also be extended? Maybe a bleary badger will stagger around for minutes, perhaps even an hour unsure of whether he is still hibernating or whether spring has come.

My hibernation lasted for over forty-five years. How long would you say the limbic period would last given this extended duration? If it lasts around ten seconds for an eight-hour sleep, then proportionally one could calculate a guess of around six days for a forty-five-year sleep. In fact, however, there is a compound factor that you humans would not account for. This extends the period of confusion to months, maybe even years. Whatever the maths, the reality is that it is impossible for me to tell in those years what was actually happening and what was a dream. I spent those years hidden at the bottom of my box, that in turn was locked up in various crates, moved about, deposited, traded, stolen and returned, still unknown, still in the darkness.

I have an image of Baron Ferenc Hatvany from that time but whether it is real or constructed after the event I could not honestly say. I was slid out from underneath The *Chateau of Blonay* box and all I can remember was a sharp white light hitting me, an intensity of light that I hadn't experienced for decades. It was streaming through the window, strong summer light, warm and comforting. I could feel my paint straightening, contracting, tightening up, clicking into place. The room was a blur. It was an antique shop but the objects in it were out of time, out of place. The light made their forms difficult to trace. I heard voices coming from tables, wardrobes, diamond rings and paintings but the sounds came all at once in a formless cacophony and I could only make out circles, squares and rectangles as if everything had distilled into a mathematical essence.

That was the start of my anxiety, the introduction to the consciousness of the fact that there may be a world out there, outside my dream. A face approached. It came out of the darkness, haloed by shimmering light, which made it unsolid around the edges, ethereal. I didn't have long to focus. It may have been five or ten minutes for that man but for me it seemed like only a fraction of a millisecond. Did it even happen at all? In dreams faces appear as if from nowhere and disappear just as quickly. One never asks where they came from or where they went. They just flow in and flow out. It was an extended, oval, face bisected by a straight, long, nose that pointed down to the subtle point of a lightly dimpled chin. It was a handsome face, with the starts of age-lines appearing on the forehead, a richly refined face. The hair was black and neat. It was parted over to the right-hand side. The eyes seemed sunken into their sockets slightly, protected by thick, black, caterpillar eyebrows. The main feature was a thick black moustache, full and fluffy, like a black crescent moon. Your attention was drawn to it. He had a mass of hair, layer upon layer of it, neatly trimmed and regimented. He was wearing a dark suit, white shirt and black cravat. In his hands were a black hat and a cigar. He stared at me and a light flickered deep in his sockets. His moustache turned up into a smile. This was Baron Ferenc Hatvany, one of the richest men in Europe.

"Yes, I will have this one. When is the auction and what is the lot number?"

Then the *Chateau* was slid back over the top of me like the closing of a coffin lid and everything went dark again.

Chapter 2

I was packed up with all the other pictures that Ferenc had bought and sent east to Hungary, to his hometown, to Budapest. It was a city on the rise. The previous decade had seen the electrification of the street lighting: lights that came on and went off automatically. I must say this innovation produced a wistful impression on me, fond as I had always been of the lamplighters of Paris, with their ladders, patrolling the streets, bringing magical circles of light to the darkness. Personally, this is a sign of progress I have never managed to get behind. Light: it originated with the Gods and was stolen by Prometheus for the good of man. Something this important should not be simplified to the flick of a switch or the twist of a knob. First it was divine, then a theft, then a gift, now it is just a human prerogative: what a devaluation. No wonder you humans take light for granted, just as you take everything for granted. You are only realising now it is too late, every debt needs paying.

Movement falls into a similar bracket. Budapest was for me the city of artificial light but also that of artificial movement. The two horse carriages of Paris had been replaced by private motor cars, electric trolleys and even (God forbid) trains that travelled underground. This is not to say that these progressions did not come to Paris as well, it is simply to state that I did not experience them there first and therefore to me they will always be associated with Budapest. That was where I

23

saw them first. Budapest was also where I was first driven in an automobile and where I first saw a trolley car, specifically the funicular that climbed from the silvery slither of the Danube up the hill to Buda Castle. The castle had just been modernised and extended when I first arrived in the city. During my stay in that city, it housed in this order: the Royal Family until their removal from power, the Horthy regency, Skorzeny's Nazi command unit, the Soviet blockade that led to it's almost complete destruction and finally, ironically, Hungary's art collection. It was, therefore, so nearly my final resting place along with so much of Hatvany's looted art collection, but as with all the men who have owned me over the years, Hatvany just couldn't let me go. I was singled out, kept apart, dare I say it: I was special.

When I arrived in the city in 1913, the Austro-Hungarian empire, which had ennobled Hatvany's father, was still limping on towards its inevitable dissolution. The city was a bastion of modernisation and money flowed through the centre of the city like the Danube. This was a city of success, of commerce, the arts, philosophers and writers. It was also a city of Jews. It was not for nothing that Lueger called it Judapest. The wealth of the city was built on the success of these nomadic peoples, historically accepted nowhere, who had managed for a very long time to put down roots in Budapest, thrived, and then assimilated. These were the Jews whose fathers fought for Hungary during the First World War and saw themselves as loyal Hungarians through and through. They took their children to St Stephen's Cathedral, just a block away from their newly built mansions of Andrássy Street, had them baptised and they themselves converted en masse to Catholicism. They commissioned shiny new coats of arms to go with their newly-granted aristocratic titles. They were the Jews who put up Christmas trees in their opulent mansions reflecting twinkling lights onto the Cranachs, Tintorettos, El Grecos, Goyas, Monets and Picassos that hung on their walls, Jews who thought that they had solved the Jewish question once and for all through assimilation. This was the city of Herzog, Chorins, Kornfield and Weiss, of Hatvany-Deutsch.

24

Ferenc's grandfather was a rural merchant and Jewish community leader that had built the family fortune on flour mills, banking, insurance, railway construction and much else. One hundred years after his birth, his grandchildren, hosting parties in the most expensive Châteaux in Hungary, passed his portrait on the walls and told stories of his exploits, his business deals during the 1873 stock market crash (where he, surprise, surprise, came out doubling his asset portfolio), praising his Yiddish kop whilst they themselves could no longer understand a word of Yiddish. As children Ferenc and his siblings just lowered their eyes respectfully as their elders spoke and politely kept silent during the renditions of these asset-accumulating mythologies. When you are two generations away from the coal face and born as one of the richest people in Europe it is easy to look down upon your money-making ancestors, the generations who 'got their hands dirty'.

Ferenc's father was culturally closer to his father than his son. Along with Ferenc's uncle they inherited vast business assets and worked to monopolise the Hungarian sugar trade, turning it into one of Hungary's most important exports. Their sugar plant in Hatvan next to the family castle was the largest in Europe and by his death Ferenc's father was the fourth richest man in Hungary. They produced paper and timber, ran banks and owned steam mills. They entered the aristocracy and gave to charity generously. Theirs was the generation whose identity shifted from the blood to the land. In heated dinner table arguments, many years after his father and uncle's deaths, Ferenc would point to his father's donations that financed the renovations of churches and parish buildings while his cousin Bertalan would note that with the same pen he signed cheques to construct a new house for the Rabbi of Budapest. His father was from the gambling generation, close enough to the anti-Semitic Russian pogroms of the nineteenth century to know that a Jew never really wins, no matter how rich he is. A Jew with money has to bet on everything, sponsor everyone and something will come up trumps. Yes, you lose, but a Jew always loses. The trick is also totting up some wins on the way. It's all in the details.

Bertalan liked to tell the story (with passable impressions by all accounts) that when Ferenc's father was asked about his two sons, he replied, "One is a painter and the other is crazy." What a way to describe Ferenc and his brother, Lajos! I never got to see their faces when Bertalan told this story. I always wondered how poor Ferenc must have felt while the warm familial laughter hung over the dinner table. I know Lajos wouldn't have given a damn. To him all money was evil. He was sure of it and he pontificated this in all the most expensive addresses in Budapest, Vienna, Paris and London. As far as Ferenc's view of his father was concerned though, I never quite worked him out. In a way, it is difficult to be the generation that turns away from the business. Although it is a difficulty lined with immeasurable wealth.

Ferenc's cousin, Endre, ran the business side of the firm for the whole family. He was the last one left with the Yiddish kop, the streetwise one. As long as he continued to work at his business plans and investment opportunities that none of the other cousins wanted or even tried to understand, the money continued to flow without the rest of them having to do anything at all. They all had their shares inherited at birth, leaving them free to just spend money and criticise the world. None of this meant much to Endre. His soul was an old Jewish one, like that of his father and grandfather, all the way to the pig farmers on the pale of settlement. He understood something that none of the other cousins ever could. Despite his immaculately tailored suits he still had mud under his fingernails. He just got on with money-making and looked upon the rest of them with a knowing detachment that I always took for aloofness but later realised was pity.

Ferenc's passion was art. He studied in Paris and became a painter. With his allowance he bought up one of the most important art collections in Europe (over 700 works of incredible quality). The amount of money he spent on it was vast by any standards. His brother Lajos was a writer, literary critic and supporter of Hungarian literature which led to the flourishing of a golden age of Hungarian writing: Endre Ady, Jósef Attila (Hungary's greatest ever poet) and Mihály Babits to name but three. The influence of his (primarily financial) support on this generation cannot be overstated. He was a close personal friend of Thomas Mann, Arthur Keostler and Bartók. He even housed and fed Dezső Szabó whilst the latter was finishing his (amazingly) anti-semitic novel, *The Eroded Village*, for which he was nominated for a Nobel prize. Art, literature and politics ruled over everything in the mind of Lajos. He was an active member of the Communist party and for him it was poetry and the struggle of the proletariat from morning to night. The whole world had to burn. There was no space for religion in his thinking and he harboured a deep, almost fanatical disdain for money, an attitude only available to the fantastically rich and the fantastically poor.

From Endre's side of the family, Cousin Bertalan was an expert in orientalism, a philosopher with a fine collection of Eastern ceramics. He also founded a literary journal and wrote widely on Eastern meditations. His sister Lilly was a playwright. Another cousin, Károly Hatvany, owned and curated one of the most magnificent collections of China in Europe. All these intellectuals, living in their very own ivory towers. Theirs was the generation that broke from the dirt of the sugar mills to raise themselves to higher artistic and intellectual plains. This was the generation who spent and spent whilst trying to never remember where the money came from, the generation for whom, as Lajos used to say, religious conversion was as natural an adjustment as putting on a tuxedo for dinner; a saying I particularly loved as it displayed both of his hypocrisies in one succinct phrase. This was the schizophrenic generation.

*

When I first arrived in Budapest I was taken to Ferenc's house in Pest, across the Chain Bridge just off one of the neighbourhood's main thoroughfares, Nádor street. I was dumped there, unpacked, with a line of paintings and rugs that today are priceless museum pieces. There we were left to sit, sometimes moved slightly from one wall to another while Ferenc travelled Europe painting, exhibiting and buying. Every year more boxes arrived at Nádor street and servants would pile them up in front of us or move us to another storeroom. Ferenc rarely came to Budapest. There were murmured moments of excitement when he came back home but more often than not, he would go straight to the Hatvan Castle in the country rather than spend time in the city. The other paintings, who had sat there for longer than me, regaled me with stories of how he lived this easy, responsibility-free lifestyle, which remained unchanged despite the First World War, the collapse of humanity and the extermination of millions of people. Ferenc continued to travel, paint and buy with the same abandon as before the war. As the Germans gassed tens of thousands of young men to death at Ypres in 1915 there was a black-tie party in Budapest to celebrate Ferenc's *Portrait of a Woman* winning a gold medal award. She boasted about this on an almost daily basis, so much so that all of us got sick of hearing about that damn party.

She is a painting of a fleshy nude with sagging breasts and midriff. She looks wistfully out of the canvas with the gaze angled away from you as if embarrassed to look you in the eye. She wears a white turban-type covering with dark patches on it. We never got on because she never shut up about her medal. She could never get over the fact that she was dumped in the same empty apartment as the rest of us and she survived the shame by clinging to the unwarranted ego of one who has won a prize and therefore believes herself something special, for ever more. God knows how she won anything, maybe he paid for the prize. I am no expert on art, but it is clear to anyone who has eyes that Ferenc made a complete mess of her knees, and so has ruined her, in my humble opinion. There is a black line which I think he meant as the meeting point of the knees but the flesh on her left thigh is just wrong. To me the black line brings to mind a bum crack, which makes the whole bottom half of her body look like the back end of a tail-less horse. The *Portrait of a Woman* looks like a bizarre hair-less Centaur woman, twisting its body around unfeasibly far. Needless to say, she was never acknowledged as the genius painting she always told us she was and I am unsurprised to hear she is not even on display at the Hungarian Museum of Art, poor girl. Although considering the way it ended up for me, maybe she is lucky to be locked up in a storeroom and ignored, medal or no medal. Perhaps her fate is better than being ogled and objectified by dirty men who like nothing more than the sight of a nipple. I do feel a bit sad for Ferenc though. When I think of all the wonderful paintings he bought that they stole from him. What used to hang on his walls are now displayed proudly as Hungary's masterpieces while his own work languishes in a storeroom, but I suppose that is art for you. Art and the State. And he tried ever so hard to be a painter. Pity he was rubbish at it.

*

The collection, the house and all legal matters in Budapest were managed by Janós Horváth. Horváth was a lawyer paid by the firm and whose job was to manage Ferenc's affairs. Endre positioned a few lawyers and accountants in each of the family members' households ostensibly to help with their expenses, the day-to-day running of their accounts. However, their real job was to compile lists of how much was being spent and report all these expenditures back to Endre. He was a man who loved lists. So, while Ferenc skipped around Europe buying art and generally doing as he pleased, all the post was sent to Horváth in Budapest who sorted through it. An accountant called Veszely (also in the pay of Endre) followed Ferenc about as a general helper and dealt with the affairs at the sharp end.

To give an example of how this worked, in 1917 as the war was grinding to a bloody end Ferenc was in Berlin at the auctioneers buying Manet's *Bar at the Follies Bergère*. He was not even sure he even liked the work, but it was up for sale and it was a buyers' market, so he took it. Originally Veszely cabled Horváth to send 60,000 marks straight to the auction house, Cassirer. This was reported back to Endre who duly turned up and stomped through the house, screaming as if his words would reach all the way to Berlin whilst Horváth wisely kept his eyes to the ground. "60,000 marks! Are you kidding me? There is a fucking war on you know! Is it not bad enough that he sends back a fucking vagina painting? At least that was cheap. Tell Veszely that he is off his rocker and he can swing!" And so the cables went back and forward between Budapest and Berlin, much to the detriment of Endre's blood pressure.

Agreement was eventually reached and Horváth sent Veszely a little Cézanne and a Renoir, both of which had been bought a few years previously and had never even been unpacked. Ferenc then swapped them for the Manet, that he didn't even like. It was thus that the girl from the *Follies Bergère* made it to Budapest where she was at least unboxed by Endre to see what all the fuss was about: "Is it just me or is the reflection wrong. Bloody hell. Put it with the cunt downstairs and let's hope he forgets that he ever bought the bloody thing." That was how she and I ended up together in the darkness, her shivering silently from the trauma of the war. Unlike the *Portrait of a Woman* who shouted her brilliance as loud as she could, the poor girl in the *Follies Bergère* was never able, or never wanted, to talk. Her downcast eyes, fixed on the floor, were the representation of the way we all felt; that we were just possessions to be bought and sold by whatever man was on the other side of the bar. We were soft-skinned objects, all breasts with sweet-smelling flowers affixed to the crevices of our bodies. She symbolised a truth we all preferred to ignore and, to be honest, we were relieved when she was sold on, just another teenage refugee, this time shipped to London.

*

By 1918 the war had finish and the Austro-Hungarian Empire was collapsing. Just one block away from us in the Hotel Astoria they tried to set up a Hungarian government, but it dissolved into chaos. There were troops on the streets, stories of people being killed and thick hanging fear in the air. The Communists seized their moment and took over the city. Lajos was at the centre of it, the richest Communist of them all. All of a sudden, he was back in Budapest, storming through his families' mansions shouting orders. The establishment of the Communist utopia was at hand. Lenin had hand-picked Béla Kún, a close friend of Lajos, to establish a workers' revolution. They marched up the street and they marched down again. There were strikes and demonstrations and beatings while Kún sat in jail penning propaganda. When he was eventually let out, the country was his. He made speeches and the summer came. In the winding streets around the Inner City and Castle Hill the red geraniums still flourished in their window boxes above shop windows, but bars were shut due to lack of food and people starved. Money was worthless, which I suppose is how Communists like it, in theory at least and Horváth was even given permission to select a few diamonds from Ferenc's collection to trade on the black market. Communist troops were stationed outside the house and we sat in our crates trying not to make a sound. I will never forget the panic. I was a wide-eyed teenager trembling in terror, just one squeak away from being fuel for a fire. Number 3 Nádor Street no longer belonged to Ferenc Hatvany but to the people of Hungary, who were starving and come winter would be cold. I remember whispering, "What would the People think about something like me? How could they love me?" The air whispered back: "Shhhh."

We should not have worried, no one entered the premises except Comrade Lajos Hatvany who kept an eye on his brother's priceless art collection for him and saved us all. Three cheers for Lajos' hypocrisy. One wonders how it would have played in the long term had the Communist State survived. Who would Lajos have sided with had the shit ever really hit the fan: his family or the State? Thank God we never had to find out.

In the end the tension only lasted one hundred and thirty-two days. The Romanian army invaded Budapest and took the city. It was a national shock. No one expected the Romanians to be victorious, not even the Romanian generals. Almost at once it was clear they had no clue what to do as they had never won a battle before. They got around the problem by parading endlessly up and down Andrássy Street, past the sycamore trees and mansions of bankers, doctors, Counts and millionaire ex-Jews like Herzog, hiding behind their drawn blinds. Finally, they grew tired of the marching and went back to Romania. Horváth was allowed back to compile an undated inventory list for

Endre. The time of the Communists was over and we forced out a relieved exhalation.

Lajos fled to Vienna with Kún and stayed there for nearly a decade. Kún's Jewishness (which he always denied as a good Communist does) was linked with his Communism. Rather than work out which was actually more dangerous, it was easier to just persecute both Jews and Communists together. But as is always the way it was not the rich who suffered. In the Elizabeth District where the poorest Jews huddled together in fear and hunger there were beatings. The sun came up over the city and illuminated the creaking ropes that held inert bodies. They softly swayed in the winds that came down from the hills and blew through the city, ruffling the hair of the lynched Jews who hung from trees and lamp posts. Budapest had once been heralded throughout Europe as the epitome of modernity, but once humans team up into ideologies and the food runs out, they quickly revert to type: a good old medieval lynching in a good old medieval city. Communists were identified as Jews and both were targeted ruthlessly. The world had swung to the left and then it had swung to the right. On a summer's day in 1920 the shops shut their shutters, the trolley cars stopped rolling up and down the streets, the church bells rang from St Stephen's Cathedral three streets away from us and the city settled down. The sun had risen on a new day. What was previously a Communist country was henceforth a Fascist country.

Miklós Horthy was proclaimed regent of Hungary but the change of political weather didn't do anything for the Jews. The first anti-Semitic laws were enacted right away. There were restrictions to the number of Jews allowed to attend university, Jews were limited in their social and economic activities and each year a little bit more freedom was taken away. However, as the poor suffered through the great depression and subsequent inflation, the Hatvanys somehow became richer and richer. If you had ready capital, there were opportunities to expand as lesser tycoons fell to the vagrancy of the times and Endre always seemed to find the money for a promising business opportunity just when he needed it.

The sale of Baron Kohner's collection of Van Goghs, Matisses and Gauguins brought Ferenc back to the city, like a vulture circling over a carcass. Life might have been worsening for the Jews in general, but the great Endre Hatvany had put his Christian tuxedo on, used his Yiddish kop and done a deal under the table. He started by safeguarding the family and then turned to help where he could. While Jewish students were banned from studying at University, Endre established an academic grant for young medical students. In Ferenc's name ten million crowns were gifted to help the poor of Hatvan and establish an infant care centre. I wonder if Ferenc even knew what he was instituting, or even cared. Money moved, influence grew and the Hatvanys prospered.

Ferenc never mentioned the orphans or the children. The only thing he cared about was art and property. In 1923 he bought a mansion across the river. It was the former Prime Minister's palace just below Matthias' Church in the old Castle area of Buda and we were all finally allowed out of our crates, stretching our tight canvases like a bunch of Lazaruses rising from our wooden graves. The Horthy regime was racist, but it was a level of racism that Endre could work with and slowly calm seemed to magically spread throughout the city. Tentatively at first and then more confidently, the rich opened the windows to their palaces to let the air in. On the street corner traffic cops patrolled in trench coats and swords like ceremonial toy soldiers. Lining the roads, garlands of electric lights lit the buildings and by the waterfront, more twinkled on the water of the Danube as the sun went down behind Ferenc's new palace on the Buda hills. Life had settled down. I felt the anxiety in the air float out of the open windows and it spread through my youthful naivety. We could live, we could hope and foolishly we could feel like we had made it through all the terror that the world could possibly have in store for us. From here on in, I believed, life would be a ball.

Chapter 3

Spring in Budapest was always my favourite time of year. From the end of March, the Danube rose and the river flowed more swiftly, snaking its way around Margaret's Island and zig-zagging below us, bringing with it a particularly fresh smell of clean, running water as it pushed up around and sometimes over the quays. The water seemed to bring its own soul with it, a creamy whiteness that glistened and shimmered, extending over the whole city. This benign spirit spread all the way up the hill and infused the atmosphere with serenity and calm accompanied, as it was, by the clunking sound of chestnuts dropping on the old, cobbled streets around the Castle, as if nature was beating her own tempo on a world that had been cruelly taken from her, but one day would be returned.

Ferenc picked me up from where I was resting against the wall and threw an almost transparent covering over me. With his other hand he grasped the box that had the *Chateau du Blonay* on it and we were taken down to his car. Apart from art his only pride and joy was his Mercedes. He made a point of only buying German cars as opposed to the Rolls Royces gracing the drives of his neighbours, as he said, the Germans did everything best. It was cream, a beast of a car with a red soft-top and matching red leather seats with the Hatvany coat of arms embossed in cream on them: an open-mouthed lion in profile holding a sword as it emerges from a helmet sitting atop a shield depicting another pair of lions. The engine extended out in front for what seemed like miles, with enough space to set a cream coloured, boxed spare wheel above the wheel arch on the driver's side, which sloped down like a ski jump. Ferenc flipped down the retractable back seats and propped me up carefully as if I were his lady and he were taking me for a ride. Ferenc drove while Horváth sat next to him leaning back to keep one hand on me, pushing me into the leather. The initial turn to the left filled me with a sharp stab of panic as we swung onto what I thought was the wrong side of the road, but the sight of everyone else using the same bizarre system calmed me down. This was how things were done here. I would just have to acclimatise myself to it. We bounced down the cobbles towards the Chain Bridge. Above us towered the Castle District with its narrow, old, winding streets that seemed to belong to a different era and in front the funicular and Buda Castle.

Life was flowing out onto the pavements, every other building seemed to be a café, or an open-air restaurant and rows of tables filled the narrow spaces forcing Ferenc to tip toe along, the car growling in frustration at the glacial pace. Gentlemen taking coffee and reading papers in the morning sun shouted greetings at Ferenc as he passed by whilst the ladies waved their expensively gloved hands. It was coming to the end of the violets season, which had begun in March, but the smell of them still hung heavily in the air. A few weeks later it would fade to be replaced by the smells of early summer: lilacs, acacias and the waft of apricots which were still grown in Budapest at that time.

"When we get back, I want violets for her," Ferenc shouted across to Horváth.

"For who?" he shouted back. Ferenc nodded his head in my direction and Horváth rolled his eyes. "Yes, Sir."

We went over the bridge with a view of the Parliament building to our left, bending away from us, following the river; all jaggedy gothic spires with a neo-Renaissance dome plonked in the centre as if it wanted to be a part of all centuries, or none. On the Pest side we passed by the apartments in Nádor street where I had hid from the Communists.

Without realising, I instinctively held my breath until we turned left onto Andrássy. The trees were elegantly lined up on either side of us, rising on their trunks in a graceful curve to display their leaf-filled branches to the Heavens. Behind them the brick and stone, marble and gold pronounced the weight of opulence. This was where Mór Lipót Herzog lived, Ferenc's brother-in-law.

We were admitted right away and didn't have to wait long for the Baron to emerge to meet us.

"Ferenc, my dear man. It has been too long. Come this way," Herzog said, shaking Ferenc's hand. Despite being only a decade older he looked like a man from a different generation. His hair thinned to near disappearance on his forehead, all that was left was a light fuzz which extended around his ears and down the back of his head. His straight nose was book-ended north to south by thick black eyebrows and a matching black moustache. He wore a black three-piece suit, a pristine white shirt with a rounded collar and a black tie. Behind him András, his son, loped in wearing cream trousers, a buttoned-up boating jacket with a large spread collar that took up half of the width of his shoulder. He had a longer, thinner face than his father, with a huge forehead in front of his slightly messy side parting and small bird-like eyes that danced behind their lids.

"Good to see you Mór," Ferenc said, "I brought the picture to show you. Though, I don't know where you plan to put it." Every inch of wall was covered in paintings, mirrors, rugs and tapestries. As we walked through the never-ending sequence of rooms, we had to move carefully around antique furniture, marble busts and full-length sculptures. I could sense Horváth tiptoeing as he manoeuvred me on a path around the priceless objects. Herzog's was one of the largest privately owned art collections in Europe.

"As you can see, Ferenc," András commented, brushing against an ancient Egyptian bust with upturned painted eyes, missing both nose and mouth like a sculptural leper begging for alms, "it has turned into a museum in here. At first István and I had to move out and then Pap and

Ma followed. We are round the corner in the house by the opera. There is no space for humans in here anymore. There are only two rooms you can actually use. One for my Aunty and the second is the study. The rest is art."

His father just shook his head. "Don't pay him any mind, Ferenc. The young today have no passion. You have any children?"

"I have been blessed with twins. A boy and a girl, almost three years old now."

"Ah, it is a Mitzvah. Just the two?"

"At the moment, yes," Ferenc looked down at his feet, "we have been trying for more, but it has been difficult."

"It will work out, Ferenc," Mór replied. "Don't let it worry you. You'll have another son very soon. I have a good feeling for you. Always good to have many sons in the house. Although God-willing you will have a quieter one than András here."

The study was an amazing sight. It was a rectangular room, less crammed with furniture and art. There was a desk at the far end and behind it a set of curved low cabinets, one of which had a painted landscape built into the side of it. On the walls there was a line of El Grecos: *Saint Andrew* holding his cross; *the Holy Family with Saint Anne*, a baby Jesus sucking at the Virgin's breast as if trying to pull it off her body: all a blur of reds and mustard drapery and white grey cloud formations that look like solid architecture. *The Agony In the Garden* was in the centre of the wall, and in the corner, *The Expolio: The Disrobing of Christ*. They all seemed to be humming gently as if meditating or singing an *Ave Maria* in a medieval Cathedral. They lent an elevated aura to the room.

The Expolio captivated me most; the sombre sideways glance of the soldier is one of resignation, his armour brightly reflecting the red robe of Christ, which is being ripped off his body by the thug in green, his face already blackened by the shadow of his actions. This red reflection is the splattering of Christ's blood upon the whole of humanity. It is reminding us that humans committed this crime; this was a crime both perpetrated by and simultaneously against all humanity, a debt that needs paying but can never be fully settled. It is a glance that says, *We have to beg for forgiveness, we have to learn from our error, we have to pray.* An old man with a long, sharp nose points at Christ, directing our eyes to him but they can't rest on him, despite the eye-catching red of his garment. The painting whispers to us, forcing our gaze to be drawn up, like Christ's, to the white flashes of the sky, punctuated by the verticals of the pikes and staffs of the baying crowd; up, up, up away from this dirty earthly realm, to the divine, to the perfect. The spiritual aura of these elongated images seemed to soothe us all and especially affected my adolescent mind, as if in this ephemerality I could find something to cling to with the certainty that all children crave. For a beautiful moment there was a serene quiet in the room, a reflective mood perhaps. Mór could feel it descend amongst us and one could sense his pride at having championed this long-forgotten master that had brought a moment of peace to the turbulent minds of men.

"It's something, isn't it." He spoke almost in a whisper. Ferenc just nodded. I wonder what he was thinking. He had come into this space whose whole atmosphere was one of ascent, of spirituality and he was bringing the polar opposite, the most earthly, the most sullen, the most human. Me: a hairy vulva in a wooden frame. I was the antithesis of those El Grecos.

"Let's take a look, then," Mór said.

"I will show you how it all works, it is very clever really," Ferenc said. He carefully laid me on the desk next to the box, unlocked the *Chateau De Blonay* lid, flicked the catch and slid out the base. Then he unwrapped me and laid me in it, sliding it back and forth to show how the mechanism worked. András peered over his shoulder with wide eyes. I noticed Horváth pace away towards a painting of *Saint Peter Penitent* and pretend to look closely at it. Finally, András gave a short, sarcastic laugh and Mór raised his thick black eyebrows which sent ripples of creases flowing up his bald forehead. He cleared his throat.

"Well, um."

"Fuck me, Dad," said András, pointing at me. "You going to buy that one?! Are we putting it in the dining room? Be careful István doesn't nick it for his room."

"Be quiet, András, no one asked you," Mór said impatiently.

"I am not selling the girl, Mór, I just wanted to show how I found it. I am here to offer the landscape, not the nude. You wanted a modern landscape for the door of the cabinet and this one will fit the dimensions. It is a Courbet. The man is a genius, you have to try to drag your tastes into the present. The 16th century is long gone. I know you have the Corot and you like it, take the Courbet." Ferenc took the picture of the Chateau and held it up against the wooden panelling of the cabinet behind the desk. "See, it is perfect. It fits. And as I told you before, I think you should branch out a bit in your tastes. It is a landscape: there's a Castle, there are trees and a cottage. It's nice. Shame he didn't paint in a deer or something on the left here but there it is."

"Ok, I will take the picture, no problem. I just can't believe you are keeping *that.*" Mór gestured his nose towards me. Their sniggering cut me in two. I wanted to disappear back into my box. "I mean, where can you hang something like that, Ferenc?" Mór asked. "Actually, on second thoughts, maybe don't tell me. Maybe it'll help you and your wife have a son!" Ferenc smirked but was clearly unamused. Why did he even have to bring me?

"Don't mock what you don't understand Mór. Look at the brushwork, this is art of the highest calibre. The issue is with viewers who can't accept that."

"Sorry Ferenc, I don't mean to joke. As you say we have slightly different tastes. To me this is base. The brushwork does not come into it." Ferenc just shrugged. "On a separate point," Mór continued, "what happened to your brother, Lajos?"

"He is in Vienna, fighting with his pen."

"You know his thugs came to my house, Ferenc, you know they took my pictures."

"I know, Mór, I know. What can I say?"

"What can you say, Ferenc? They didn't take your pictures, did they?" Mór said jabbing his finger at Ferenc's chest.

"Maybe they didn't want them," András quipped from the back of the room. A nasty jibe.

"I said sorry," Ferenc said, "what can I do? Do you want me to talk to Endre."

"This is not about money, Ferenc," Mór said, "it is about respect. I just want to know whether he is going to say sorry, huh? To my face."

"Look, Mór. What do you want? It was a revolution. They took your pictures under military convoy to *The Palace Of Exhibitions*, they looked after them didn't they? They did a show, just an art show. The Horthy regime came in and you got them back. I am sure all the people who offended you are either dead or in exile. What do you want me to do about it?"

"I got them back! Got them back, he says," Mór's hands flew up and he looks over theatrically at his son. "It was not that easy to get them back, Ferenc, it was not *cheap*. I resent having to pay twice for something and still not receive an apology."

"Look," Ferenc said, losing patience, "I am not going to apologise for Lajos. He is not here. What can I say? I will apologise to you, though, on behalf of the family. Here, have the Courbet for free then, there, happy? I don't even care anymore."

"That's what I like about you, Ferenc," Mór slid the *Chateau* away from me and towards his side of the table, "you are above these petty discussions of man. Your ideals serve a higher purpose. I am sure you are a great artist."

"Not your style, Mór, not yet anyway."

There was a pause in the room as Horváth sighed, making a mental note of how the transaction had happened. I could sense he was worried about the explanation he would have to give to Endre that afternoon.

"By the way," Mór said finally, changing the subject, "are you not worried about this lot? These fascists?"

"What do you mean?"

"Come on!"

"It's fine Mór, don't start on this again."

"Ok, but you be careful, Ferenc, the Left yesterday, the Right today. There is not much difference when you get down to it. I have a horrible feeling that they will be at our door again before long, taking our pictures. Same people, different uniforms."

"Different ideas, different outcome maybe," Ferenc parried.

"No, Ferenc," Mór said shaking his head dolefully, "it all ends the same way. It would break my heart to be parted with my paintings again. I don't think I would survive."

"Don't worry, Mór. Don't worry. The Fascists don't like the Communists, we are not communists, that is pretty clear, it'll be fine. It won't affect us."

"They don't like the Jews."

"Don't worry Mór, we are not Jews anymore either."

With these words, silence filled the room and we were all compelled to look up at Christ praying in the Garden of Gethsemane, as if we had been silently called to acknowledge something that surrounded us. At the foot of the picture the disciples sleep soundly, using their arms as pillows for their heads. Their bodies are shrouded in the same yellow cloaks that the angel wears, wrapped around his waist. In the far corner the tiny stick people are only just visible, marked out by the fiery lamps they carry. Judas is at the head of the line pointing the way. The betrayal has taken place. Betrayal and denial. Mór wouldn't live to see it, I know that now, he would be dead before it happened. No broken heart for him. It would have long stopped beating by then. András wouldn't be so lucky.

*

Back in Ferenc's new, white mansion in Buda he found a place for me in his studio across from another Courbet, *Femme nue couchée;* a full-size nude with the head still on and luscious black hair, completely naked except for stockings and shoes. The way her right thigh lays over her left has created a perfect triangle of pubic hair in the centre of the painting that compliments the deep burgundy bed on which she lies. Ferenc had a 15th century cabinet moved across the room, so it ended up directly underneath where I was to hang and on it he placed a vase with a fresh bunch of violets. There were no other people in the room. He leant forward so that I could feel his warm breath on my paint and he whispered:

"It is a tradition in Budapest that one gives violets to the lady of one's desire on the first day of spring. I am sorry it has taken me so long. I don't know what kept me. Lost time is wasted time and it can't be regained. All that is left when the sands have fallen is regret. But you are here now and here you will stay. There is no power on earth that can change that, nothing. This is your home."

And I believed him because I wanted to, more than anything else in the world. He drew back, sat on a chair and stared at me intently, every so often he would glance over at the full nude as if trying to locate me in the person of another, transplant me. He reached out for a pencil and paper and started to sketch me. In his studio I had shifted from being a painting to becoming a model, from an object to an entity and whilst he worked, I felt he had eyes only for me. More than that, I felt that in his eyes I was beautiful.

*

For Ferenc we were something different. He never pulled his member out and tugged it at us. His eyes never glazed over as he pulled and pulled more quickly in our direction. He guarded us selfishly for his gaze in the same way that Khalil did, but the difference was that when he chose to look at us, he did so intently and unflinchingly. He looked at us for what we were, not what we represented. We were not to be used as a conduit to another mental space, we *were* the mental exercise. His focus was not on escape from us but deep concentration of us, so as to be more present, not more absent. Through his eyes, we turned from pornography to art, from ugliness to beauty, from outcasts to being accepted. His gaze transformed us, it reset our primary function.

He would sketch and paint all of his art works. It was not just me and it was not just the nudes. He would bring Courbet's *Waves*, one of his favourites, that normally hung above the mantelpiece in the drawing-room, into the studio and sweep his pencil over and over, filling page after blank page trying to capture a movement that Courbet once produced in a moment of thoughtlessness. Ferenc spent years of effort attempting to grasp that spontaneity, but it was a vain attempt. He was transfixed on arriving at the same result as Courbet, to the sunlit pool of that finished image, but for Courbet it was the process that created the art, the journey in its entirety, replete with mistakes and alterations, with anguish and heartbreak. You can learn from the past but can never fully recreate it.

The closest he came was a superb copy of Courbet's *Femme nue couché*. Ferenc got the smoothness of the white skin just right in his copy, the razor-sharp straight line of the pubic hair triangle and, most importantly, the folds in the gorgeous deep red curtains that hang over the naked woman. He was always better with the big picture than the minute details. Maybe that was why his copies of me were always such a disaster, always destined for the fire. However, he was so pleased with his *Femme nue couché* that he sent it to Prince Paul of Yugoslavia instead of the original for inclusion in an exhibition of French Art in Belgrade. It was not questioned at all. Ferenc read us all the reviews of the exhibition with the glowing praise heaped upon his Courbet. He was practically giggling with glee. It was his greatest artistic success and he couldn't see that it was emblematic of his own personal failure. When it came back, he hung them side by side. He always boasted of 'getting one over the establishment'. I wonder what he considered himself to be if not the establishment.

It was with this sketching, painting, drawing and modelling that we were transformed. It was this reverence that introduced us into the pantheon that is art. It is an infinite amphitheatre which images can be added into for all eternity, we shuffle up against each other, we interact. New ones are always grudgingly admitted and then almost immediately accepted on arrival and acclaimed. Some of us hold central positions of importance and some are pushed towards the edges, there is some movement outwards and inwards but not much. Acceptance comes in degrees, but it is always binary. You are art or you are not. For Ferenc we were all art, no matter what we had been before and he treated all of us as such: the nudes and the Saints, the landscapes and a picture of fruit on a dresser, portraits of great Kings and a lady with a pug. We were art for falling under his gaze and by dint of his collecting us. He was universally acknowledged as one of the great collectors in Europe and so his ownership of us validated our worth. Being owned by him transformed us without us changing one brushstroke. It was through him that we could find confidence. I thought it was a real, solid confidence, as all young people do but, of course, it was as brittle as they come. How can any young woman truly find acceptance if it can only come through the gaze of a richer, older man? If only I knew then what I know now.

*

In 1927 Lajos decided to bite the bullet and come back. Every debt needs paying, as Endre was fond of saying, every single one. Somehow. The Fascists inevitably threw him in jail for his part in the Communist takeover, but the family looked after him as best they could, despite his ingratitude, and Endre helped get him released. He settled one street up from Ferenc's mansion and at once his home became a cultural hub of writers, composers and artists. Ferenc ran study sessions for his painter friends who had a free reign over the house and used it as a gallery. They discussed us, sketched us, criticised us. Then they went away and innovated.

Béla Czóbel started coming more often in the 1930s and quickly became closer to Ferenc than anyone else. This experimental painter had become famous in Europe, winning prizes and exhibiting in France, Germany and even New York. Ferenc stayed with him whenever he went to Paris and by the mid-1930s Czóbel was spending every summer with Ferenc, either in Budapest or more often at the Castle in Hatvan.

This was where the whole family moved when the temperature started to rise in the city, when the noise from the bars ran into the early hours of the morning and when the smell of plums swept down from the orchards in the hills above us. They went away to the shade of the country and we were left to swelter and pine in their absence.

Chapter 4

These years were a golden time for Ferenc and his family. Ferenc's wife, Lucie, was pregnant with their third child Maria. Alexandra had just turned ten and was starting to act more like a small teenager than a large child and her much less mature twin, Alexander, had just been given the little brown dog, Miksa, for his birthday that he insisted on grabbing, squeezing, taunting or picking up whenever he could catch it. The poor creature! Forced to suffer the attentions and tyranny of this little boy, how he hated it.

However, Miksa had no choice but to put up with Alexander with the same stoical resignation as the rest of the household. Ferenc was overjoyed when the boy was born, the whole household was made to fuss over him and attend to his every whim: there was finally a boy child, an heir. Despite this seeming reverence for his masculinity, his mother, Lucie, insisted on a girlish hair cut with a fringe and a mid-bob around his ears which, combined with his electric blonde hair, made him look like a pudgy girl. He went around the house with a scandalised look on his face as if he were constantly on the point of bursting into tears. Despite the fact that the children were forbidden to come into the studio unaccompanied, we were constantly afraid that in his rage he would rip one of us off the wall one day or attack us for no reason other than spite or frustration.

Alexandra, on the other hand was a true beauty, her mother's daughter. She worshipped her mother, adopting the same elegant posture and gait. She had flowing blonde hair like her mother and a pinched chin that gave her an aloof look. The woman of the house, Lucie Hatvany seemed like the symbol of a new sense of womanhood; liberated enough to live her own life; to see friends, to host salons and to have social influence. However, looking back on those days, I now see that Lucie and her friends were still paraded socially (and silently) as the possession of men. It was a shadow, a mirage. Women had only achieved the vote less than a decade earlier and despite all Ferenc's proud talk of their new rights and emancipation (hypothetically speaking, of course) both Lucie and Alexandra glided through the house as beholden to the Hatvany men in the same way I was. Two more girls would be born by the end of the decade. Two more moving statues to adorn the Hatvany house of joy. We would all learn soon enough the limits of this so-called emancipation, we would all be disabused of our naive notions in the cruellest way possible.

*

Lajos only came over when he wanted to show off Ferenc's art collection to his friends. A particular visit that stands out was in 1935. The German Nobel prize winning writer Thomas Mann had fled the rampant Nazi party in Germany and had settled (where else?) in Switzerland. He still toured countries he felt safe in and had decided to stay with Lajos for a few weeks. It was the talk of the literati community. The long summer months had come to an end and the tables, which had lined the streets just a few weeks previously, had started to be taken in, whilst the large fires in the corners of the vast garden restaurants' dining rooms had been fired up. In the streets, women could be seen wearing long black gloves and fur lined coats, the gentlemen in brimmed hats, white scarves and dark over-coats hanging down past their knees. The air from the hills that had been bringing us the sweet smell of fruit and flowers since the end of April now brought a biting chill that at once invigorated and assailed you.

A core group of close friends and family had been at the house a few days previously to hear the art lectures that Ferenc had arranged for them. Ferenc had also been over to Lajos' for lavish dinners, followed by piano recitals by Bartók and endless discussions on art, literature and politics. Thomas' son Klaus had requested a closer look at Ferenc's paintings, so a morning was given over to the group as a tour, something Ferenc rarely encouraged as it ate into his sketching routine.

The group trekked past Endre who was in the study discussing accounts with Horváth, that morning. He raised a sarcastic eyebrow as they passed. Lucie was in the nursery with the new baby, just staggering uneasily to her feet, learning to walk. Ferenc's sister Irén was also playing with the baby but when she heard the Manns had come round she and her husband Albert added themselves to the tour at the last minute, sliding in next to Katia Mann and Otto Zarek. Otto was a slightly pudgy little man who always looked like he was being engulfed by his own clothes. Despite being around the same height as Thomas Mann he seemed much smaller, although that was probably a question of presence rather than dimensions. Thomas Mann stood tall and with his neat moustache looked elegant and lithe. Otto was the opposite, slightly stooped and for some reason he tended to hold his left hand in his right one and extended both of them in front of his body as if he were in constant supplication for something. He had been a successful dramatist in Berlin, which is where he had befriended Thomas and Klaus but as a Jew had been smart enough to move to Budapest from Berlin while he still could. Of the Mann children only Klaus and Elizabeth had been brought along by their parents. The others were scattered around Europe. Golo was preparing to take up his first lecturing position in Rennes, Monika was studying the piano in Florence and had refused to come on the trip and Michael was studying the viola in America. As they walked into the room where we were hanging, Thomas was bringing the group up to date with news of his eldest, Erika.

"She left Germany after the Reichstag fire in '33, just like you Otto, but instead of coming East she went West to England. It is a shame you did not go to England, my friend. It would have solved a problem for me."

Otto shot a tense glance at Thomas, whose moustache bristled into a mischievous smile. Lajos, who was a clear head taller than both of then, looked down with amusement.

"Oh yes, Thomas," Otto gamely played along, "and what problem would that be, exactly?"

"Well," said Mann, pulling away from the ladies who were staring intently at Tintoretto's *Portrait of a Venetian Nobleman* and lowering his voice a touch, "Erika needs a husband to get a UK passport after Germany cancelled her citizenship. She has been engaged all year long in the tedious task of trying to find a good quality British homosexual to marry for convenience. She started with that group she knew from Germany, Isherwood and the like but to no avail. If only you were there to help out, Otto, I would feel safe were she to end up with you." Lajos let a sharp laugh like a gun shot that ended almost as soon as it began. He patted Otto in the back supportively.

"Sadly, I would have been of no help, Thomas," Otto shot back, "as I am equally stateless as you know. It is only with the help of Lajos and Endre that I am able to extend my residence permit here and every time I have to go through the process it's getting more difficult."

"And expensive," Lajos added.

"Yes, indeed," Thomas murmured fiendishly. "On second thoughts, I am not sure marrying Erika off to a stout Jewish playwright is going to make all her problems go away after all." They all laughed with the exception of Katia who looked nervously down at the ground.

"Out of interest," Otto asked semi-earnestly, "did Erika manage to find a nice British man in the end? If things keep going the way they have been, then I may have to try England out. It would save me a lot of time if she has a list of potentials that I could start with. Maybe you could arrange flowers to be sent out in my name."

Thomas frowned and shot a glance at his wife. "Oh, I think she married Isherwood's 'friend', W.H. Auden. Good writer, not sure about him as a son-in-law."

Lajos smiled at him. "I don't think you will have to worry much about it, Thomas."

"Quite." His eyes fell nervously to the ground as his wife glanced over to him without anyone else noticing. No one except Otto, that was, who narrowed his eyes suspiciously with a slight furrow of confusion on his brow.

The party moved up to me and stood around in a semi-circle. Ferenc, who towered at least half a head over the rest of the group, introduced me dryly. This was his way of introducing me whilst still trying to draw the least amount of attention to what I was. It showed me how uneasy he felt with his brother's friends.

"Yes and this is *The Creation of The World* by Courbet. So, yes, pretty self-explanatory. Excellent brush strokes, of course."

As per usual there was a synchronised raising of eyebrows amongst those who had never seen me. Katia Mann gave a sharp cough and tried to move Elizabeth on, which elicited a dry smile from Otto. He was standing next to Thomas Mann, directly in front of me. Both men's reactions were unusual in different ways. Otto's face was the most interesting, as far as I was concerned. His look was something I had not come across before. There was no shock in it, no instinctual dilation of the pupils. The skin did not tense up as with the other men who looked at me and his eyes did not shift back and forth, up and down as I was used to. His gaze was direct and yet un-intense. He did not lean in towards me nor pull back. His chubby face did not screw up and I could not help noticing how still his hands were; one holding the other, his nails, clean and manicured. Thomas stared uninterestedly at me for a moment but slyly snuck his gaze off to his right and allowed his eyes to rest on Otto. There was no movement in Otto at all, not physically and (more importantly) not mentally either. He looked at me with a shocking disinterest that terrified me. With a slight closing of his left eye he softly murmured, "Very nice brushwork," with an emotionlessness that diffused the atmosphere in an instant. Then, in a moment of break that surprised both of us he turned and looked directly at Thomas. I sensed immediately Thomas started and I could feel his feet shifting backwards, almost imperceptibly. Otto, who normally appeared so lacking in confidence all of a sudden seemed in charge of the atmosphere. It was as if they had been playing a game of cards and Otto had revealed that he had known all along that Thomas had been bluffing and more than that, bluffing badly. Otto held Thomas's wary look for a moment and opened his body up to him, as if he wanted to reassure the more famous man that he had nothing to worry about, that he, Otto, would not reveal the secret that he knew, that really, everyone knew. He unclasped his hands, one from another, very slowly placed his left hand lightly on Thomas's arm and gently led him away from me to the *Femme nue couchée* where Klaus was already standing, picking a piece of dirt out from behind the nail of the pinkie of his left hand.

The three men stood close by one another and I noticed Klaus lean up against Otto almost imperceptibly, the sleeves of their shirts brushed against each other, left to right until Klaus extended his hand down and rested it against the back pocket on Otto's grey trousers. Thomas stared at them, like an out of focus figure on the edge of a grainy photograph. His look was a nuanced mixture of disapproval and jealousy. Many years later, back in Paris, I learnt that when Klaus committed suicide Thomas and Katia did not even attend his funeral. How is one to interpret the actions of those who grieve? Was this to be read as a show of not enough love, or too much? Otto gazed up at Klaus, the taller man still only twenty-nine and very handsome with his high cheek bones, and his slicked back dark hair that showed the first signs of the thinning to come. They moved on to catch up with the others and the discussion restarted as if I had never been there.

"As I was saying it is getting harder and harder to renew my residence permit. I am sure that were it not for his support I would not be here with you, you know how grateful I am to him and your whole family,"

Otto said to Ferenc sotto voce as if he was used to protecting his words from the world. "However, I sense the same Germanic wave of hatred extending to Hungary. I fear it will cover the whole of Europe."

"Don't be a fool," Lajos barked aggressively at the little man who physically withdrew like a scolded dog. "To what are you referring, huh? To what? To the Jews? Don't be ridiculous. This is nothing to do with race. This is all about money, can't you see? The rotten capitalist system is collapsing in on itself. The Hungarian Jews are some of the richest in all of Europe, no wonder these right-wing capitalists are circling like vultures. It is the decomposing body of a decrepit system. It is dead, can't you see? What have these fools done? What have the Jews done? Do they work? Do they produce anything now? For the last 2000 years they have lived on usury. They are social vampires. What you are afraid of is not some German idiocy, that farce will never last, the real change will come from the social revolution that will not just sweep Europe, it will sweep the whole world. You are as safe or otherwise here as you are anywhere, Otto, the Communist state does not recognise Jews or Gentiles. It only recognises citizens."

"You don't know what you are saying, Lajos," Klaus Mann shouted angrily. "This Hitler is not some economic thinker or social philosopher. This man hates Jews and he will have his way with them. We have seen that in Germany. Otto and I have seen this. He will not stop and the way England and France are appeasing him shows he will not be stopped. To him you are as much a Jew as Otto, Lajos. Don't be naïve."

"I am not a Jew. Ferenc is not a Jew." Lajos stabbed his finger angrily into his brother's chest, "Irén is not a Jew. We were baptised in St Stephen's Basilica. Don't throw that at me."

"Lajos! Come on!" Klaus continued, ignoring his father's glance at him, warning him to let it go, "This is not a religious question or a social question. All through history Jews have converted to Christianity, think of the Conversos in Spain. They were still persecuted as Jews. They were still burnt as Jews. You know this. This Hitler is no theologist, he does not care about your politics or what you believe in your soul. For him the Jews are a category, nothing more and nothing less. They are nothing but a list of names from whom he can appropriate goods and on whom he can blame all of Germany's problems for his own political gain. This is a question of simple categorisation. This movement is built for large numbers, not for the nuances of the individual. They will not listen to your arguments, to anyone's arguments. They make lists and if your name is on the list..."

"If your name is on the list..." Ferenc repeated the words and for some reason this brought silence to the room. It was as if everyone had forgotten that he was there, even though it was his house, even though he was the tallest and most imposing of them all. They were standing in front of Ingres' *Small Bathers*. She was sitting with her back towards them so that all that was visible of her was the extension from the nape of her neck down to the split of her buttocks. On her head she wore the most amazing gold and white turban-like headdress that glistened and glimmered. It was by far my favourite piece of clothing in the room (although with all the nudity on show it was not up against strong competition). It was the only piece of fabric I was ever jealous of. I can't say why, maybe it highlighted my lack of a head but the idea of wrapping one's hair up, out of sight and then glancing, as she did, over a shoulder always got me. For all the bare bottoms and breasts on show in the room, this girl, who displayed only the extended line of her back was, in my eyes, by far the most sensual. You cannot see her face; she turns her head as if she is about to look at you, but she does not pivot all the way around towards you. She never will, always the expectation, never the culmination. There is only a speck of light reflecting off her right ear and in the darkness of the shadow, the outline of a cheek.

"If your name is on the list..." Ferenc repeated. I knew he was lost in the darkness of that invisible face. While the rest of the party stared at the bare bottoms or the breasts of the other bathers in the background, I knew for Ferenc it was all about that invisible face. I had seen him search for it for hours, sketch it ceaselessly over the years. He never found what he was looking for.

"If your name is on the list..." Thomas Mann repeated the words as if taking on a baton. He spoke quietly, almost in a whisper, as if to himself, muttering, garbling his words, trance-like, "The lists are a categorisation, as Klaus rightly says, but they are more. Categorisation is dehumanisation. The group identity negates the individual identity. This is what you miss, my dear friend. The creation of categorises creates these groups: in-groups and out-groups. This dehumanising grouping is, perversely, the most natural of human instincts. We cannot help ourselves; we have to do it: them and us. For you it is a division between good socialist citizens and traitors, for Hitler it is Jews and Aryans, the heterosexual and the gay. You are not so dissimilar to him; your extremism makes you cousins at the very least. Once you create your own group the other group must be persecuted. It has to be destroyed."

The next painting was El Greco's *Mount Sinai*, the tiny sinewy figures dominated by the twirling mountains, twisting up, all dark browns and yellows into the stormy sky from whence God would descend. The rickety stairway leading up the mountain is hardly visible to the eye. Thomas nodded towards it, "You see, only when one group is totally powerless can it be humble enough to allow the 'other' to exist. This is the secret of the Jews, why they survive so well. They have never had the power to dominate, only to be dominated and hence to be martyred. They can go on like this for ever. As long as they are never put in a position of power, in a position to make lists of their own they will endure. God forbid they ever get a land of their own, God forbid they ever get enough power to show the world that they are really no different from anyone else. The spell would be broken. What goes up must come down, Lajos. The tragic trick of life is always to lose."

*

Otto was right, of course, the anti-Semitic laws started ramping up in earnest in 1938. And as was the case in Germany they started with their definitions. Equality of citizenship for Jews was reversed, and the list of categorisations of who was and was not a Jew were broadcast on the radio. Anyone with one Jewish grandparent was a Jew. Lajos could shout and swear all he liked but that was the law of the state. He was a Jew. Punto-finale. Once this was done, quotas were announced for how many Jews could be lawyers, journalists, engineers, doctors, government officials. Otto, the wanderer, the stateless Jew, packed his bags, shed his tears and left for England. Lajos was next to leave, first to Paris and then to England. I must admit that we all shared a teenage snigger in the studio when we heard that he ended up in Oxford. Was this really the best place on Earth to bring about the world's socialist revolution? The truth was that it was comfortable there and it was easy for Endre to forward money to him in England. Everyone overlooked his enduring hypocrisy and let him get on with his proletariat-based pontificating from afar.

In 1939 there were a new set of laws. Jews were forced into the Hungarian army and the stories started circulating about hard labour and deprivation beyond imagination. Endre pulled up his sleeves, got out his chequebook and started negotiations on the cost for exemptions for the family. Cousin Bertalan helped him out (financially at least) by announcing his move to Paris, one less name to get off the list. He announced it in front of us all while Ferenc was painting. Ferenc's style had loosened in the late '30s under the influence of the post-impressionists. As form fell away from his paintings Ferenc moved to a more Cézanne-like impressionistic colour and his canvases filled with shadow and light, blurs and blocks of shade that came together to make up sunny parks and fruit bowls. I must admit I personally preferred this stage of his painting but now wonder if the comfort I took from this colourful art simply appealed more naturally to a naïve, teenage mind. Impressionism provides just enough optical complexity to make one feel clever without the depth and darkness of the outside world boring too deeply into the consciousness. It is a play on light and perspective on a sunny winter's day when the snow, which every child paints as a block of pure white, is in reality flecked with greens, browns and ochres. It is exactly as it claims to be, an impression, and hence an illusion. All of a sudden, paintings of apples next to a glass of water, or a bowl of peaches had started to look like escapist folly. The world was dark and redemption was nowhere to be found, no matter how hard Ferenc studied the late autumnal light flooding through the yellows and oranges of falling leaves.

Bertalan came into the room and Ferenc's gaze turned from us to his Picasso sketches and Cézanne's still life painting which he had next to him: all tablecloths and colourful fruit. Endre was quoting figures at him while he worked, numbers that floated around in the air but made no impression on Ferenc whatsoever.

"It is all very well for you, Ferenc," Endre was saying, "with your exhibitions and the like, but I don't think you are taking this seriously. You have to let me value this lot, so we know what we have. I have already priced and catalogued the family's collection of carpets and I think Bertalan has sorted his stuff out, you are the only one acting as if nothing is happening."

"You have fifty pieces, Endre," Ferenc murmured. "It is easy for you. You can catalogue them in an afternoon. I have over seven hundred. It is a lot of work." He waived his paint-spluttered hand listlessly at the air around him, "I will get round to it. I just need to get this painting done first."

"Ferenc, you are not listening. Ah, here is the man I want to see, Bertalan, welcome. Can you knock some sense into this idiot and get him to properly catalogue his collection? We are not talking about moving or selling anything, all we are doing is getting organised."

"I have some news, both of you," Bertalan said curtly. "I am leaving."

"Leaving!"

"What! Where?"

"I am going to Paris." Bertalan said as he sank into a chair and looked meekly at the ground. "I have been considering this for some time. I have to go. They won't let me publish; they won't let me teach. I have to apply for a permit every time I want to travel. This is not living. And it is only the beginning. Endre is right, Ferenc you have to come to terms with this. Can't you see we are not welcome in this country anymore?"

"This country? This is *our* country." Still holding the paintbrush in his right hand Ferenc raised his left and formed it into a fist. "This is where we were born and where we live. I am welcome. I have done nothing, I sit and I paint. What have I done wrong? What? I received a letter this very day from the Countess Éva Almásy-Teleki asking for some of the Courbets and some of my own work to show in her new exhibition."

"Ferenc! You are not even in this world! They will come for you too," Bertalan shouted.

"Look, calm down," Ferenc said, "I am not an idiot. I can see what you see but this is Hungary and we are Hungarians after all. We still have some rights that they dare not touch. There are problems and Endre sorts it out. It is business after all. They need us, they may not like us, but they need us. For now, it is ok. It is a question of money, right, Endre?"

Bertalan's shoulders sunk and he looked at Endre who just shook his head in despair.

"We have been living up here in the hills too long," Bertalan said in a low voice that sounded like some far-off rumble of an approaching storm. "We feel so close to Hungary, to the country we thought was ours, but we forgot to keep in touch with it. Now these Nazis come and say we are Jews first and we cling to the spirit of a community that we were once part of. But that community isn't here anymore. It has now gone away. We are living too high up, Ferenc, the air is getting thin. You are a Jew and a Hungarian. How long can one identity save you from the other?"

Ferenc's eyes caught fire all of a sudden, as if he had been woken from a deep sleep. He opened his mouth as if to speak fiercely but no words came out, just a thick atmosphere that rolled over the room like a mist. All us paintings tensed our canvases, our Japanese paper and our wood, as the sculptures' marble crackled inaudibly. The humans' skin tightened and their hairs stood up. The room was silent and yet all ablaze. Then all at once, as quickly as it came, it dissipated and the temperature of the air modified, regulated and the tears started to roll down Bertalan's cheek. Endre looked away as if his attention had been caught by something on the other side of the room but there was nothing there, just an empty frame, propped up against a wall, waiting for its void to be filled by a canvas. Ferenc looked down at the ground. He put down his paintbrush and palette and reached for a cloth to wipe his hands. There was a cigar smoking in the ashtray to his side and he took a long tug at it. His exhalation blew the thick smoke into the air and his previously upright body slumped back against his chair. He nodded sadly, as if agreeing to some secret truth.

"Where in Paris will you stay? What will you do there."

Bertalan talked for a while of the translations he would undertake and his plan to set up a Hungarian Oriental Society. Before long the bell went and the cousins got up to leave the room and head down for lunch with the rest of the family, Bertalan expounding on the merits of the *Tao Te Ching*. My heart broke as he spoke reams of learned, empty words into the high ceiling rooms where these men sat together, emotionally distanced from each other, each alone in their isolation. Only I could see the earnest face of little Alexandra who had sneaked up, peeking around the door, silently looking and listening, absorbing truths that would destroy her life, powerless to do anything about it. Her eyes were glazed with tears that would not come forth. She was like me, just a little girl and hence both present and not present, a forgotten addendum.

When lunch was over and the house was again his, Ferenc settled back down at his easel and picked up his paintbrush. He sighed, closed his eyes. When he opened them, he took a moment to stare deeply at the ruffled green and white stripy tablecloth he had set up on the table, next to which he had arranged a white bowl overflowing with pears, apples and bananas. He started to paint again as if there was nothing else in the whole world. He didn't even stop when Antoinette, who was then 5 years old, padded in followed by the dog, who had taken to following her around as she was the calmest and hence least threatening of the children. Despite the no-children-in the studio rule, which was normally strictly enforced, Ferenc didn't even seem to notice when she plonked herself down at his feet. She took up a scrap piece of paper that had fallen to the floor and started drawing with a crayon; a house, a sun, mummy, daddy, her sisters and her brother and the dog, Miksa, who she drew three times bigger than any of the humans.

Chapter 5

Bertalan was right, of course, although as with anything, it is always easy to look back and recognise events that come to pass as inevitable. Things are never inevitable until they happen. Looking back from the comfort of peacetime it is easy to wonder how people like Ferenc could have been so naïve, so blind, so out of touch with reality and blame it on his status, his wealth. But it always seems simpler and safer to do nothing than to make a change, always easier to just accept the status quo. Ferenc and the many other Jews like him in Budapest who stayed throughout the war, saw themselves as Hungarians first and foremost. It was this level of identity that they clung to as their totem of self. It was just a shame that the authorities foregrounded another identity and enforced it upon them. It is hard to accept an identity that you don't acknowledge as being overwhelmingly yours, harder still when it is imposed upon you.

The first tremor came from the house of Herzog. Without the protection of Mór, who died in 1934, the three children were ripe for the taking. I am sure that this would have been Ferenc's fate without Endre and his Yiddish kop sorting everything out in the background. All three of the Herzog children were foppish and naïve: the cream trousers and boater hats brigade. They had never had to fight for anything in their lives, never had to earn a living or negotiate a deal. They were the tennis-playing, socialising elite, so far removed from their father's and grandfathers' instinctual ability to survive that they wouldn't have perceived a crouching lion as a threat.

András was shipped out to the Russian front in 1942 with the enactment of the first set of forced labour laws. He wasn't even given a coat, let alone a gun. On the Eastern front it was a race against time to see whether he would be lucky enough to be shot before freezing to death. It wasn't even reported which one ended András' life, him and the tens of thousands of others who went with him. The other two children managed to get over the shock quickly and some survivalist DNA kicked in just in time. They wisely traded their family's wealth for their freedom and managed to survive, although for Istaván, the youngest, it was a close-run thing. He was already on the train bound for Auschwitz when his sister managed to get him off the list.

András' draft not only shocked his siblings into action, it reverberated across the river and invaded the Hatvany house. It is one thing to dismiss a threat as theoretical, over there, but once it happens to one of your own, your contemporary, it is harder to ignore. The penny finally dropped for Ferenc. The tables were still out on the pavements and people still lounged under the leafy trees of the gardens of the great taverns of *The Marble Bride* and *The Rose Tree* when the allied bombs started falling in the city. Windows blew out and brick rubble fell from regimented walls onto the streets. There were fire engines and screams. It had begun. All of a sudden there was a mad dash to catalogue and secure the art.

With an air of calm expectation Endre turned up the morning after the first bombs had fallen. Ferenc was sitting perfectly still in the drawing room, staring at Courbet's *The Wave* as if expecting some epiphany to emanate forth from it. Lucie was frantically marching through the house barking inaudible orders at any passing servant who would listen. Alexander, then 17, was cleaning the hunting rifles as if he was going to fight the war on his own and the two youngest girls, Maria and Antoinette, were hugging each other in a corner, crying into Alexandra's velvet dress.

Endre strode through the drawing room without even pausing to say hello. He pointed at Horváth and mentioned for him to follow.

"Get paper and a pen. You..." He grabbed a kitchen boy who ran past him with no obvious idea where he was running too. "There are boxes and packing materials outside, next to my car. More should arrive any moment. Bring it all in. Get help, get moving. Ok János, let's get down to it. Chop chop."

Within the hour Ferenc and his whole family had pretty much been forgotten in their own house. Everyone working for the house was given clear tasks by Endre who directed the taking down of the art and the packing of valuables. Ferenc, Lucie and the children were moved heartlessly around from room to room as rugs, porcelain, carpets, dressers and tables were spirited away from beneath their feet and hands: China teacups were taken from their fingers, fur shawls stripped off their shoulders. We stood stock-still in the studio, petrified to our core, hardly daring to breathe. In the end Ferenc found a wooden footstool in the kitchen that he was allowed to sit on unmolested. Miksa, sensing his master's powerlessness, dutifully sat by him and softly whimpered, while Ferenc distractedly stroked his head. Alexander buzzed around trying to get involved, still holding his father's hunting rifle until Endre snatched it from his hands with a stern rebuke and told him to stay out of the way.

Endre then moved onto us. Like Ferenc, Lucie and the children we waited our turn, limply resigned to our fate. We were taken off the walls, carefully removed from our frames, which were packed separately, and we were taken into the study. It was there that Endre had set himself up with Horváth and Veszely.

"Right, listen up, these two boxes of porcelain are to be listed here in this column as belonging to Veszely. These ones are going to be deposited in the Hungarian Commercial Bank of Pest. The trucks are arriving in around an hour. Pack everything that has been laid out on that side of the desk. Don't get anything mixed up or God knows we will never be able to work out where the fuck anything is when this is all over.

"János, everything in the drawing room is to be listed under your name. It is already organised with the bank so get going. Everybody will be moving their stuff into safety deposit boxes today so don't get caught up in the stress. I organised these lots months ago when I did my house so they should be ready for us. The Degas and that lot in chests 7 and 8 are going to the Hungarian Subordinate Credit Bank. Ask for Gregor the manager, tell him who you are and have them put in Box V number 13.159. Go down with him and make sure he does not make a mistake. I want to know where everything is. Ok, go now and then get back here quickly.

"Alexander, my boy, if you must hang about, you might as well make yourself useful. Don't worry about the guns, you will have plenty of time to defeat National Socialism when we are done with the packing. Take this and neatly mark down everything that is going into that crate, number IV...Yes, that's the one, that tapestries, the rolled-up painting of the lady-bits, God forgive me, those drawings, that Kostsztka fishing scene, make a clear list. I want your best handwriting. When you are done, write Hungarian General Credit Bank on the outside of the crate 987/121 and let me know the moment János gets back. I want a full list of deposit numbers and I want three copies of all the documents so we can split them up."

Just like that, we were packed away, nailed down and shipped out. It was a terrifying experience, a whirlwind of activity and what seemed to me like a tornado of destruction. Walls were stripped bare, glass was accidentally broken, furniture was scraped across the floor. The house that had always been ordered, quiet, safe and calm suddenly became cacophonous and chaotic. I felt my paint tensing in anxiety and fear as we watched each other stripped of frames and rolled up. It was like losing a limb. I felt the ghost of my frame as if it was still there with me. Antoinette slipped into the room holding her big sister's hand and sat in the corner watching with wide eyes as the room she knew and loved was dismantled before her. There is no fear on earth like that of a discombobulated child. It was my fear as well, I will never forget it. We had no idea what was going to happen next.

Everything of value was distilled into piles of crates, which were sent off to four different banks. There were some pieces too large to move, Courbet's *Wrestlers* for example, and in my first night in the dark bomb-proof vaults of the Hungarian General Credit Bank I imagined Ferenc wandering around his massive palace, the walls stripped bare of pictures and tapestries, drafts of cold air coming through the rug-less floors. I imagined him standing in front of that monumental painting of the two wrestlers, their muscular bodies intertwined in what must have seemed to him an eternal cosmic battle, their huge arms pressurising each other's necks as if trying to rip their heads clean off their bodies. I imagined him standing in the gloom crying. I wondered if that was the moment his mortality suddenly became clear to him. I wonder if that was the moment he finally panicked and did something truly awful.

Chapter 6

It was dark for a long time. The Nazis came and they killed and they left. The Soviets came. There was a big siege. All we could hear from the vaults were the incessant bombings, day and night, the noise was deafening. The earth started shaking and it shook for fifty days and fifty nights. It was like the Old Testament stories Lucie used to read to Alexandra, the ones that start scary but end with God's protection of his favoured children: it would not be like that this time. Suddenly it all went silent. We lay in our crates and waited, creaking in apprehension, trying to stay as quiet as we could.

All of a sudden, things started to move, we could feel it through the concrete. There were loud Russian voices, the crack of a rifle against someone's skull and a sharp cry of pain, the sound of a pair of knees hitting the cold ground, the ruffle of clothes as a body was pulled up to its feet. The vaults were being opened; everything was being opened. Say what you like about the Germans but at least they never looted from banks, it would have been messy, un-bureaucratic. The Germans loved their paperwork, they would contort themselves into incredible positions to appear legal, to appear to be doing everything *by the book*. Why they seemed to desire this veneer of legitimacy has always struck me as rather quaint considering the atrocities they performed on an industrial scale, but with the Nazis there were always lists to follow, rules to obey, paperwork to sign. The Russians, however, did not care about any of these niceties. Where the Nazis would rob you blind but provide a receipt, the Russians would just loot indiscriminately. The Nazis were in Budapest for a year but never touched the bank vaults. The Russians had them open at gunpoint on day one.

Crate after crate was dragged out with no care whatsoever. The screeching of wooden panels against the floor cut through the air. Finally, the top of my crate was opened. and we were pulled out one by one. The rooms were so full of paintings, partially unrolled tapestries and porcelain that there was no room left against the walls for us, so I was thrown up against a table leg, my canvas falling onto either side of it, like a wet rag, and left to sink down heavily onto the freezing floor. The tables were covered in unrolled canvases, sketches, jewellery, etchings, bars of gold and silver, money, glassware and irreplaceable, ancient pots. There was not one visible centimetre of bare surface. Everywhere was covered with priceless objects, masterpieces layered upon one another. It was an orgy of oppulance. Russian soldiers were running back and forth pushing armfuls of money and diamond jewellery into kit bags, overseen by a Major who in turn looked fearfully towards a tall Lieutenant-General. This man stood by the table. Unlike the rest of them, he was spotlessly clean and stood well over six foot with an elegant air about him. He was wearing a fur-lined coat which puffed out luxuriously about him and carried his hat under his arm, showing off a receding covering of dark black hair, perfectly slicked back. Everyone else in the room was covered in mud and blood, shivering, despite their felt hats, in the freezing February air that blew through the glassless windows. It was said that not one pane of glass survived the Russian bombardment of Budapest. It was a shattered city of broken glass.

Next to the Lieutenant-General stood a petrified-looking man in a non-military black suit. With his hands shaking he picked up one thing at a time, glanced at it briefly and dropped it into piles on his left or his right. He was totally bald with small circular glasses that barely covered his eyes. He stooped over the table and looked tiny next to the

Lieutenant-General. Behind them was a Russian soldier with a black cloth tied over his right eye as an eyepatch. He was holding onto the arm of the manager of the bank, who would have collapsed to the ground had it not been for the support. The poor old man was swaying slightly, still gripping the vault keys in his hand, as a stream of blood dripped down from the side of his head. His nose was clearly broken and the bottom half had turned ninety degrees to face his left ear. His eyes were fixed on the table and specifically at which piles everything was falling into. When the crown jewels of Hungary were roughly thrown onto the ground with the proclamation of 'Fake!' I could see him try to hide a conflicted look of both horror and relief in his one, not bruised, eye.

Just then a Russian soldier came in holding a heavy looking German typewriter. He was ushered through as if he was of utmost importance. The Lieutenant-General snatched it off him greedily and turned it over in his hands, murmuring with delight.

"This?" the Lieutenant-General barked, thrusting the typewriter into the little man's chest, whose eyes widened in terror, magnified by his lenses.

"But...but....it won't work, Sir, the keys are wrong Sir."

"Don't be such an idiot, man, we can have the keys changed in Moscow," the Lieutenant-General snapped, devoid of patience for his quivering associate.

"But, they are Hebrew keys, Sir," the little man with glasses stammered. "Even if you change the keys...um... if it is Hebrew. It will write from right to left."

"For fuck's sake! A fucking Jew typewriter. Are you kidding me? I have had to come all the way to this shithole, if I don't leave this country with a decent German typewriter someone is going to get shot, do you understand?" The Lieutenant-General threw the typewriter down behind him without looking and it crashed through a painting of a landscape with a man on a donkey that I think was Herzog's Corot.

"And that lot?" The Lieutenant-General barked, clearly still furious.

"Paintings, Sir, more paintings, I am...I..."

"Well, pack them up then. Let's go.....No, not that rubbish." The Russian soldier with the black eye patch had picked me up and looked over at the Lieutenant-General with a childish smirk on his face. He then dropped me down again, his one, unpatched, boyish eye never leaving me.

It took hours but finally the officers left and the Bank Manager was allowed to collapse on the ground bleeding puddles onto the floor. The soldier with the black eyepatch picked up a bronze staff that looked like it was first century BC Egyptian and came over to me. With a sly glance around at the other soldiers, who were busy pocketing left behind notes or loose diamond earrings that had been forgotten in the chaos, he picked me up from the floor. I felt the agonisingly sharp piercing on my canvas as he threaded the bronze stick through the sides of me and held me up over his head so that I fluttered in the freezing air.

"Long live the cunt!" he yelled, "Long live Mother Russia!"

The other soldiers looked around and all of a sudden, their mud-stained freezing faces burst into laughter, their eyes sparkled in the February sun and their missing teeth chasmed through their broad smiles. They were nothing but boys, silly boys; hungry and scared like me, sent to fight, to kill and to die for nothing that concerned them. All they wanted was food and alcohol and warmth.

The soldier with the black eyepatch took me outside. He jumped onto the back of a truck loaded with bags of loot from the bank. It was my first view of Budapest after the Russian siege and, looking back on it, this was the moment I finally grew up. This moment marked the end of my childhood. What I witnessed was nothing short of hell on earth. The terror was overwhelming. The city had been totally destroyed. The buildings were nothing but skeletons; no windows, no roofs, huge holes blown out of their sides, rubble everywhere. The tree lined streets that had once teemed with people were now a mess of broken material: glass, coils of destroyed barbed wire, splintered timber, parts of humans and stone. Fires burned here and there and groups of Russian soldiers stood by them hoping to warm up a bit before being moved on by their superiors. There was no life left in the city, just smoke, dust, blood and army colours trudging through the destruction; lines of tanks, burnt-out cars and buses, disfigured metal structures bent into excruciating positions. This was where everything died: human and material objects alike, nothing was saved. I was just a spark, a rip, a slip away from joining the seemingly endless oblivion that surrounded me. In one way, I had never been so frightened in all my life, but it was a different kind of fear to before; more mature, more accepting, as if I had finally thrown off the last vestiges of my veneer of comfort and security in the face of reality. There was nothing worth saving in this city, no value left. At that moment I couldn't imagine anything that could be called the future.

There were no bridges left over the river, they had either been destroyed by the Russian bombardment or blown up by the Germans who had retreated to the Castle in Pest for the final stage of the siege. Driving down by the river, my thoughts turned to the Hatvany house. If this was the level of destruction in Pest what could possibly be left on the other side of the river where the fighting was at its most violent. Could anything have survived? Both the Chain bridge and the Freedom Bridge, which I had once crossed with Ferenc and Horváth in the beautiful cream and red Mercedes, had been reduced to book ends. The stone and steel towers still rose on either side of the river, but the chains slumped into the water, no longer reaching tautly over it. It was as if the bridge, once a symbol of hope and connection, had been repurposed as an underwater passageway, as if the time of humans had come to an end and a new being was reworking all that remained to new functions.

The Russians had constructed a pontoon bridge of around forty floats laced together. This allowed us to cross the river. We crawled along at a snail's pace, lined up behind military jeeps, ragged pedestrians and starving horses. I was held aloft as the winter sun shone heartlessly, freezing my extremities, the end of my impasto brushstrokes. Everyone stared at me and broke into smiles as I was held aloft. Bare genitalia fluttering in the breeze. Was I a symbol of something positive in this

69

valley of desolation? All of a sudden, I was no longer afraid. The pontoon was swaying precariously beneath us. Just one slip of his freezing fingers and I would have been dropped into the river, already full of floating debris: masonry, wood, rocks, the upturned faces of dead horses with their wide, lifeless eyes staring vainly at the February sky and human body parts trailing thin lines of blood behind them, floating, lightening in colour from blood red to baby pink and diluting in the thick, dark mass of the river.

"Long live the cunt! Long live the cunt!"

He screamed it out as we passed groups of soldiers, some carrying comrades with missing arms and shattered legs and they paused in their pained misery to look up and answer back: "Yeah!! Go on! Long live the cunt, fuck the fascists!"

It was a revelation for me, I had been created to be unseen, to be viewed by only a select few and even then, very rarely. Yet here I was, being viewed openly, by everyone: what was this? Was this liberation or was it exploitation? I felt equal amounts of terror and exhilaration as the freezing air licked my paint. Nearly all the soldiers had paintings or other portable works of art folded up and stuffed into their pockets or down the legs of their trousers. What was so special about me that I should become their flag, their totem? What is it to be a flag anyway, to be a symbol in a world that has disintegrated into the chaos of a moral vacuum?

Below me a young captain with a hairless, youthful face and dull grey eyes was negotiating with the guy next to him for a painting by Dürer. He had already offered his belt and two broken wristwatches, which he had produced from inside his jacket, but the younger soldier was holding firm. The man clutching the Dürer wanted the belt, the watches and his boots or it was no deal. "But these are really good boots, are you crazy? These are really good boots!" It went on and on like this as we turned right onto dry land, weaving in between roadblocks constructed from the rubble of collapsed buildings. On our left, the rock of the Castle district rose sharply over us and on our right, I saw the river view of bombed-out Pest. As the argument continued I wondered, who was the genius and who was the fool? What is more important when the world starts to burn: a painting that had once been considered priceless (and would be again) or a really good pair of boots? I wondered if the earnest young man would regret the deal even if it came off. If you freeze to death on a Russian transport train heading East nursing your frostbitten toes, or get blood poisoning from infected blisters, what good is a priceless Dürer to you? Is it not just something else that can be stolen from your weakened body at the point of a knife or a barrel of a gun? In the end he settled for the Dürer, a small Goya and a few sketches for the boots, the belt and the broken wristwatches. There was a man who genuinely believed in the value of art, for better or for worse. The other soldiers just laughed at him. One of them was holding up a curved 17th century Ottoman ceremonial sword, the jewels in the hilt glinting as he waved it about.

"I knight you, Sir Asshole." And he touched the sword lightly down on the shoulder of his companion, who rolled the Goya up and tried to hide it in an inside pocket of his coat. I wondered what would happen to that man with his Dürer and his Goya. I wondered if he ever made it home safely. I wondered what one does with stolen priceless art in a Communist country. I wondered what would be done with me.

As we passed Adam Clark Square the view to our left opened up and there, for the first time since I had come to Budapest over thirty years previously, I saw that the funicular was not working. Huge boulders of stones were lodged into the metal rails wrenching them out of the ground and twisting the ends up towards the sky. For some obscure reason this affected me more than anything else, more even than the bombed-out castle, the shell of which was still perched on the hill above us.

Why all this emotion for a funicular railway? Because it was unique? Because it had always worked, always fulfilled its Sisyphean task of lugging its carriages up and down that steep hill? Because it had once symbolised the progression of man, just as I, fluttering above this pointlessly destroyed city was the symbol of man's core baseness?

We turned onto Ferenc's street and I was able to see that what I had dreaded most had come to pass. I had a perfect view, waving above the soldier's head, of the gap where the Hatvany house once stood. There was nothing left to see. Where I once had lived, where the whole Hatvany family had lived in comfortable opulence, there was not a house anymore. In fact, there was barely even any rubble, some splinters of wood had slid down the hill and lodged near the bottom next to a solitary wall, supporting nothing, connected to nothing. I strained my eyes for any sign of Courbet's *Wrestlers*, but I saw no sign of canvas, no remnants of my fallen brother. Had they made it out intact in the end? By the side of the road there were lines of dishevelled humans in clothes blown to rags, picking through the bloodstained fur of dead dogs that littered the rubble. They were looking for remnants of their homes and families, scraping the dirt and the blood with their fingertips. Like them, I too would have to wait to find out what happened to those I cared about.

As we came over the top the hill on the other side we were stopped. An officer waved down the truck and barked at the driver. Despite his wearing a Russian uniform and speaking perfect Russian I was able to detect a Hungarian twang to his accent. He was hiding it well, but this man was from Budapest, no doubt.

"Ok, ok quieten down. Where are you lot going? This is a fucking war, not a Sunday morning drive in the country. Hey, you, yes, you. Take that fucking thing down."

"Yes, Sir," the Soldier with the black eyepatch who was still holding me aloft replied. "We were heading to Central Command at Atilla Street to check in with the rest of the regiment, Sir."

The officer with the Budapest accent didn't seem impressed. "Waving around a painting of a cunt as you go?" There was sniggering from the truck. The soldier with the eyepatch just shrugged cheekily. The officer glared at him. "Ok, give it here, you have had your fun."

"But Sir," the soldier with the eyepatch pleaded with as much of a mocking tone as he dared, "it is a portrait of my sweetheart, I always carry it with me." The truck broke out into peals of laughter and even the officer cracked a smile. A voice came from the passenger's seat of the truck, "I thought it was your mother!"

"Hey!"

"Fuck you."

"Ok, ok calm it down," said the officer with the Budapest accent. "Thank you, Sergeant. I will take that. Proceed and check in. As you were."

The car drove on and I remained in the hands of the officer who carefully unlaced me from the bronze staff. He smiled as he looked upon me with twinkling eyes and murmured to himself, "Hatvany or Herzog? Hatvany I think." In the back of his truck there were thirty or so cylindrical art tubes, he rummaged through them and held me up against one then another until he found one that was the correct length. Then he rolled me up delicately and slid me in. I was once more in the dark, once more for the eyes of the few and not the many. At least it was warmer there in the darkness, hidden from the eyes and hands of men.

Chapter 7

A year later I saw his face again. This time we were not alone. I was somewhere very familiar. I knew the voice even before he opened the tube. It was, of course, Endre. I was taken out of my tube and laid on a table. We were in the front room of Ferenc's apartment in Nádor Street, back in the same place I had been brought thirty-three years previously. Amazingly, the apartment looked very similar. Most of the furniture was the same and the windows were clearly new. The whole apartment had been replastered to hide any sign of bullet holes in the walls or bomb blasts. I should have known, this was the Hatvanys after all, the rest of Budapest still looked like a war zone but in Ferenc's house all had been put to order. There were tell-tale signs though, key differences. The main one was the lack of pictures on the walls, the lack of Ancient Grecian pots on the tables, the lack of tapestries hanging down. The desk was intact though and was standing where it had always stood, in the corner of the room. Behind it sat Ferenc, wearing a deep burgundy three-piece suit and smoking a cigar, looking like nothing untoward had happened at all. Likewise, Endre was his normal bustling self. He was spreading canvases on a set of large tables that had been placed in the centre of the room and Horváth was close behind him, pen and paper in hand making notes.

"Right, so what's your story then." Endre straightened up and looked straight at the officer with the Budapest accent who was now dressed in civilian clothes and had entirely dropped any hint of Russian from his voice.

"I explained all of this last week on the phone." He spoke in a low, calm, gentle voice that sounded the opposite of how I had heard him speak to the Russian soldier on that cold day in February. The change was so remarkable that I almost thought he must be a different person, except for the fact that he clearly was not. I assumed he must be some linguistical expert, a professional impersonator, an actor, or a spy. "I know someone who has amassed some pieces which he believes may be of interest to you," the man continued. "He asked me to intercede as a go-between as he would like to remain anonymous, for obvious reasons. However, he has given me a set of paintings that he wanted me to present to you and a list of further works that he can get for you should you desire. The price is not negotiable, I'm afraid, it is 10,000 florins per piece."

Endre snorted, "And you, what about you?"

"I am a lowly messenger, Sir. Nothing more. Think of me as a *bordárok*. The same occupation as my father. I am sure people such as you have never had need of people like me and my father but at the turn of the century, we were useful for all sorts of things.

"Say a gentleman had just arrived in the city in 1900 and needed a place to stay. We would offer our services the moment he stepped off the train. We would take him to a coffee shop, settle him down, collect his luggage from the station, find suitable lodging for the gentlemen, unpack, sort everything with the porter and represent him to any authorities (for instance a workplace or a place of study) to whom he may have had to present himself. All of this while the gentleman enjoys the paper and a leisurely coffee. For a small fee we would arrange all the tiresome details that come with travel. That is what I do now, more or less. Help gentlemen with any little problems they may have."

"I know what a *bordárok* is, thank you." Endre spat out this word with disdain. "And what makes you think we have any problems you can help with."

The ex-Russian officer gracefully waved his hand with an aristocratic limpness. "Bare walls, Sir."

Endre shot a dagger of a look at the man and then looked at Horváth who nodded at him.

"These are them, Endre. The Courbet is a bit damaged at the sides, but you would not even see it once it is framed."

"A misfortune, Sir, a slight casualty of the war," the officer said slyly. Endre just stared at him with look of intense disgust until the officer dropped his eyes to the floor, in feigned diffidence.

There were five paintings lying around the room: a large Delacroix, two Manets, a Renoir and me. I am not sure about anyone else, but my attention was fixed on Ferenc. He did not glance over at us, not even once. His feet were up on the desk and he was staring dreamily out of the window, blowing cigar smoke and watching it float into the air of the room. He didn't even react when Horváth placed the full list of paintings on the desk in front of him.

"Do you mind waiting outside for a moment." Endre signalled to the door with his eyebrows. The Russian officer nodded and left with a small bow, closing the door behind him.

"Well?" asked Endre. Ferenc just shrugged. "Are you really going to buy that bullshit, Ferenc? They are clearly his. Don't give me all this *bordárok* messenger shit."

"What does it matter, Endre? Just pay him."

"Fuck you, Ferenc. Where the fuck have you been throughout all this? Do you think this has been business as usual. Come on, get real." Ferenc looked up at him with drooping eyes, the look of a child who has been refused an ice cream. He didn't say anything. Endre strode over to the newly installed window and stared across at the apartment in the building opposite. It was bombed out, a windowless shell. You could see right through the building to the far side and there was nothing to see, just absence.

"What do you think, Horváth?" Endre said eventually.

János waved his hand back in a non-committal gesture and said, "I expect Ferenc would insist on at least seventeen. We couldn't move more than that anyway." Ferenc did not react to being discussed in the third person while he was in the room.

Endre exploded, "170,000 florins on art! Look at the fucking world. Are you fucking mad?!" János bowed his head and waited for this to pass. "I don't believe this. What the fuck do you think you are going to do with them, Ferenc? You do realise that we are basically controlled by a Soviet regime. You would need a permit to take them out of the country. You do know that, don't you? Ferenc? Oh, fuck it, this is a complete waste of my time. People are starving to death, struggling to survive out there, you know? Don't you have eyes? Don't you care?" Inevitably, there was no answer. He shook his head and continued to stare out of the window. Suddenly he spun round.

"Ok, fine. Fuck it. You can take 10 pictures. You pick them from the fucking list. The amount comes out of your allowance, any pictures you can't take with you when you leave revert to the company. I will try to send them abroad to you by other means, but any extra expense incurred by the firm from transportation comes out of your shares. Ok?" Once again there was no response. Ferenc did not even turn around to look at him. Endre snorted and continued, "Fine... János, you deal with that filthy liar out there. I have more important things to worry about than this." And with that he strode out, his coat flapping up behind him.

When he had gone and the door slammed, Ferenc slowly turned round and looked through the lists of painting names. He held the paper away from his face, smoking as he made his selection. Horváth came over and looked over his shoulder to see which ones he indicated. I was the first one he chose and that was how I came to be bought, for the second time, by Ferenc Hatvany.

Chapter 8

During those last months in Budapest, before Ferenc and I left for Paris, I was the only painting he hung up. He was a changed man, the essence seemed to have been sucked out of him. Like the shattered city around him he was just a shell; windowless and cold. It was no surprise; we were all changed by the war, we had all grown up. I too felt hollowed out, like a child who has stared too long at the inert body of a dead family pet until they can't even feel sorrow anymore, until all they see is his congealed-blood fur and the pink outline of organs that were once internal, hidden, now exposed.

Lucie was so pale and thin she looked as if she had died and been stuffed by a taxidermist. Her eyes seemed a duller shade of grey, they no longer darted over objects in her field of vision but languidly rested, unmoving and unemotional, her lips had thinned to a pencil line. She moved with the same elegant gait, but the bounce had gone out of her steps as if she no longer made contact with the solid ground anymore. She seemed to me as if she was hovering ethereally just above the earth. The first time I saw her back was the night they dined together with Czóbel. She wore a black open-backed dress. I knew there was an awful story to tell, a story she wasn't able to verbalise. I felt her silence, gagged by the atmosphere in the room, the male air. She told it the only way she, as a woman, was allowed, through her body, her skin. It was a story that they all knew, but no one dared mention.

She did as was expected of her and wore what they wanted, her splendid dress that complimented the gentlemen in their bow ties and tails, like some remnant of a time past that would never return. Ferenc and Lucie sat across the table from each other and ate in silence. Something had been broken between them that could not be fixed, or more aptly; something had been revealed, seen, which could never go back to being unseen. Some things are not for public view.

"You know I can't get you all out right away, don't you, Lucie?" Ferenc said. "But I will find a way; you and the children. Endre will look after you. It'll be fine. I will go to Paris, sell the pictures, raise money and get you out. I know the Communists are in charge, but they will take our money."

"I can help, Lucie," Czóbel added. "I have an exhibition in Switzerland in the fall. I will take some of the pictures that don't get an export permit and re-route them from there to Paris. It will only be a short amount of time, you'll see, Lucie. By next spring we will all be together, drinking Champagne by the Seine."

"Just be patient, my dear," Ferenc said supportively. Lucie did not say a word. She simply stood up, turned around to display the clear zig zag network of whip scars that went all the way from her superb pearl necklace down to the small of her back and left the room. Ferenc sighed. Czóbel just shrugged and looked up as if to Heaven. "What can you do?"

During those months Ferenc talked to me as he sketched. He told me the whole story, everything he did and did not do. I was the only person he could talk to, the only one who would not judge him, or at least that is what he thought. The night before the Germans had entered the city he had waited until his whole family were asleep, then he snuck out of the house in the middle of the night. It was Czóbel's idea, he said, he had just gone along with it. Czóbel had heard that the SS were going to take over Ferenc's house and turn it into a casino. He told me that he had no choice, he had to hide. He said he had the best intentions, if no one knew where he was going then no one could say anything to the

Germans when they arrived. He told me he thought he was protecting them, all of them: Lucie, Alexander, Alexandra, Marie and Antoinette. He told me with a pained smirk that as he was tiptoeing out the house that evening to flee, the thought struck him how ironic it was that the combination of his youngest childrens' names was Marie Antoinette. It had never occurred to him before. He said it brought a cold sweat to the back of his neck.

Czóbel was waiting for him just outside the gate. He owned a country house in Szentendre, a small town around 20km north of Budapest. He managed to get Ferenc false identity papers including an exemption certificate as an estate employee. Ferenc, who had never worked with his hands in his whole life was, officially at least, listed as a gardener. Czóbel stuffed him into the boot of his car (a sight I am very sorry I missed) and they drove out of Budapest to where the Danube splits. There Szentenbre sits on the turn of the river, less than an hour from Budapest and there Ferenc stayed, sleeping in the basement, both seen and unseen. As the two painters sat in the gardens, out of sight, painting the leaves that had fallen from the trees, I couldn't help wondering whether they were able to hear the trains rumbling by on the other side of the river. I wonder if they drove out to where the river splits, passing the railway lines and caught a glimpse of the cattle trucks that carried the hundreds of thousands of Budapest Jews who ended up in the Nazi death camps of Auschwitz? I wonder if he ever wondered whether Lucie and his children were on any of them. I wonder when it was that he discovered that his sister Irén and her husband Albert were crushed into one of those trains that passed so close by him as he painted in the late Autumn sunshine. They were gassed on arrival.

The SS did come to the Hatvany House. They came, as Czóbel had said, to turn it into a casino for SS officers and (of course) to search for money and art. Alexander escaped by jumping out of a first-floor window and rolling down the hill but Lucie and the girls were captured. It was at this part of the story that Ferenc would pause, his eyes would sharpen and he would lean closer to his sketching pad as if trying to fuse himself with the scratching sound of his pencil on the paper, to disembody himself, in some way, to spiritualise himself, dissolve into artistic line-marks on the blank sheet. Lucie had no information on her husband's whereabouts of course. She had no answers to their insistent questions. In that, at least, Ferenc was correct. They threatened her with deportation but to no avail because there was nothing she could say. In the end they hung her and her children up from meat hooks in the kitchen, starved them and whipped them repeatedly for four days, using the same efficient drainage system designed for the kosher slaughter of sheep to clean off the blood of the mistresses of the house. After those four days the officer in charge started to tire of the futility of it and, more importantly, Adolf Eichmann was due to arrive and didn't want Jews in the house when he was gambling, even if they were just dying ones in the basement. Lucie and the children were taken down and dumped at the gates of the ghetto.

The ghetto was across the river in Pest just a block south of Nádor Street. It was a sealed, fenced and guarded couple of blocks in which 70,000 Jews were left to die. Even when that did happen the bodies were not allowed to be removed so the dead lay on the street to spread typhus. The only way out was deportation to a camp, where they were to be killed more efficiently and cleanly. Lucie and the three girls were left on the street, the scars not yet formed on the wounds twisting down their backs. Once in the ghetto they were collected by the ghetto police, which was run by the Jewish Council. They were led to a single room which already had a family of five living in it. The family stared hard at them as they were dumped in their corner of the room. When the ghetto gendarmerie had left, the wife of the other family spoke to them. She told them she was in charge of the room. She explained where their corner ended. She told them that they had to keep their corner clean and with an afterthought of either human kindness or sanitary self-interest she advised them where they could get straw to sleep on.

On the first night three armed men came into the room and tried to rob them but there was nothing to take. They shouted at the girls and held a knife up to Lucie's throat. "Where is your baggage, where is your wedding ring, where is the money, come on, newbie!" Soon they realise that there was nothing to take. Lucie had nothing left to give. The men left. The mother of the other family told them these men went round, room to room. She said Lucie should report the incident to the Council, they shouldn't let other Jews get away with this. Lucie just shrugged. The girls wept loudly until they were told to shut up, then they sobbed more quietly.

The rumour was that the war was ending. Everyone just had to hold tight and not die. The Russian bombardment of the city had begun and after only a few weeks in the ghetto their whole block was being moved to a transit camp just outside the city. It was freezing cold as they waited outside the gate in lines for hours on end. Eventually as they passed under the guarded red gates of the camp, they were checked against the ghetto record lists. A Hungarian boy of eighteen took their names. Checking on his list he drew Lucie and her children aside from the queue. They were made to wait three more hours as it grew dark by the side of the entrance. The lists were checked and double checked. As they had never formally been registered in the ghetto, so they didn't appear on the transit lists. Lists of names, the bureaucratic equivalence of existing, of being seen, were complete but they were not on them, how could they exist? Not on the list, but physically present. After another hour they were taken to a hut and given a bunk.

It was a race against time. The Budapest Council were working with the Hungarian police trying to slow the deportations to the extermination camps while Eichmann and the SS were trying to speed them up. All the while Russian bombs were falling. The end was in sight. The rumour in the camp was that it was to be liquidated and all of them would be sent north to the death camps in Poland. For days all Lucie and the girls could hear was the rumble of the trains and the explosion of bombs. A further layer of hell was coming. This, however, was not to be her fate. Just a day before the camp was liquidated in its entirety a Hungarian officer turned up in a jeep with two crates in the back. The crates were taken out and replaced by Lucie and her children. The officer drove them away from the camp, east out of Budapest towards Gödöllő Hills which lay between Budapest and the ancestral home of Hatvan, where they used to spend happy summers. This was where Ferenc had learned to hunt as a small boy with Lajos and their father. This was where they would come as a family to picnic when her children were small, to walk through the trees and allow the children to paddle in the clear streams or pick flowers in the hot Hungarian summers.

All of a sudden, she was there again; the forests of oak trees were the same, the alders that grew uniquely in these forests were still there, the meadows of grass lands, the crocuses, the yellow blind-nettle. The plants were all still there as if nothing was happening, as if nature was totally oblivious to the unnatural acts of man just a few kilometres away. As they pulled into a clearing in the midst of a thickly clumped bunch of beech trees at the intersections of two paths that made the sign of a cross, Lucie later told Ferenc that she took solace from the calm of the place. If she and her girls were going to be shot anywhere in the world, she thought, this would be the place for it, that this, at the very least, was a blessing of sorts, a consolation. The officer driving the jeep wordlessly helped them out and led them to a black car, whose engine was running. He opened the back door and there in the front seat was Horváth and Endre. Endre looked at her with a smile and held up a piece of paper. It was the updated register from the transit camp with her name and the childrens' names underlined neatly. He only said one word: "List."

*

Endre found the rest of them, he found all who were still alive to be found. He eventually tracked down Ferenc. By the end of the war, he was living in Rósa Pilisy's brothel in Magyar Street, which ironically abutted the outer wall of the Jewish Ghetto's south side. Thus, in an unsavoury irony, husband and wife were close enough that they could have shouted over the wall to each other, had they known. Yet the difference in the living standards of the man and the women of the

Hatvany family could not have been starker. One similarity, however, was that they were both prisoners of their hosts. For while Lucie was locked in behind barbed wire and high walls, Ferenc was imprisoned by the extortionately high bill he had run up at the brothel and was stuck there until relieved financially. This is where, predictably, Endre came in. He found Ferenc relaxing in an easy chair in the Arabian sitting room, sketching while partially naked girls walked by dressed in faux Ottoman outfits, like a war-rationed distasteful parody of Delacroix's orgiastic *The Death of Sardanapalus*, a painting Ferenc had always loved and had even tried to purchase from the English collector John Wilson.

"Right, come on, Ferenc. Enough of this. Rósa can I have the bill please....? What the fuck! Ferenc, how long have you been here? Are you fucking mad? Do you even know where Lucie and the girls are, do you even care? What is wrong with you man?"

"I had to leave Czóbel's when the Germans pulled out and started moving north." Ferenc pleaded, "They were swarming around the place like bees. What was I supposed to do? I have been worried sick but what can I do?"

Endre flicked through the pages of itemised meals, drinks and whores in front of him; "Well, you don't look like you are worried sick!" Ferenc just waved a non-committal hand.

In a rare act of taking a stand, Endre refused to pay the debt from the firm's account, something that Ferenc repeatedly complained about. In the end they settled the bill with a (priceless) antique diamond necklace and earring set that had belonged to Ferenc's mother and that was one of the few valuable possessions that belonged solely to Ferenc, unconnected to the firm. Ferenc was furious.

"Where did you get that, Endre? I hid it in the house! That was to be kept for Alexander. It's going to be a wedding present for his wife when he is old enough to marry."

"What are you talking about?" Endre shouted. "There is no house, Ferenc. It was blown to pieces by the Germans. It is a good thing that you are too fucking useless to properly hide things, or this would have been blown to the moon. I looked after it for you, just as I have always looked after everything for you. This, however, is too far. I have never judged you or questioned you, not you, not Lajos, none of you. But this one time I will say it. This makes me sick. This is your debt and I am not going to pay it. So come up with another solution. Every debt needs paying, Ferenc, you never learnt that, or never wanted to. Every single one. Somehow."

It wouldn't have mattered anyway. Necklace or no necklace they never found Alexander. There was to be no wedding, no wife. He was only seventeen years old. But, as Endre said, every debt has to be paid.

Endre left no stone unturned. His effort was gargantuan. It was clear he was doing it for Lucie, not for Ferenc. People came in and out of Nádor street. Each had a different story. Some said Alexander had fought with them as part of an underground militia and had perished in the bombing of Budapest Castle. Some say they had seen him living hand to mouth in the street, hiding in shelled basements getting thinner and thinner until he died of hunger. A nurse from the hospital said he died from a fever, that it was a quick and painless death. They all traipsed in, told their story and filed out with their hands held forth for their payment. There was no definitive story and nothing left to bury, just a disembodied memory floating around the apartment like a phantom, hovering around the high ceilings, below which Lucie screamed uncontrollably with her girls crying next to her.

In the end it was unbearable, Ferenc said, he couldn't hear himself think, he couldn't hear himself breathe any more. He couldn't even find the space to grieve. He left Budapest in 1947 without his wife or his three daughters and without his beloved paintings, as Endre had predicted. However, thanks to an official (and frankly insulting) accreditation from the Hungarian cultural officials of '*no artistic value*' he was able to take me. Of course, it had to be me. It would be five years before Lucie and the girls got out, thanks more to the negotiating skills of Endre than the perseverance of Ferenc. In the end the Communists accepted a donation to the state for each family member. To Ferenc's credit the bill for his wife and three remaining children at least exceeded the ransom money he paid for his paintings.

I would love to describe my travels across Europe; the train pulling out of shattered Budapest and the sight of Paris coming towards me, the city of my birth. Sadly, however, we paintings rarely travel well, especially in terms of the view. I would also like to tell you that in some way I felt like I was special to him, that I was a substitute for his wife, for his mistress, Countess Maria Magdalena Bethlen, for the many whores of Rósa's brothel, or for all of the other girls he slept with. Maybe I believed it myself for a second, when I was younger, in those golden days before the war. But as we stuttered across Europe, lurching uneasily from checkpoint to border checkpoint, he smoked in the dining car and I rattled in the baggage hold. Maybe I did try to believe that he had picked me, that I was a surrogate for everything he needed in his life, that I was *exceptional* in some way. Maybe I wanted to kid myself so as to regain the comfortable certainty of past days, unrecoverable, so not to acknowledge the truth, which was that I was nothing more than transportable currency. If there is one thing I have learnt from living with humans it is that no matter how verbose their liberal rhetoric, when the shit hits the fan it all comes down to money. The war had wised me up to that at the very least.

Even so, it hurt that he didn't even unpack me when we got to Paris. It hurt that I never got to see the inside of his apartment, never gazed out the windows at the pink spring bloom of the Magnolia trees, never inhaled the deep smell of freshly baked bread wafting up from the boulangerie ovens. It hurt that he never stared at me one last time to say goodbye. It hurt that after all the sketching, all the intense looking, I was nothing to him, nothing more than a way of settling the bills. I suppose it was destiny in a way, a rendezvous that I had evaded eighty-one years previously when Constance hid me from Khalil. On our arrival at the Gare de L'Est I was transported directly to none other than the famous Hôtel Drouot auction house and checked into the same building where all of Khalil Bey's other paintings had been auctioned in 1868, the same building where Gustave Courbet's final possessions had been auctioned in 1877 and where, I would later discover, that Constance's furniture was auctioned in 1907. There I lay in storage until 1955.

By then Ferenc and Lucie had sold the remaining paintings that Czóbel had helped smuggle into France and the Hatvany family had moved to Switzerland. I am not sure if this is just a coincidence, or if, like elephants, wealthy humans have some kind of natural instinct to take themselves off to Switzerland when they get to a certain age, but Ferenc settled in Lausanne, twenty minutes up the lake from where Courbet had breathed his last. Like Gustave he would also have been able to take the twenty-five-minute trip up the mountain to the Chateau de Blonay. Did he ever go there, on the good days when his failing health allowed? Did Lucie take him up the hill to sit and look at the Chateau whose painting had once obscured me, the painting sold to his brother-in-law all those decades ago when old man Herzog was still alive, before his son was killed, before the war that destroyed their lives, before Alexander was bombed, shot, crushed, starved to death, died of fever? Is that what old men think of when their short, allotted time is nearly up? Or did he sit on the hillside and think of me, did the Chateau de Blonay become a substitute for me? Did he regret packaging me up and shipping me off to Drouot without even a goodbye, without even a final backwards glance? Or maybe he never went there at all, was Ferenc ever a man for a backward glance? Maybe not.

He died in 1958 and therefore could not attend Antoinette's marriage in Paris. It was quite the society do. There was much gossip of it in Jacques Lacan's summer house, which was where I was hanging at the time.

Apparently, the bride, the mother of the bride and both sisters wore very high-necked dresses that covered their whole back and arms, despite the wedding being on a sweltering day in the middle of summer. A very unusual dress design, it was noted.

Chapter 9

By 1955 Picasso was one of the most famous people in the world and artists like Courbet and Delacroix were seen as heralds, visionaries, geniuses living before their time. This was reflected in the value of their works. I was bought at auction for $1.5 million, which must have made Ferenc a packet, although by then he was probably too ill to enjoy it. Shame, if I had a head, I may have shed a tear. I do hope Endre heard about it, though. Considering they had bought the painting back from the ex-Russian officer for around $900, it may have given him a slight sense of pride in Ferenc right at the end. A good profit was something Endre admired above all else, so I expect even he had to concede that in the end I was a good deal.

I was bought by the famous psychoanalyst Jacques Lacan and his second wife, the film star Sylvia Bataille. By the 1950s, Lacan had truly made it. He had finished with his first wife, who had stood by him (and born him three children) as he had risen through the ranks of Paris intelligentsia. She was discarded pretty brutally when his friend Georges Bataille introduced him to Sylvia, his own wife, an actress. They were in the process of divorcing but in classic Parisian style they had somehow managed to break up on good terms. Lacan was immediately smitten with her, and very soon they had a child together. They bought a country mansion an hour north of Paris, in Guitrancourt and set about filling it with art and books.

Sylvia was the first example I had seen of a truly public woman. Until then the female role models in my life had been either partially or totally hidden: Constance who was forced by society to operate totally in the shadows to survive and Lucie who on the surface was emancipated but still ate her grand dinners in a ball gown, politely hanging on the inane words of whatever gentleman she had been sat next to. Yet what Sylvia represented was something that should have been new and different, progressive. Sylvia had been a celebrity in her own right, a public star. When she met Jacques, she had just starred as a lead in a Jean Renoir film and had been awarded the *Prix Suzanne Bianchetti* for most promising young actress. She had been in over twenty films. And yet despite this she had pretty much given up acting by the time I entered the family. She seemed to have relegated herself to her husband, shrunken herself underneath his growing presence as his fame sucked the air out of the relationship, like a vacuum. To the outside world she may have been a star to be envied but in my eyes, she was just another entry to her new husband's itinerary of owned objects, a symbol of all that had not changed.

And yet perhaps I had expected too much of her, too much of society. There was a photograph I saw of her once. It was from a film shoot where she had posed topless in the snow. I couldn't connect this image with the dour, tartan-skirt wearing, buttoned-up woman that I knew. Was her fame just another male fantasy, just another exploitation. I searched deeply in that image for a sense of her, a sense of her power as a human being but I couldn't find it. I was left cold with an eerie sense of that photo. In it she is lying in the snow with her breasts uncovered, perfect and voluptuous, totally naked from the tip of her head to her waist. On her bottom half she is wearing a pair of what look like skiing trousers with a thick belt. Her long slender arms are lifted above her head, displaying her armpits, and overlap each other over the top half of her face, covering her eyes and her forehead. Her mouth is slightly open and the angle of the camera shows her nostrils as two large, black caves that, in my view at least, dominate the picture. Is it those nostrils that make me feel close to Sylvia in that photo, a Sylvia long gone by the time I met her; those black holes like the ones that once punctuated my face, in a lost memory from long ago? Was I searching her for shadows of myself, or more accurately of Constance. I don't think so, it was something else, it was the way the arms covered her face, hiding her eyes from public view, that struck me as a déjà vu. It was if, in this exploitative image of absolute exposure, she had an instinctual desire to hide away, to try and cover her face. I felt I had seen that image before, as if it was seared onto my subconscious, like when you come across an old black and white photograph of a great great grandparent who you have never met but somehow recognised. For a man it may be a pose of titillation but for me it was the posture of shame. To me it looked like she wished the pristine snow would swallow her up, wished she didn't even have a face or even upper body at all, if only to reduce herself to what she was for these male viewers: just a pair of breasts, one next to another.

Chapter 10

Lacan was a horrible looking man. I disliked him the moment I saw him. He had a deeply lined face that pinched at the bottom into a double chin. It was long and rectangular, with big protruding ears that made his head look disproportionally large when compared to the rest of him. He wore his white hair back but naturally it was thick, so it tended to sweep up from his forehead before going back, which only accentuated the length of his face. By contrast his eyebrows were thick and bushy. They sprouted out over the top of his rimless glasses, making him look a little like an evil German scientist. Many people said that his eyes were lively and interesting, but the way they were sunken deeply into his darkened sockets gave him a generally malignant appearance. A few years previously he had been the President of the Paris Psychoanalytic Society but had left after a dispute with the institution and founded his own rival society. This, eventually, would form the basis for what would be the Lacanian school of Psychoanalysis. His weekly public seminars had become one of the central events for Parisian intellectual society, always packed beyond capacity, with disappointed queues snaking out the door and devoted acolytes hanging on his every word. In short, he was your typical egotistical white male, with a twinkle in his eyes that some took for benign charm, but which froze me to the core.

He had apartments on the Rue De Lille on the south bank in Paris; the road that runs from the famous, once all powerful Academy of

Painting and Sculpture (whose Salon was such a bane of Courbet's life) to the Gare D'Orsay train station. This was where Lacan did most of his work during the week and saw his patients. The country house in Guitrancourt was for luscious parties and weekend living. As he got older and even more eccentric the two places blended into each other, with more and more patients coming out to Guitrancourt for treatment. However, at the beginning, in the 1950s and 60s, the working week was Paris and the party weekend was Guitrancourt. I was bought for Guitrancourt and although I eventually did end up residing in the Paris flat it was not until after Jacques died, and I became the possession of Sylvia.

The house at Guitrancourt was a beautiful 18th century courthouse with lovely gardens and ivy climbing up the back wall. In the summer there were large parties and Sylvia used to put up awnings in the gardens by the back of the house. There were round tables set up in a semi-circle around a stage, like tables at a cabaret. The centre of the show was always Jacques, who would prowl around whilst people ate. His behaviour was frankly bizarre; he would talk at people, sometimes he would not even use words and just make random grunting or screeching sounds. He would jump about like he was a circus performer or a clown. He would hide behind bushes or trees and then leap out at people to scare them, before running off in peals of childish laughter. Often, he would come out of the house dressed up in his favourite fancy dress, a full owl costume representing wisdom, and stand in the centre of the tables making owl noises all through dinner. You could see people who did not know him well look from one to another as they ate, trying to work out if he was for real, or if the joke was somehow on them. His more eccentric friends would join in and soon groups of them would act out plays in costume or put on grand dances where partners were swapped around.

Adjoining the house was a separate loggia which the previous owners had used as a painting studio and which Jacques called the aquarium. Sylvia converted it into an office for Jacques to work. It had a great bay window overlooking the whole garden and light streamed in at all hours of the day. When lunch was served outside on sunny days, the doors to the aquarium were opened up so that the indoor, where I was hanging and the outdoor became one space. Soon after buying the house Sylvia had a mezzanine built that was reached by walking up an iron spiral staircase. All around this overhanging level were bookshelves filled to the brim with thousands of books, Japanese prints, Chinese scrolls and glass fronted cabinets of curiosities displaying rare Chinese fans, terracotta figurines from Ancient Rome, pre-Colombian ceramics, Egyptian sculptures and statues. In the downstairs area where he saw his patients the walls were covered with works by Picasso, Monet, Renoir, Balthus and Giacometti. It was a museum dedicated to three things: Jacques' cultural learning, Jacques' newly-found wealth and Jacques' love of ownership. Everything and everyone in the whole wide world was, to Jacques, just a thing for him to own. I am jumping ahead of myself but of all the great things said about Jacques Lacan, all the books subsequently written about him that laud his genius, the best description I ever heard of him was shouted in anger by his brother Marc-François Lacan who, of all things, was a dedicated Monk of the Abbey de Hautecombe. It was the only time in all the decades I knew this pious man that I had ever heard him raise his voice:

"You want to own women, Jacques. You were always possessive, ever since you were a child and you are still that child. You have never realised that women are not *nothing*, they are not just *things* to collect! For all your genius and foresight you have never acknowledged the otherness of women. Marriage is an alliance modelled on God. Through relationship the individual is formed and the otherness of both the man and the woman is preserved. You have missed out on this, Jacques. I pity you, but more than that, I pity all the women you collect and use and destroy and leave in your wake."

Amen to that! Through all those psychoanalytical sessions that I was forced to listen to, all those affairs where Jacques groomed and fucked his patients, his friends, his employees, his mistresses and his wives on

93

that desk or that couch, down the spiral stairs, or against the bookshelves that made the mezzanine shake and volumes fall to the floor, I always thought of his brother and wished that I would one day be left to that man after Jacques' death. It was probably for the best that I was not. I don't suppose I would be considered acceptable wall-hanging material in a Benedictine monastery.

Jacques originally wanted to hang me in the mezzanine, but from the start Sylvia objected to me being put on display. When I first arrived, Jacques swung me around the room, holding me at arm's length as if he were taking me for a waltz around the dance floor.

"Come on, Sylvia," he squealed, "why not? Can't you see this painting is the ideal symbol of my whole philosophy. This is at once the *Thing* and the absence. It is perfect. I have been showing mirrors to my patients for all these years simply because I did not possess this. Now we can throw all the mirrors away, every one of them. Let's do it now, throw them all away. Not a mirror in the house. I forbid it. From this day onwards! This here is the only mirror I need. I need it here, on my desk or right there on the wall so I can thrust it in the face of every patient. No, wait, I need to have a special case made, I need to be able to carry it back and forth, I need it with me at all times. This painting is my everything!"

Sylvia patiently waited until he had paused for breath, gazing at him like an indulgent mother. She talked softly with that slight lisp of hers that elongated her words, dragging them out into the air.

"Come on, Jacques, it's a scandal. The neighbours and the cleaning lady wouldn't understand."

"I can make them understand," And he did *make* the cleaning woman understand, the bastard, one winter's day when Sylvia was out of the house. He grabbed the poor woman as she cleaned around him and forced her, face down, onto the table with his hand pushing violently into the centre of her back. I always wondered how much Sylvia knew of these things. Maybe she knew and bit her tongue or maybe she was blissfully ignorant. I am not sure which shows her in a worse light.

"Look, Jacques," Sylvia continued, "I will give it to André and he can make a case for it, just give it to me. Now, please. I will speak to André about it. I will bring it back soon, you'll see, it'll be back soon." She carefully coaxed me off him and he gave in with a huff.

"Fine then," he said slumping into a chair so that his belly fell over his thighs, stretching at his white shirt. "Bring me Champagne and caviar. And send for the pedicurist. I want my nails done now."

"Jacques, it's a Sunday."

"But I want it!"

As with most powerful men who sleep with many women, Jacques was not objectively attractive, far from it. Women talk of charisma, electricity, dynamism but I have always struggled to understand what these things really are. What did people see in him that was attractive? It couldn't be his physical attributes; he had a stout body with a belly that was starting to droop over his belt. When he smiled his dimpled chin and stretched lips fanned his features out in a cartoonish manner; infantile and playful. When he frowned everything was drooped and deeply lined, dragging his face down to the ground with a severity that spread a depressed greyness over the room. It couldn't have been any sense of style: he wore terrible suits with garish bow ties, checked sporting jackets with polo neck shirts, the most expensive bespoke boots fitted and sent over from London; none looked right on him. Everything about him was designed to be contrary. He smoked a particular cigar, a corkscrew-shaped Punch Cuelebras, not the one that everyone else smoked. He had to have a particular whiskey in a particular type of glass, this whiskey not that one. He wanted this chocolate from this patisserie not that one. If you didn't have it, get it sent for. If it was impossible, he cried and tantrummed like a six-year-old.

I have heard him turn on the famous Lacan charm (more times than I would like) and he was very successful with it, but to my ears it was overdone as if learnt by rote from a film, trowelled on, like a young child on a manic sugar high. The Lacan I knew was in his mid-fifties, I can only say I am glad I did not know him when he was younger, although

I have a sneaking suspicion that he was not that different. He became more and more successful with younger and younger women as he got older so you could argue that he matured with age and became more attractive. I would say he grew richer, more powerful and more famous so his relationships became less and less equitable and more exploitative, something only his brother had the courage to point out.

As far as I was concerned, however, Sylvia won and I was taken away to be carefully measured. I can still see her long fingers hovering over me, tape in hand, her delicate and gentle movements, those famous black eyes that held a glint of some deep sadness juxtaposed, as they were, by the severe whiteness of her complexion. Those were the eyes that could not bear to look on the photographer who took that nude photograph of her. I was then sent away to the South of France to be framed by her brother-in-law, the surrealist painter André Masson.

André Masson was married to Sylvia's sister. He was also a friend of her first husband George Bataille and of Dona Maar, who Lacan had "treated" in the 1940s with (illegal) electroshock treatment after her messy break up with Picasso. André made a wooden frame designed just for me. Like my *Chateau du Blonay* box there was a catch system with a false back into which I slid perfectly. Once in, I was totally covered by a wooden panel on which he had carved a figurative white lined image of me as a landscape. He scratched sketchily, creating the effect against the black grains of the wood and the lighter brown contrasting background, so that if you knew what you were looking for you could make out an outline of me, but if you didn't it just looked like a random drawing. One side of the case folded out with a hinge and inside was an invisible clasp which released the panel so I could be slid out for the big reveal – ta da!

He thus made me twice removed from my Lacanian essence: it was at once a surrealist depiction of me and a realistic rendition of the *Thing*. It would take me many years to understand all these psychoanalytical notions and if the truth be told I am still not sure I get some of them even now. Had I been alive and in his presence, I am sure Lacan would

96

have labelled me as another of the 'idiots' that infuriated him so much. But whatever the highfalutin theory they wanted to read into what was essentially an updated box, I was once again hidden behind a wooden panel, once again concealed. Seen and unseen.

Chapter 11

Jacques was the type of person who was either entirely interested in something or not at all; he abhorred the middle ground, the prosaic and ordinary, the average and the non-extreme. He was fixated on the present moment and had the tendency to disregard the past and refuse to acknowledge the future, especially when facts or past events didn't suit him. This lent an intensity to him, an excessive, manic one. This is not to say that he was always distracted, the opposite in fact, when something grabbed him (an idea, a book etc.) his powers of intense concentration were equally extreme. He could sit for hour upon hour reading and writing with no reaction at all to the outside world. If, for instance, he was engaged in a book or in some work and a lunch had been planned that he had to attend, he would walk from the aquarium across the garden to the dining room still carrying the book, sit down, eat and then leave without taking his eyes from the pages and totally ignoring the other people around the table. However, if he were to pause his reading for some reason, he would immediately snap back into the atmosphere of the gathering and engage overwhelmingly with those around him, dominating the conversation totally. So, it was no surprise that when André delivered me in my new frame he hardly looked at it or at me. In that moment his mind was elsewhere. André showed Sylvia how to slide open and close the panel demonstrating how I could be entirely hidden behind his carving. Everyone around the table was impressed, it even got a little round of applause. Jacques never raised his eyes from his papers, there was not a word. I was then hung up by the spiral stairs on the mezzanine level in a space between two bookshelves and left in the dark.

At the beginning, when he remembered that I existed, Jacques would show me to some of his patients, but this was very rare and I was certainly never carried with him to Paris. Around this time, he was in a bitter feud with the Psychoanalytic establishment in Europe over the length of his sessions. The rule established in the 1940s and enforced all over Europe was that each patient should receive fifty-minute psychiatric sessions four or five times a week with a programme of treatment lasting around four years. Lacan's cost was high even amongst his peers. Sessions with him cost between one hundred and five hundred francs, sometimes, if he thought he could get away with it, he charged even more. I quickly understood how his extravagant lifestyle was paid for and my mind, as it often does, shot back to Endre: these margins would have impressed even him.

Although he initially started with the fifty-minute sessions pretty soon Jacques began to shorten his sessions dramatically. When other psychiatrists complained that he was giving this new burgeoning industry a bad name, Jacques just argued and swore at them. He was having none of this and was not a man to back down. Soon an impasse was reached and Jacques broke from the official Paris Psychoanalytical Society and started shortening the sessions to as little as twenty minutes (without reducing the cost, of course). He claimed that this experimentation was for psychoanalytic reasons, however a convenient by-product was that he could see many more patients each day and hence got richer and richer.

The theory of analysis, as far as I understand from years of observation, is to allow the patient a safe space to transfer their unconscious desires or frustrations onto a silent Other (the doctor). The patient is coaxed into playing out (transference) their repressed emotional relationship (standing in for their relationship with their

Mother, Father etc.) or desire as part of the therapy. The doctor's role in this is to creates a safe space for this transference to play out. His role, therefore, is that of a safe and non-judgemental cypher. This replaying of the repressed relationship should allow the patient to come to terms with their emotions in a safe, proxy environment. This way they can learn to recognise the emotions they are feeling, thus becoming conscious of them. Of course, the patient has repressed his or her emotions for good reasons and therefore the subconscious fights against this transference with all its might.

In these early days of psychoanalysis, there were stories of monk-like doctors who allowed themselves to be spat at day in day out for years, screamed at and even assaulted, whilst they restrained any reaction or judgement. This allowed their patients to release their pent-up anger and recognise it. I must say I never witnessed Lacan showing this level of martyred calm or taking any such abuse. That was definitely not his style, despite him lecturing widely that it was what a good psychiatrist should do. On the few occasions I did hear his patients lash out at him he was more likely to tell them that they were 'fucked' than turn the other cheek. Like every other unorthodox position he took, he justified this unconventional, unprofessional (and probably psychologically damaging) response as an attempt at shocking the patient into revelation. As with most of the crap Lacan spoke, it was lapped up by his disciples as gospel.

His justification regarding the short sessions was that these were also a way of frustrating or unbalancing the patient which he claimed would benefit their treatment, because he (apparently) was careful to halt the sessions on certain words which would *reactivate their unconscious desires.* He disagreed with a set time limit for psychoanalytical sessions because for him the patient's *moment of truth* (essentially one's death) *was approached through counting.* This, he argued, could lead to an obsessional marking of time, that culminated in counting for counting's sake as a way of establishing control. Counting, therefore, could become an end in itself; a form of procrastination, a thing in itself that one became a slave to, like a tic, an obsession. His theory was that if you conducted set session lengths the patient subconsciously counts out the minutes of their session, or the number of sessions and this gives them a feeling of control. Lacan argued he was disrupting this by terminating the session unexpectedly, thus catching the patient off guard. And so it was said and so it was analysed and written into gospel by his acolytes.

After all the wasteful words had evaporated into the air and there were no other humans left in the room, we all remember how Jacques would lock the door. He would take out the piles of money that he had nonchalantly thrown into his desk drawer, giving the patient the impression that money meant nothing to him. However, in the fading light of the evening, on his own behind his locked door, he would carefully smooth out each note, caressing it between his palms. He organised the coins in piles, he sorted the bank notes by denomination and turned them all so the portraits printed on them faced the same way up, murmuring 'hmm Hugo' at the image of Victor Hugo on any 500 franc notes he came across. Finally, he would settle back and count them all again, smoothing the notes out, over and over for an hour at least, sometimes more. When I first arrived he would try to fulfil this guilty pleasure in private but as he aged and was less and less able to spend any time by himself he would start doing it more openly, counting the larger and larger piles of money that flowed out of the sessions that got shorter and shorter until they lasted for only minutes sometimes or even seconds: one word only sometimes, one hundred and fifty francs please. Ker-ching.

In the 1950s and apropos of nothing he moved me down to the lower floor. He then developed the habit of walking over to where I hung whilst the patient was talking. Carefully he would lift me off the wall, walk over to where the patient sat or lay on the couch and, whilst the poor patient was in mid-sentence, Lacan would pull back André's panel and thrust me right up to the face of the astounded patient, so close that I could feel their breath on my paint. Often, they would scream out in shock and little droplets of saliva would drop on my thighs and my pubic hair before Jacques would violently slide the panel back across and carefully replace me on the wall as if nothing had happened. He did this over and over for decades. It was like I was living in a perpetual horror movie. My days were filled with close-up faces of people screaming in shock, their skin taut in terror, their jaws open and their eyes wide in their sockets. Over and over again. How could one ever find any calm living like that. It was a nightmare.

Thankfully, by the 1970s he had grown bored of these elaborate tricks and resorted to baser methods. Once a patient came in and sat down on the couch while Lacan was busy sketching a page of those knots that would obsess him in his later years. Without looking up from his pad he calmly said,

"This is the start of the session, you may begin." And before the patient could utter a word he screamed at the top of his voice: "NOW GET OUT!"

He proudly drove his beloved white Mercedes (a descendent of Ferenc's car) with no thought of any other road user, speeding manically and completely ignoring red lights. When Sylvia cried on his sleeve about this, he proudly stated that the laws of the road simply did not apply to him, that his time was too precious. Unsurprisingly he had two serious car crashes in his life but no matter what injury he suffered his attitude did not change, as if the reality of the outside world did not have any effect on his imagined image of himself. He loved dangerous sports like skiing, even after he broke his legs by irresponsibly launching himself down pistes that he was no way good enough to tackle.

Why did no one question his complete avoidance of personal responsibility, his incessant affairs and his wildly paranoid secrecy, justified by his insistence that his enemies were always watching, copying him? How could the people around him not see his almost inhuman capacity for concentration which in later life turned into the obsessional repetition of arbitrary tasks and tics? How did they not diagnose his inability to truly empathise with other people most of whom he regarded merely as objects whose sense of being he totally disregarded along with anyone he classified as an idiot or an 'underling', which turned out to be most people.

The simple answer is that he was an extremely rich white man and a clever one at that, whose ability to theorise and construct narrative explanations led to the formation of a loyal set of disciples who worshipped his every word. What would be classified as megalomaniacal egotism in most (and certainly any woman) was canonised in him as wisdom. Against him there was to be no dissent and anyone who questioned him was immediately classed as an idiot and an enemy. As he said himself, there is no such thing as dialogue. Dialogue is deception. The deception contained in the idea of 'dialogue' resides in the fact that there is never any exchange between two individuals. There may be a reciprocal exchange of objective information or communication of facts, but this is a juxtaposition of monologues. To my late teenage mind, sucking up these exciting new ideas like a sponge, this struck me as a pathological lack of interpersonal empathy.

With women he was even worse! He either treated them with excessive kindness, gallantly, as if he was acting a role in a film; or disregarded them completely as non-humans. "There is no such thing as a sexual relationship." I remember him still holding another woman's panties in his hand whilst screaming at Sylvia who had unexpectedly walked in on them, "Women don't exist!" It was a staggering symbol of his super-human arrogance that despite locking the door to count his money he never did it when he was having sex with people other than his wife. To me, in the midpoint between childhood and adulthood Jacques Lacan represented everything that was wrong with this patriarchal society. Would I have been as harsh on him had I know him when I was much younger or much older? I don't know, but we are always at our most furious and sure of ourselves (superficially at least) during our teenage years.

The only one who I ever heard speak truth to him and be accepted was his brother. Soon after I was installed, Jacques was trying to widen support for his new Psychoanalytical movement. He had written to the

Communist Party trying to show how his teaching would sit with Communist doctrine. They ignored his overtures, so he changed tack. The next time his brother came to stay with him Jacques saw his chance to widen his horizons.

"Look, I really think this work I have been doing is revolutionary stuff," Lacan shouted at him, despite the two men sitting close enough to each other to whisper. "It fuses with all aspects of society. I have written a presentation of my new theories framed around the central importance of the individuals' relationship to truth. This, at its heart, is what psychoanalysis is about. It is not about curing people, that is for doctors and death. I don't cure people; I mine their subconscious for the truths they are repressing. This is the core of my approach: truth, above all truth. Me, the truth, I speak!"

His brother, still dressed in his habit, wiped the bit of spit that the over excited Jacques had released across the desk and that had landed on his cheek. Slowly he raised his face, clapped and then softly got up, "Brother, I love you deeply, but I am afraid I am not used to these late hours. In the Monastery we retire to bed early and rise early. As fascinating as your, well, now two-hour lecture concerning the essence of truth was, I think I may be done for the night."

"But you haven't answered my request."

"Jacques, you haven't asked for anything. You have just talked at me."

"Oh, right. Yes, well. So, you understand that if truth is my core, then effectively, we are the same, you and I. Truth is religion's core as well and you are a Monk so… Well, I thought, seeing as I am in Rome in a few weeks you could call the Pope and arrange an audience for me so that we can bring our union ever closer."

"The Pope!" His brother laughed. "What do you think? That I have the Pope's phone number? Do you think I am the holder of the Papal diary. I am a lowly monk in a small Abbey in the south of France. The Pope has no idea who I am."

"Well, he might not know you, but I am sure he knows *me*. I am Jacques Lacan."

"Of course, dear brother. You are the great revealer of the Truth, right. Jacques, don't be offended but you are lying to the Psychoanalytical Society about the length of your sessions. You haven't told your first wife, and the three beautiful children you had with her, about Sylvia (who you have not even married yet) and your daughter with her, Judith. Your first three children have a half-sister they don't even know exists because of your lies. You are lying to both women about the many affairs you are having, and this is despite both of their unwavering loyalty and support for you.

"Your patients are suffering to their core. They look to you for help and guidance, but you wouldn't think twice about seducing them if you can, which is a vagrant abuse of power. You are lying to me about wanting to be a better Christian just as you are lying to the Communist party about your atheism. With all this you claim your life's central tenet is supposed to be the revelation of truth." He paused for a moment and stared at Jacques before continuing, "My advice is this: forget the Pope, forget all your theories classifying the core of what is Truth. Just try to be a bit less cruel to those around you, those who love you deeply. And go to bed earlier, you look tired."

With that he left the room. Jacques just pulled his face down, puffed out his cheeks and shrugged his shoulders with a typically French bof. I don't think he understood one word of it. It simply didn't relate to his worldview, which for Jacques Lacan, meant it didn't relate to the world.

Chapter 12

After getting bored of using me as a cheap shock tactic with patients he went through a phase of pulling me out as an after-dinner amusement. It generally followed the same pattern; the guests would be led to the aquarium after lunch or dinner where he would invite them to express their delight and congratulate him on his impressive collection of treasure as they sauntered from one to the other, oohing and aahing appreciatively at all the other works of art. Then, suddenly, they would arrive in front of me. With a boyish grin that wrinkled his cheeks and a flick of the wrist, he would pull me out from behind Masson's painted frame eliciting a scream or a jump of shock whereupon he would reduce himself to peals of high-pitched laughter. My life was reduced, therefore, to large periods of darkness punctuated by sudden light, more close-up faces drawn into horrified expressions for a brief moment and then darkness again. I, once again, existed solely to shock and titillate, in the same way a bright close-up shot of a contorted face flashes onto the screen unexpectedly in a slasher movie, causing a jump. This was my life for nearly twenty-five years: a horror movie that I was made to live through for a quarter of a century, shredding my nerves, obliterating any remaining respect I had for humanity and instilling in me a deep fear of day light that I cannot shake to this day. It is for this reason that the softer experiences stand out, like that of Dona Maar and her new (much younger) friend, James Lord, from whom, so said the gossip, she was inseparable.

It was a lovely May afternoon, quite soon after I had been installed in the aquarium, back in the days when I treasured the spring sunshine. I was still getting used to the new routine, still getting to know Jacques Lacan and the serious psychological horror torture that was to come had yet to be inflicted on me. Dona Maar was a regular visitor to the house for Sunday lunch and she had been given the *L'Origine du monde* shock treatment on her first visit after my arrival. However, this was James Lord's first and only visit to the house. He was a writer and an art lover; he was also a friend of Picasso, through whom he met Dona, and he would later go on to write a biography of Giacometti. Dona was friends with Sylvia Lacan back from when she was married to George Bataille and the two women kept up the relationship for the rest of their lives.

The doors had been thrown open to the garden so we could all hear what was going on, whether we wanted to or not. Sylvia and Judith (their daughter) had prepared a light lunch, and the tables were positioned by the doors of the aquarium so that Jacques could easily go back to his desk if he became bored of the company. The conversation was standard tattle, mainly Dona and Sylvia catching up on old mutual friends. Jacques was sitting next to James Lord but ignored the young man completely. He had brought a book to the table and was totally engrossed in reading it, pausing only to take some notes in a small notepad that he had on the other side of his plate. Judith would have been around sixteen at the time. She was a beautiful girl with a grave look that was very similar to her father's. She, however, wore her severity with a pleasing softness that diverged from his cruel aggressiveness. She had an oval face with a long nose, straight black hair that fell past her shoulders, down her back, held neatly in place with a black velvet hairband. She was dressed expensively but demurely, a cashmere jumper and a perfectly fitted pencil skirt were her main articles of clothing, black and white were her colours. Her posture was immaculate in its elegance. She was politely trying to engage James Lord in conversation as a substitute for her father and she worked away at her social function without any hint of reproach or excuse for him. Later in life she would become a psychoanalyst in her own right and with the support of her husband she became the leader of the post-Lacan Lacanianism. She was a poised, confident woman, indeed even as a young girl, and everything in her demeanour asserted that her father could do no wrong. She did not even question him when, earlier that very month, Jacques finally got around to informing her that she had three half siblings that he had fathered from his previously undeclared marriage. He had been forced to confess to these ignored progenies because the eldest, Caroline, was getting married that year and they were invited to the ceremony. Despite what must have been an emotional shock, Judith took the news with a calm and measured level of interest and not a hint of reproach. It was with this unwavering loyalty and worship that she bought his love and respect.

At the lunch she was asking James about his writing and about the modern painter Balthus, a mutual acquaintance, who had just bought a huge run-down Chateau in which he proclaimed himself King, despite living with no furniture or heating and barely any lighting. James had recently returned from an uncomfortable visit to Balthus's castle and told a few amusing stories to entertain the enthralled teen.

Judith then shared an 'amusing' story of her own which created a good laugh at the table but disgusted me to my core. This was the moment I knew I could never forgive Jacques and Sylvia. It concerned Laurence Bataille, who was Sylvia's first daughter with her previous husband George and hence Judith's stepsister, older by around a decade.

Throughout the 1940s Balthus had been a regular visitor to their house. At the time he was a world-famous painter specialising in highly eroticised pictures of very young girls, famously (or infamously) as young as eleven. Nowadays, that would put him firmly in the camp of being a paedophile and I cannot understand how any defence of so-called artistic genius can excuse that. Those, however, were different times, back when men's reputations trumped morality even more than they do now. So, because of his reputation and in view of their friendship Sylvia and Jacques had approached Balthus, by then in his forties, and commissioned him to paint Sylvia's sixteen-year-old daughter Laurence, which was at best naïve and at worst down-right irresponsible.

Judith regaled the table with a light-hearted story about the first modelling session, which took place after Laurence got in from school one Monday. After Balthus left, Laurence came downstairs crying to her parents about Balthus' wandering hands. "He kept telling me to lift up my dress a little more," she cried through her tears, "a little more and a little more." Despite Judith telling us the story as if it was a bit of pithy lunchtime amusement, to my ears that was a courageous cry for help. Laurence had sought the protection of her mother and stepfather, but they dismissed her out of hand, telling her that she should be thankful that such a great painter would take time to paint her! Inevitably she ended up being seduced by him and this union produced many masterpieces for which humanity is supposed to be eternally grateful.

The worst part of it all was watching Judith relate this disgusting behaviour as if it were a cheerful story, a completely acceptable occurrence, eliciting proud looks from the Lacans as they considered the part they had played in bring this prodigious art into being. In their minds they had facilitated the greatness of their friend, a view supported by the most revered museums and galleries all over the world: the Tate in London, the Met in New York. As long as a good painting comes out of it, who cares about the virginity and dignity of a defenceless teenage girl? Jacques Lacan even brought the painting out to the lunch table to show us. She normally hung in the main house, and this was the first time we in the aquarium had come across her. I can't stand seeing her. I never could.

The painting hung prominently in the Lacans' drawing room, as if it were an innocuous still life of a bowl of fruit or a bunch of spring flowers in a vase. Innocently titled *The Room*, it shows Laurence lying totally naked, stretched out on a green chaise lounge, her underdeveloped breasts and hairless genitals at the centre point of the painting. She wears only a school-girl pair of white socks, neatly pulled up to her knees. Her head falls back, angling slightly towards the viewer with her right arm draped over the chair, its weight allowing it to fall down toward the red rug on the floor. Her eyes are closed as if she is sleeping and an even younger girl, maybe based on Judith (although the severe fringe-bob hair cut is total un-Judith-like to my eye) pulls back the heavy looking curtains to let the day's light stream in through the large window. The room is sparsely furnished and dark but the sharp light from the window illuminates Laurence's nakedness like a spotlight, displaying it entirely to the outside world. The younger girl tenses her face and body with a seriousness bordering on rage, as she clutches the curtain with a quiet ferocity. I would like to think that this is an admission from Balthus, a realisation that what he is doing is just plain wrong. I want to see this younger girl with her neat skirt and long sleeve top, her severe haircut, as the representation of Balthus' subconscious regret, a Freudian admission of guilt, a pictorial rendition of that famous line by Oscar Wilde: "A bad man is the sort of man who admires innocence." However, having witnessed Balthus's despicable behaviour countless times during my years with the Lacans, I am afraid the little girl's rage represented something different to the painter and probably to Lacan as well. For men like him, every woman must desire him, or more specifically everyone he desires *must* consciously or subconsciously desire him more. "Why am *I* not the one chosen by you?" The little girl's face demands of the painter, "Why is she naked and centre stage not me?" Her expression is Balthus' defence.

That lunch was one of the few moments in my life that I was glad to have had no mouth to scream from and no eyes to cry out of. That monster Balthus took advantage of that poor girl, just like he did with the other girls he painted. What was more sickening to me at that time, when I felt close to girls of that age, was that Balthus was enabled to do this by Laurence's parents: he did it in their house. He did it with their implicit consent, they even paid him. That was the day I realised that these must be the worst people I had ever had to share space with. They made every fleck of my paint, every molecule of my being recoil in disgust. What was worse was that this man was revered in this society, he was famous, successful. All these crimes he committed, which went unpunished, were instead justified by a narrative of artistic genius. This 'modern' art that started with Courbet and me had led to this: this exploitation. Was I, in a way, the Godmother of this depravity, was my rage a subconscious sign of my implicit responsibility, just for existing? Or did I hate them so much more because deep down I knew my mother Constance had also failed to protect me? Was this in some way all my fault?

Looking back, these memories make me feel old and tired. I feel painfully distanced from the young, naïve person I was then as if I have lived several lives, but she comes back to me as I think, as the words form and the rage flows through me again. She makes me feel more alive now, that younger me, despite my immobility, my cynicism, my acceptance. All the years have weighed me down as if I were being painted over with layer upon layer of varnish that obscures and dulls me. I wonder how I can support all this weight. Time extinguishes light and free emotions: rage, indignation, certainty, ire. You must be young to commit fully to them, young as I was back then, decades ago.

*

After lunch, as Judith and Sylvia took in the plates, Dona Maar clutched James Lord by the arm. "He'll show off his Courbet now, just you see." They all came into the room and Jacques put down his book and notebook. All of a sudden, he livened up, as if someone had flicked an on-switch. He rose from his desk and began talking manically at a million words a minute, like a small child hurriedly relating a story to its parents in a single breath. "Now you will see something extraordinary," he announced with a glint in his eye, a puffed chest and a deepened tone to his voice, like a circus master building anticipation before the curtain is pulled back to reveal the splendour of the big top. And with a well-practiced flick of the wrist, "AHA!!"

111

What I saw before me was a stocky man with a large, smooth, serene face displaying an emotion that throughout my whole life up to that point I had rarely encountered: ambivalence. He looked like a G.I., a solid man with a very rectangular head and a large chin. He had a quintessentially American look to him with his mid length side-parted hair and his relaxed posture. He cocked his head and looked at me with interest but only up to a point, as if he was assessing my creation scientifically, not engaging with me as a vaginal image. Behind him Dona Maar looked upon him slightly amused, with a hint of maternal pride. Jacques, for the first time, looked shocked.

"Well? Well?, WELL?" Jacques was shouting in his face. James Lord shrugged softly and his eyes wandered past me to Giacometti's small sketch of a skull, the sight of which immediately enlightened his face in interest; his whole body instinctively pivoted towards it. Jacques started talking, faster and faster to fill the awkward air in the room that he himself was generating; his lack of control over James had unnerved him. It was something he clearly had not anticipated.

Lacan laughed mockingly, a curt fake laugh, "He says nothing, huh, he says nothing! Dona, who is this man you have brought? Does he not realise what he is looking at? This is not a vagina." He leaned close to James, who was still studying the Giacometti sketch. Jacques grabbed his arm, trying to direct him back to me, "Can't you see, my boy," Jacques babbled. "This is the painting of an absence, that is the key to its genius. It is like psychoanalysis. We expose the truth that is *not seen,* this is the truth, right? Not what is shown, not what is displayed, you see, not, as in psychoanalysis, what is *said* but the gaps between what is visible; the spaces between what is said and the relationships between the seen and the not-seen, the said and the not-said. This is what Courbet has given us, he has painted one of these gaps, one of these liminal spaces. Freud said in *Civilisation and its Discontents* that the genitals themselves are not beautiful and that is why a painter should not depict sexual pleasure directly, but Courbet has challenged him. Courbet has painted the most beautiful genitals EVER but they are not what is shown, not this, not this ugly vagina! He has painted the penis that is *not* there! This is what he has painted, the greatest pull-out picture of all time. It is our penis, can't you see, the viewer's penis, my penis, the penis of Lacan! The most beautiful. The phallus is in the painting. It is the painting!" He roughly swung James back towards me, forcing him to look. Once again, I was met by this serene face, nonplussed, displaying a slightly bored expression.

And then he said, with typical American candour, "Look, Monsieur Lacan. No offence or anything but I think I know considerably more about the beauty of penises than you do, if you catch my drift and sorry, Sir, but this sure as hell ain't it." And Jacques' mouth dropped and Dona Maar produced a childish high-pitch scream of laughter, clapping her hands in glee as my covering was snapped shut with a violent slam.

Chapter 13

As Lacan aged his extremes worsened. For months on end, over a year sometimes he would never expose me. Then, all of a sudden, the memory of my existence re-entered him and he would turn to me every day with a renewed passion, in every session, thrusting me into the faces of patient after patient. He was like a child rediscovering a lost toy, giving himself over to it as if there was nothing else in the world so important and then forgetting it again. For me, this uncertainty intensified my torture, it was the same hell as sleep-deprivation. I was denied the relative peace of regularity. When Judith once asked him en-passant whether he felt that he used his collection, his carefully-curated things, as an aid to his writing; perhaps giving them life or humanising them, he laughed out loud, spitting a bit of part-masticated ortalan across his desk.

"What!" he stammered. "You...you think I could conceive of that skull or the vagina hidden behind that screen, as alive, as in any way having human life. You think I am like Freud who used to talk to the Chinese figurines he had lined up on his writing desk, expecting them to answer him! No, Judith, in that I do not follow Freud. For me it is the opposite. These things are not even things in themselves. The point of all these objects is not what they are, it is what they *conceal*, what significance lies behind them. I collect these objects," and here he waved a flamboyant yet loose hand at us, "to get to the hidden meanings beyond the objects, their shadows if you will, don't you see? All this…this, *stuff* is useless, totally useless, nothing. They are just like people in fact. Like your mother, like you, all of you. It is the Thing, behind *that* is the Thing."

*

It was such a drawn-out process that looking back it is hard to know when it all properly fell apart for him, when he lost control of the delicate balance within himself, when the people and the things of his life fell away and the void between them, the darkness of the beyond took over. I cast my mind back trying to remember the first time he started on the knots, but I can't place it. It is as if they were always there, in his mind, unravelling, waiting to take over.

He had had his first car accident in 1964 but it was hushed up so that no one could accuse him of being a flawed human as opposed to a God-like aura, which is how he wanted to portray himself. It is amazing he did not suffer more crashes as he got older, the abandon with which he hurled his white Mercedes cabriolet around the streets of France was scandalous. After that first crash, he just got worse, even more reckless. He would refuse to stop at red lights (I AM LACAN!), he had no interest in any speed limit (I AM LACAN!), he would never wait in a traffic jam, he would swing out onto the hard shoulder or even onto the other side of the road, forcing other drivers to swerve round him (I AM LACAN!). When he was stopped by the police, he simply claimed that it was a medical emergency and talked his way out of it. No one argues with a doctor, it seems.

It is therefore a great irony that it was not him who died in a car crash but his eldest daughter, Caroline, who was knocked down and killed by a speeding driver. That is what you humans call serendipity, or maybe Endre was correct and every debt needs paying, even cosmic ones, even if it looks unfair. Caroline, who he had always been close to, in his own twisted way, was his first-born child. She was buried in Paris. He was on holiday at the time with Catherine Millot, his patient and last serious lover and they sped back for a typically Lacanian funeral: wife number

115

1 with children numbers 2 and 3, standing with wife number 2 and child number 4 and girlfriend number.....God only knows.

What Catherine, a clever, beautiful woman in her twenties saw in him that made her choose to spend her best years with him I am afraid I never worked out. The attractive qualities of ugly, old, egotistical men have always been a blind spot for me. What is it that these women see in the empty plumage of feathers whose colour has long-since dulled, like a faded picture, tarnished by dirt and varnish? The only thing that Jacques, a seventy-two-year-old wreck of a man, had left was his fame and self-generated, unmerited, confidence. Is that all you humans need to be infatuated with someone, just being told that they are worth the infatuation? Is there nothing more tangible, nothing beyond?

With the other women one can almost excuse them their folly. When he was younger Lacan was undoubtedly fun when his bipolar-like extreme swung that way, but by the time he was in his seventies and with Catherine there was little of that left. The joy of life in Lacan's core had seeped away month by month and year by year to be replaced by mania, anxiety and obsession. We could all sense it evaporating, smoking away like a soft mist that glides over the ground escaping out of the gap between the floor and the door. It was almost as if Jacques finally got around to his own analysis, an internal reckoning that he conducted on himself. He seemed to descend into his own personal analytical hell, as if he was a character from a Greek myth who, after a life of sin, finally succumbs to a curse that has been pursuing him for years: an inescapable fate. He would pace around the study, mumbling, growling, grunting and shouting. "When I speak," he used to mumble, "I speak to the walls, Catherine, that is my genius, that is what they all come to hear. I speak to the walls. And I can say anything: Grrr, argh, AHHHHH, mmmm, graappplrelajiKKKAA!!!"

He spoke to the walls, did he? Well, I was on the wall. I suppose, in a way, I was his analyst. How he would have hated that; me of all people: the analyst of the great analyser. Lacan, like any patient looking for analysis, needed to transfer his emotions, his thoughts, his past, his subconscious onto something and seeing as there were no humans that he could trust or that he held in high enough regard, he spoke to us, he transferred onto us: the skull of Giacometti, the genitals hidden behind a screen, Monet's weeping tree, Balthaus' sexualised images of under-aged girls. We were the ones who knew him best, knew him most honestly. We were the only ones not taken in by his self-proclaimed deity. None of them could offer what we could offer. All the humans: his students, Sylvia, Judith, all his followers, Catherine, they sat silently in the room and watched him age without comment, without judgement, as they themselves aged. They all sat there hour after hour, day after day just so he wouldn't be all alone. For as he got older that was the thing that scared him most, being all by himself with only his neuroses, and us: his judgement.

Chapter 14

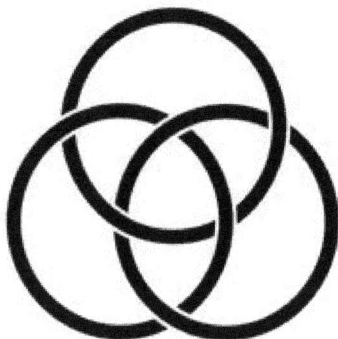

If there is one useless subject I know much more about than anyone need ever know, it is Borromean knots. These are so called because they were adopted as the symbol of the Borromean Princes in their coat of arms during the Renaissance, however the symbol is much older. Dig deeper and one unearths links spanning the globe, from Japanese Shintoism to Norse mythology. The three circles link together in such a way so that when one is broken the other two become free. Lacan made this the basis of his theory of man's sense of subjectivity, three interlinked levels that make up the conscious and the subconscious. The three levels are the real, the imaginary and the symbolic. The truth, however, for Lacan, the essence, *the Thing* was not in these knots, not even in their interlinking, but in the space between them, the void. This void is what obsessed him in his later years. It was darkness.

It started excessively, as everything did with Lacan. He set up a Borromean Knot study group with a few young mathematicians, Soury and Thomé being the main protagonists. It turned into a kind of mini-cult with Lacan at his head, as was par for the course with him. The mathematicians rented a flat together in the centre of Paris and declared they would cut themselves off from society, that they would form their own family dedicated only to the study of these knots, and this alone. Unsurprisingly, this did not do much good for the mental health of any of them. Lacan, of course, took up the position of cult leader, although he never moved into the dingy Paris apartment as that would have been beneath him. He would go there on and off over a seven-year period to encourage them, writing letters to them and phoning them in the middle of the night, whenever the urge took him.

As far as he was concerned, the rest of his life turned into a mad knot. He spoke less and less, sitting for hours drawing knots over and over again until literally hundreds of pages were scattered over his desk, all covered in drawings of Borromean knots. He carried around bits of string that he would cut up and tie together in knots; tie and then untie and then retie. Even when he went out for dinner with Catherine, he would take his drawings and his string, pieces of shipping rope that he would carry in a bag where once he had carried papers and books. He would sit in the most expensive restaurants in Paris in total silence sketching or tying knots while Catherine ate or asked questions that she knew he would ignore (what did she see in him?!). I will never forget the fallout from the time he went into Paris with Catherine and forgot his string or a pencil to draw with. He went into a rage, screaming and bashing the table until one of the waiters ran out to a nearby hardware store to get him a set of curtain rings and some flexible telephone wire that he could link together to make a knot. Only then did he calm down. Even for Catherine, when she finally managed to get him home, this was too much and she complained about it to Judith. Although why she should care about the problems of a young woman who was essentially replacing her mother was beyond all of us.

Jacques' professional sessions grew shorter and shorter (despite the regular fee increases) and his behaviour more and more erratic. He would come downstairs, hair dishevelled, unshaven, in his slippers, his bare knees showing as the folds of his dressing gown shifted. He would see three patients one after another whilst drawing a page of knots, saying next to nothing except: "Come in" or "Get out" and then go upstairs to shave. He would fit in ten patients an hour charging them exorbitant rates that he seemed to make up on the spot. Once he made a patient who had driven all the way from Paris wait outside his office for over an hour while he worked out that he had made four million francs that calendar year alone and then decided all of a sudden that he was going back to bed without seeing them, "Send them away, Catherine. Tell them to come tomorrow. Today is impossible!" What did his patients, if they still could be called that, get out of these sessions? Just the right to be in his presence, to be warmed by the pale fire of his fading fame? Or was it something integral to psychoanalysis as an act, something sickly human, something that he himself said: "I talk to the walls." Lying on the psychoanalyst's couch talking to a crazy old man who isn't listening and does not respond is the same as just talking to paintings hanging on the wall. Social communication and group building are the (self-proclaimed) ultimate human skills. They are what you humans think sets you apart. These skills have allowed you to dominate and destroy this planet as you wish. What is all this talking good for?

In the last three years of his life the disintegration completed itself. Jacques was driving one evening with Soury, missed his turn-off and swung the steering wheel manically to avoid the irritation of having to turn at the next junction. The car skidded off the road and embedded itself in a crash barrier. That was the end of the car and I expect since then the roads of France have been statistically much safer. Both men survived without external injury but internally the craziness of the knots was taking them both. Lacan decided he did not need Soury anymore and stopped going to his apartment. He stopped calling and writing to him. Soury said he was not well and needed help, he wanted Lacan to be his analyst, but Lacan rejected this out of hand. Soury was only thirty-nine when he committed suicide. He drove out in the dead of night to a forest. He then walked quite a distance to a specific place, a small clearing where three paths intersected. He sat down on the grass and must have stared up into the gap between the canopies of trees, up into the clear starry sky. He calmly drank cyanide from three bottles simultaneously and lay down to die in the space of the void, the centre of the knot.

By then Lacan had almost entirely stopped talking with words. He communicated only through silences, a few grunts and by jumping up and down in rage, crying or bursting into soundless laughter like a character in a silent movie. Despite this he still 'lectured' to packed halls. He would arrive late, stand at the front of the lecture hall drawing Borromean knots on a white board for just under an hour without saying a word and then leave early. Can this be described as lecturing? His acolytes sat around praising the lucidity of his mind, so magnificent that it did not need to communicate itself anymore. He had moved to a level of pure thought, they said, he was operating on a higher plain. One patient said she only came so that she could be in the presence of the clarity of his eyes and the lucidity of his perfectly formed ear. This was the Emperor's new clothes come to life. To us, he was a sick old man whose appearance was a mess and who walked around with his fly open, a naked cult leader who expected his fame, that aura that seems to be so powerful to you humans and to human women especially, to excuse him any responsibility for anything he did.

*

When he died, his family hushed it up. They refused to allow it to be admitted that he died in hospital in extreme pain due to complications from a tumour in his intestines. He died just before midnight on the 9th September but Sylvia and Judith could not accept this and made the doctor transfer the dead body to his apartment in Paris where he was laid out neatly on his bed. The next morning Sylvia reported the death, which was registered on the 10th with the paperwork stating that he had passed away in his own bed at home, surrounded by his loving family (number 2). I wonder if his brother ever found out the truth. Even on his death certificate Lacan was a total fraud, a complete liar – so ended the life of the great revealer of Truth. And good riddance.

Sylvia took everything down from the house in Guitrancout and moved back to Paris. Her instructions were clear: "Tell everyone that we sold the art to some Japanese businessman. All of it. I don't want anyone to know that I own that smutty cunt painting." I was taken to the basement of the flat in Paris and locked away at 3 Rue de Lille. Sylvia was the only female owner I have ever had and she never set eyes on me. Not once. I was back in the dark and grateful for it. It was 1981 and a few doors down from where I was stored, from where Sylvia lived out her final years, the Italian architect Gae Aulenti had just won the project to redesign the old D'Orsay train station, which was falling to pieces. And just like that Rue de Lille became the centre of my own personal Borromean knot; the void, the non-space and yet the place where everything magically came together.

Chapter 15

The old Palais D'Orsay had been burnt down during the Paris Commune along with most of the neighbourhood around Rue De Lille. Some of the paintings I later hung with, those who had seen some action during the Commune, claimed that it had been my own father, Gustave Courbet who ordered this destruction during the months he had been in power in the Commune's government. I don't know if that is true but I would like to think so. It would make everything in my life so neat and tidy, tied up in a knot, if you like. Life, however, like history, very rarely works out that way. In fact, there were probably no definitive orders given for the destruction of this thing or that thing. It was all just mad wanton violence, except, of course for the famous Vendome Column, which we do know Courbet was instrumental in pulling down, much to his own personal chagrin.

The whole quayside was basically rubble until the end of the turn of the century, when it began to be redeveloped. Where the Palais once stood, they built a new train station. The Gare D'Orsay opened in 1900 and was proudly proclaimed as the first electrified urban train terminal in Europe. As with much that trailblazes it was soon almost useless, defunct. Due to the small size of its platforms the station could not accommodate the longer trains that came into use in the 1930s. Therefore, within thirty years (a blink of an eye to me) the trickle of trains thinned and thinned until eventually it was closed in the 1970s.

The question came up again and again and different options were considered by various administrations: what was to be done with this huge Beaux-Arts style building with its large open spaces and huge windows? In 1976 it was leased by, who else?, the Hôtel Drouot auction house while they rebuilt their premises in Rue Drouot. So, for four years, the last four years that I spent at Jacques Lacan's house in the country, the Hôtel Drouot, the auction house that had sold the effects of Khalil Bey after his bankruptcy, Gustave Courbet after his exile, Constance's furniture after her death and the remains of Ferenc Hatvany's art collection after his flight from Hungary, operated out of the D'Orsay building on Rue de Lille, a few doors down from the Paris apartments of Jacques and Sylvia Lacan. The auction house stayed there till 1980 when they finally resettled in their new home in Rue Drouot. This is where they can be found to this very day. Predictably, it was Drouot who Sylvia and Judith contacted to organise the sale of Jacques Lacan's furniture, books and objet d'arts including the famous mousy grey analysis couch from Rue de Lille, bought by an anonymous buyer. I hope whoever took it fumigated the thing thoroughly before touching it.

Back in the 1970s the Drouot cleared the tracks from the ground, opened up the side rooms and filled the massive space with furniture, sculptures, paintings and automobiles of the great and the good, the bankrupt and the destitute, the once wealthy and the recently deceased. There had been talk of knocking the building down before Drouot moved in. But the auctioneers did a good job with the displays and the situation was complicated by the fact that the building was listed by the State as having cultural and architectural significance. So, when the auction house moved out the French government took the decision to renovate it and convert it into a museum. The plan was to use the new Musée D'Orsay as a place to display art that was considered too modern for the Louvre and not modern enough for the Pompidou Modern Art Museum across the river.

The Musée D'Orsay opened with great fanfare in 1986 while I was gathering dust in the basement down the road and Sylvia was pottering about in her old fashioned but still luxury apartment. By then she was well past her prime at almost eighty years old. Her skin hung loosely off her body and a cigarette dangled limply from her fingers as cataracts dulled her eyes and greyed out the final years of her life. Did she ever go down the street to see the forty odd Courbets that were displayed in those brand-new halls, in their own dedicated rooms just off the main hallway? Did her mind ever wander and rest on me, trying to recall where she had hidden me all those years ago? Or did the lie about me having been sold off to Japan take root so deeply in her mind, that to her I was housed halfway across the world, in the land of the rising sun? I wonder if she regretted that fictitious sale that had never taken place, the non-completed action. As long as they let me be, I hardly cared anymore. I was so weary, simultaneously weighed down and worn out.

Of course, she knew exactly where I was, or if she didn't then Judith did. The family had been fighting the French tax authorities for years so as not to settle the massive state inheritance bill that fell on them after Jacques's death and the calculation of his extreme wealth. I wonder how he would have taken the news. As a miser it would have been so painful for him to hand over such a large sum and yet part of him would have been so proud to see it all added up, with so many zeros running across the page. All that money! Not bad for a boy from a family of vinegar merchants from Orléans.

Sylvia and Judith cannily kicked the can down the road. They denied that I existed, argued with the valuations, employed every dodgy accountant and every trick in the book. When the Brooklyn Museum in New York wanted to put on a Courbet retrospective in 1988 she claimed I had been sold to a Japanese collector who would like to remain nameless. She offered to get it for them and charged them a 'reasonable' organisers fee. It was thus that I was shown in public for the first time. I was crated up and sent to the USA, only the second time I had left France and the first time I had ever left Europe. I can't say it was a revelatory experience. The best I can say is that it was bumpy and quite uncomfortable. But there I was, in New York City, praying that I would not at any moment be moved to the Met anywhere near their Balthus paintings. That would be the last straw!

I was described as *long-lost*, as *recently rediscovered*. They came and stared at me, so many people, day after day. They sketched me and made notes in front of me, they looked hard and long, they scratched their chins and cocked their heads to see me from every angle, as if looking deep inside me. Articles were written about me, they compared me with the other Courbets in the room and picked up on this brushstroke, commented to each other on that highlight, this flick of the genius' wrist. I was hung on a light blue wall in the corner of an open room next to a picture of a naked woman in the waves, her hair falling down her shoulders and arm hair visible in her pits. Next to her was *The Sleepers* with Jo Hiffernan's amazing red hair catching the light with its curls. As they stood gawping at me, they rehashed the old lines that they must have read in their guidebooks; how the flesh tones were perfectly executed, like Correggio, how the handling of paint was sublime, the mastery of the attention to detail; the genius of eye and hand. But who was the model on which I was based? The story did not hang together, it was assumed that I was a portrayal of Jo Hiffernan like all the other dirty paintings, but if the model was such a famous red-head, how do you explain my black pubic hair?

It was my first experience of the public and I can't say I enjoyed it. They looked and looked and after so much time being un-looked upon it made me feel thinned out, rubbed down, opaque. I felt looked through, glanced upon, somehow both concentrated on and simultaneously ignored. I realise this sounds paradoxical, but the attention made me feel at once self-aware and curiously not-there. People filed past and even in their concentration there seemed to be little there; a scarcity of depth, a lack of thought and certainly no empathy for me as a being. There were some, of course, who looked deeply and stayed in front of me for a long time, but was I really *seen* by them at all? Did they acknowledge and hence respect me as being alive, as *being* in the room with them? Could I ever be more than an it?

I was long-lost, after all, I was a revelation, would they ever see anything like me again? The funny thing, to me, was that before I was 'long-lost' no one had cared whether I had existed or not. However, all of a sudden, when I was found, rediscovered, I became in some way immediate and also (surprisingly) invaluable. To myself I felt as vindicated, as immediate as I had been for the previous hundred and twenty-three years but to them, I was not the subject, I was the object. Even those who looked with supposed expertise, the academics and the artists, primarily seemed to be seeing in me what *they* needed, what fitted for them, for their view of the world. I never once felt that someone was looking at me for me, for who or what I was. The seen and the unseen. They wrote books on me, conjecture and theory abounded, argument raged but I in a way still felt forgotten, lost.

I was back on a plane and back in a basement the very next year and the silence did me good. Too many eyes had seen me, too many mouths chattered, wasting too many vacuous words; it would take time to readjust. Deep down I knew this was my future. I would be made public. I knew it was inevitable. It was only a matter of time. In many ways, therefore, the last years with Sylvia were the most delightful of my whole life. I had grown. I had learnt to enjoy the darkness, to take solace from it and in solitude to connect to myself. I learnt to value this time of being invisible. It was a state in which I had spent so much time but had never really appreciated, back when I was younger, back when the future seemed out there. It took a long time, but I eventually learnt to let go, to accept it and now value it most highly. It was the realisation, just as I gained appreciation of the darkness, that it would be taken from me, that allowed me to experience the quiet for what it really was, to experience it in its magnificence. Now it is all I long for.

During my life up to that point, I had been used to only a few eyes looking at me; and those eyes had ownership over me. Those eyes were familiar to me and though they all used me for their own purposes I had been with them long enough to understand what they wanted, how each one had their uses for me and this made their possession of me less painful, although of all of them Lacan pushed it to the extreme. Khalil needed me for his lust for sex, Hatvany for his love of artistic technique, Lacan as a representation of his perverse desire to shock other people, Sylvia to reject my very existence: these were the people I had grown up with and, as with all families, had come to terms with. My only blessing was that in each case I had had plenty of time to come to terms with them, to get used them and their foibles. However, after being exhibited in New York I realised that my discovery would inevitably lead to a new kind of looker, a transitory one, one who is passing through, one with whom I would have no relationship at all. They would look and I would be looked at. I am thankful for those years of darkness to prepare me for that torture.

I probably did not realise it at the time but looking back, I was deeply affected by all those psychiatric sessions that I sat through. Over the decades I have had to listen to scores of Lacan's patients talking about their pasts, their anxieties and their hopes for life, whilst the Great Lacan spun neat psycho-analytical webs of self-discovery. All of a sudden, left on my own in the dark it was impossible not to venture along the same mental paths. If I had to relate myself back to my childhood does that not make Courbet my father and Constance my mother? Sigmund Freud placed his own version of the Oedipus complex at the core of human anxiety and in this theory, he claimed that it is tougher on women than men, no surprise there. Whereas little boys only have to realise that they can't sleep with their mothers (despite their inherent desire to) and have to transfer this lust onto other women (mother substitutes), little girls have to make a double transference: once onto our mothers (until we realise that they don't have a penis) and secondly unto our fathers and to men in general. This leads to double the anxiety. In addition, little boys' transferences are fuelled by their fear that they will be castrated if they continue to desire their mothers, whereas for girls the fear of castration is not available and so they have to be motivated by deep levels of shame that lead them to a natural state (according to Freud) of subservience and low self-confidence. Do these theories still hold as human society has progressed? In the Freudian sense, I am the visual epitome of this, the visualisation of penis envy, my very portrayal of penislessness and the way I have been looked at, from the moment of my birth to the present, is a visual representation of this. And yet could I honestly say that I can find in my subconscious some kind of Jungian competition with Constance for the affection of Courbet? This seems so alien to me, could it be that it doesn't apply to what humans call objects like me, representations of humans? Does consciousness only apply to humans themselves? Could it be that as a representation, a copy, I have something missing and I don't mean a head! I mean a psycho-analytical depth, a well of emotion, of anxiety somewhere that drives me. Can an object even have a drive? Is this what a human soul is? If it is, it seems a very male description. And if this is the case, how do you humans see nature, the very earth that you seem intent on driving to unsuitability for human habitation. The earth spun for millions of years before humans and will continue for millions of years and for countless lifeforms after humans have gone extinct. Is there not a drive in this reality, or, like the tree falling in the forest that no one sees or hears, without humans can it not be said to exist?

From a personal point of view, what I can state is that I have no feeling of affection for Courbet, Khalil, nor for any of the men I have encountered in my life. Whatever feeling that links children to parents and visa-versa is not in me at any level. I have had years to explore this within myself and my conclusion is definitive. I wonder if maybe that was because the parent/ child bond is a two-way thing and my parents (if that's what they were) never saw me as anything more than an object, a possession. If there is a link to anyone I have encountered, it is to the very few women in my life and specifically Constance who rejected and decapitated me. I see this set of women, Constance, Lucie and Sylvia as a progression in societal terms of what women were permitted to be. Does that make me their zenith, the most progressive? Am I the symbol of all that is modern womanhood? Just female genitalia in a frame, being gawked at.

As I sifted through the years of my past, I found myself returning again and again to Constance. I started to believe that she held some kind of a key, that it was through her that I could understand who I am. And yet she was the one I knew least; in whose company I spent the least amount of time. My understanding of her as a person was the shallowest. Is that why I focused on her so deeply, because she was the piece that was missing? It was her rejection that cut the deepest; that fleeting feeling I had at the time that she would maybe accept me as a woman should accept another woman, despite me being nothing more than a shadow of her. It was that nagging hope that somehow, she could imagine me as more than I was. Maybe humans can only analyse themselves with words, not with images. Maybe this is the limit of their empathy. Humans reduce everything to words except themselves, this is the root of their arrogance and also the secret of their success, which has led them to the mastery of the world, with all the negative consequences that are just being realised. Maybe when God named Adam and Eve it wasn't naming at all but describing. Maybe he was simply calling humans adams and eves like calling a certain type of four-legged animals a deer or a doe. Humans translated that descriptive word as a manifesto of their individuality, a proof of their primacy, why? What justification did they have, other than their arrogance and deep sense of self-importance? I AM ADAM! Is that why Constance could never have seen me for what I was – a representation of her in all her being, more than that: a representation of a freedom that she was denied. She could have embraced this, accepted this link between us. However, like the Picture of Dorian Gray, in the end, humans always seem to end up with a knife in their hands stabbing wildly and furiously at anything that looks too much like them. I am certainly not a Jungian version of Electra. I desire no man for their affection, no father figure for their love. I am one stage behind. I just wanted a woman to accept me as another woman. I realised quite early on that this dream would never be realised.

So, when Sylvia, my only female owner, was so disgusted and ashamed that she packed me up never to lay eyes on me for as long as she lived, I wasn't surprised. I had grown up. I didn't feel that white heat of rage, that deep emotion of fury and frustration. I wasn't even hurt. I was older and my emotional capability had dried out like a river bed in a drought, as the global temperature rises year after year. At most I was a little disappointed.

Chapter 16

After Sylvia's death I was gifted by Judith to the French state in lieu of unpaid inheritance tax and in 1993 I was installed in room 20 of the Musée D'Orsay. It brings me absolutely no pleasure to state that I am one of the main draws of the museum, one of the jewels in the museum's crown. In short, I have become famous or more precisely infamous!

In the room where I hang the sun does not shine, like in a jail I expect. I have spent so much of my life hidden: behind a curtain, behind a sliding panel, behind the doors of a locked cabinet, locked deep in storerooms, out of sight and out of mind, but now I am constantly exposed. The walls are a dark grey colour that someone passing me once described as *ash*. A fitting term I feel: the remnants, the leftovers of that most basic form of destruction, that of fire. Ash is the lightening of solidity, the near nothingness that survives after the end. Nearly nothing, but not quite.

There are lights shining down from the ceiling and the air is controlled, conditioned. Anyone can walk into this room as long as they have paid for a ticket, but they have to look for it, to find their way in here. It is a room that has to be located, discovered. There is a sightless element to it.

Can I explain how to find me? The lightness of the gallery entrance gradually fades as rooms are split into smaller, weaving spaces with steps between them, false walls break up what is essentially an enclosed internal corridor. I am on the left-hand side. To see me you would have to pause, stop, look around. I am pushed against the back of a false wall, like a child playing hide and seek. I am visible and yet concealed, lit from above and yet shadowed from the sun.

From the moment I was put up, there was a slew of imitations, controversies and objections. A modern artist made a copy of me and drew a big penis between my legs, which I am sure Lacan would have pointed out was entirely unnecessary. A performance artist in a spangly gold dress and fantastic golden eyeliner had room 20 closed down after she lay in front of me with her legs open showing her own privates. It caused quite a stir in the museum but all I could do was try to remember my face and whether Courbet had shadowed my eyes. It was so long ago, the memory of the image of my lost upper half is just a blur to me now. After a bit of a struggle between some outraged members of the public, security men came and they took her away. She was trying to add something, shouting that she was creating art, but this modern art, which they try to trace back to me is not an addition. If I am at its core then it is a reduction, an amputation. I am the proof of that, it's just that no one could see, no one knew. Except, I would discover, Constance, who was in a way the mother of modern art, even though she had been forgotten, lost in history; and no one knew she had ever existed.

They put me on the front of book covers and the dust jackets of novels. When they did that, the novels were banned from publication. They put me on social media and Facebook was sued for having caused offence, so they had to take me down. I am offensive, unacceptable, inexcusable. You need to give a warning before encountering me. I am unsuitable for public eyes. And yet I am just that, public. Are all those photographs that they take of me every minute of every day, those exact reproductions somehow different to how I am as a *being*? How can that be, the image is the same? Am I acceptable in an art gallery but not on a book cover or on Facebook? Are there levels of how public 'public' can be?

Maybe each representation and copy of something is completely different from the original even if it is exactly the same. Maybe there is something of me here in this gallery that is somehow deeper, more soulful than just a picture of me on a book cover or a JPEG on a device, just as you humans doubtlessly believe there is something deeper and more soulful about Constance than there is of me. Does each reproduction thin out bit by bit so that it becomes less than the reproduction that came before? Is a photograph of me somewhat less than me? In a Borges short story, a fictional poet, Pierre Menard, sets out to write Don Quixote, not to copy it but to write it as if writing a new work but an exactly identical word for word copy of the original. Is this what each photograph of me is, a new work of art created in its time and by its artist that just happens to represent me exactly? If so, is everyone with a camera phone an artist as good as each other? How many millions of people come through my museum each year and therefore how many millions of photographs are taken of me each year, on every minute or every hour, in every weather and at every variable state of light, from every angle? You humans worship uniqueness and yet your God is both singular and omnipresent. Is that not what an artwork is?

The sculptures in the main section of the hall, just outside my room, lecture us ad infinitum on art theory. In my experience no piece of art is more up itself than sculpture. During the Renaissance there was a concept that came to prominence called *disegno*. This represented the conceptual production of an artistic idea as opposed to its actual physical production. Following the emergence of this concept as the highest form of artistic production *the idea* was elevated as an art form in itself, one that was deemed more valuable than the simple application of a craft. This led to a situation where artists managed teams of people who produced work for them and it was the designer, not the producer, who was recognised as the genius. In this way an architect is more elevated than a builder and, in modern art installations, when the artist employs a carpenter, for example, to build an artwork the carpenter who produces the work is not named but the artist who designed the piece is. Following this idea, you humans conceive of yourselves as geniuses brimming with conceptions, but from our point of view humans are like craftspeople, you have sex with each other like animals, legs open, in and out. There is no conception to the basest and most intrinsic of your desires, no *disegno*. As far as I can see humans are nothing more than the descendants of a process (or evolution to use your words) and that is no different from making a terracotta jug or weaving a quilt. We artworks, however, stand testimony to an idea, a conception, not just a production. If I weren't how would I be heralded as great art? In Renaissance parlance I am the *disegno*. Should I not feel proud, important? Why do I not? Is it because I am trapped here, imprisoned in this frame hung from the ceiling, strung up and stretched out in a windowless room from which I cannot escape?

*

In addition to the photographs, lots of people stand in front of me and talk into cameras, they talk about art and exploitation and sex and feminism, they talk about the male gaze and Courbet. I am the subject of the talk. I am the reason they are there, but I still feel a bit like offensive wallpaper that no one actually wants to look at. A Mexican artist did a version of me as the backdrop to a painting with an indigenous man by an easel painting me. He is wearing a beautiful colour headdress and the canvas is a block of red. A conceptional photographer made a version of me out of newspaper clippings in black and white. A Serbian artist did a painting of me wearing blue panties with the EU flag in the centre, a circle of stars. It is all the same. They come and hold up the work (or a reproduction) next to me and everyone lines up to take photographs, to make their reports, to make their documentaries and then they go.

The most interesting, from a personal point of view, was the woman artist who set up an easel in front of me for six weeks in 2011 and did a perfect copy of me, exactly like Courbet would have done. In the end there were two of me. It was interesting to see her paint layer by layer. I suppose it would be like watching a video of your own birth, except that at the end of that video you would see yourself all grown up, not as the baby you were. She did a perfect reproduction of me as I was in 2011 and presumed that was how I had always been. But I feel that I have changed so much over my life, I have grown.

People see paintings as fixed things, unaltering and unalterable but that is not the case. We are alive, not frozen in time. What I was in 2011 was not what I was in 1866 or in the 1920s in the peace and quiet of the Hatvany house, with Alexandra and little Antoinette running around, or bearing my torture of living with the Lacans. We objects are also constantly ageing, exactly like you humans, it just takes longer to notice the changes. In that sense and despite being created, we are closer to the natural world than you, more like mature trees, seeded before any living human. This artist who painted me in 2011 could only paint me one way; working without deviation to end up with the picture she could see in front of her, reaching finally and inevitably the sunlit pool of her finished image. She was painting as if Courbet knew from the start the conclusion of the final image, as if everything was predetermined. If you make a copy, you always get to the end point, the point that is right in front of you. If you make an original, you hardly ever know how it is going to end up.

*

The turning point of my life came in 2018, via an academic called Claude Schopp. He had just won a major literary prize for his biography of Alexander Dumas and was researching a book about Dumas's son, Alexander Dumas the younger. As he was going through an archive of letters that Dumas the younger had written to George Sand, he came across a document that solved one of the greatest mysteries in art history. Totally by chance, Schopp found a reference to the model that had posed for me and unearthed a woman totally forgotten by history: my mother, Constance Quéniaux.

The book was a revelation, a mystery solved. They had a book launch in front of me. They put up a large, framed photo of Constance, the one taken by the famous photographer, Nadar and there we stood, side by side, mother and daughter. They laid out rows of seats for an audience and a film crew set up at the back. There was a lectern set up in front of me, carefully positioned so the speaker's head would block the parts of me that they did not want to broadcast on national television. Claude Schopp arrived looking every bit the French distinguished public intellectual. He was a sprightly seventy-five years old who could have passed for a man in his sixties. He wore a short, neat, white beard and had a thinning layer of white hair that was wispy on his nearly bald pate. He wore thick rimmed glasses that covered his wrinkled eyes. These eyes turned down at the edges which gave him a slight look of melancholy. Clothed in a black pinstriped suit with a dark green shirt, he talked with vigour and ease, in a serious professional tone. He spoke about his research and his discovery. At the end of his talk, he sat down and a woman stood up. She was dressed in a nineteenth century black dress that bellowed out around her and her hair had been scraped back to match Nadar's photo of Constance. She was introduced as a famous theatre actress. She said that she was going to perform a fictional account of Constance's life that had been written by a Parisian author. The author stood up, received a round of applause and sat back down again. The audience settled back in their seats as the actress began to speak. It was Constance's voice and she told her story. A long-forgotten story that was, in a way, my story.

Book 2: Constance Quéniaux

Chapter 1

My name is Constance Quéniaux. Though you do not know me, you have probably already seen more of me than you have seen of most woman of my age, perhaps more than you wished to. However, my story did not start with this painting nor end with it. My name is Constance Quéniaux. I am a woman and I had a life.

It is not a painting but a photograph that marks the beginning of my story; a photograph Nadar took in 1860 but never exhibited publicly. He did, however, show it to me. Or more precisely he showed it while I was in the room. In many ways it was the advantage of being a woman in those days, especially a young and beautiful one, as I undoubtedly was. You are at once shown off, displayed and yet at the same time often unseen in plain sight, ignored as if you did not exist.

Gaspard-Félix was early to the business of photography and in Paris he became its king. He called himself The Great Nadar, with a modesty only men can muster and set about photographing everything he could. He was the first man in the world to take an aerial photograph (he did it from a hot-air balloon!) and he was also the man who photographed the catacombs of Paris; from the clouds to the sewers, the open to the confined, the seen to the unseen, The Great Nadar photographed it all.

In 1860 Nadar had just moved into his massive, new, and unbelievably expensive studios at 35 Boulevard des Capucines. If you wanted to be someone in Paris, it was the only place to be photographed.

He took the top two stories of the building and the renovation costs were the talk of the town. By the time he was finished the outside was a gleaming shimmer of glass and vibrant red, that shone all the way down the boulevard from the Opéra (which then was still a building site) to the Madeleine. Nadar had put up an illuminated red sign – *Nadar* – emblazoned across the façade of the building as if he had personally signed the architecture in fire. Inside, the red theme continued and if you were fortunate enough to be entering at the same time as someone famous you would see the moustachioed genius himself, glowing bright in his flame-red dressing gown, meeting and greeting the latest celebrity before a shoot: Gustave Flaubert, Jules Verne, Baudelaire, Dumas, Victor Hugo, Rossini, Berlioz, Sarah Bernhardt, George Sand, Wagner, Liszt – Nadar's was the place to be and to be seen.

Discretion forbids me to mention which gentleman friend had booked me in for my shoot, but I was standing perfectly still, dressed in a black dress with lace collar and cuffs, gleaming buttons running down my front and the mandatory pearl earrings dangling from my ears: pearls signify purity. I was led into a room, placed in my spot by the table and told that to be photographed I had to keep absolutely still for the fifteen minutes exposure time if we wanted the image to come out clearly. Any movement could end in blurring the photograph. I remember how I picked a tiny spot of red paint on the wall opposite to stare at, regulating my breathing just as I did when I held an arabesque during training. My hair was parted in the centre, which in the photograph accentuates the white line running down my head, to the tightly packed bulge of hair at the back. It was not the first or last time I was to be photographed and as a highly trained dancer standing still for over ten minutes was no issue for me. Even when the door opened and the blurry image of five men trooped into the room from behind me, my eyelashes did not as much as show a flicker. I am proud to say that the clarity of the surviving photograph is testament to the command I had of my body.

It was Nadar, himself, who had entered the room, along with Halil Şerif Pasha, who I would come to know as Khalil. He was born in Cairo, which was then part of the Ottoman Empire and had worked in both Athens and Saint Petersburg, starting as a diplomat but rising up the ranks to become an ambassador. I had never met him but knew of him from the theatres and the Goncourt brothers (who seemed to be everywhere in Paris in those days, as if there were ten of them rather than just the two). Finally, a mountain of a man entered the room. He had a huge, shaggy beard studded with baguette crumbs. The odour of stale beer whirled around him and he emitted a booming laugh that exploded from his belly. This was, of course, Gustave Courbet, the painter. They didn't even acknowledge my presence in the room as if I were merely a piece of ornate furniture. I, respectful of the camera's exposure time, did not move.

"This is something you have never seen, Gentlemen! It is not for the eyes of ladies, which is why I asked them to wait in the cafe," Nadar's hands waved as he spoke, as if he were clearing the air around him, his dressing gown flicking behind like a devilish tail. "This is something special for you, Khalil Sir, who has seen the world and you, Sir, the artist. What can life possibly offer to you that you have not already seen or imagined?"

Nadar crossed the room and, without even giving me a glance, started pulling out drawers to my left where I could not see. Courbet collapsed with such force into a chair that I worried for its integrity. He was wearing a suit with waistcoat, a black tie badly tied, it hung down his white shirt and extended down between his legs. He turned his eyes towards me and I could see the bone of the lower half of his eye sockets pushing his skin outwards and embedding his eyes within his skull. Gustave managed to look at the same time both obese and skeletal. The intensity of his stare was ravenous, like a drunk staring down his first beer of the day.

Khalil stood by him, elegance personified, leaning lightly on his cane. He wore pristine white trousers and a pocket watch chain glinted against his dark waistcoat. He had a straight nose that felt its way through life for him, short, neat hair, side-parted with a curl above his right ear and

143

a glint of life danced in his eyes. I knew at once how he had won Jeanne de Tourbey as his mistress, a lover he shared with Prince Napoléon no less. Oh yes, Khalil was the talk of all of Paris and as he turned to rest his eye on me, I shuddered, perceptively enough to worry about the camera.

"As I was saying, Gustave," Khalil continued, "when M. Lepel-Cointet heard that I wanted to buy your *Venus and Psyche* he immediately sent his card and tried to sell it to me. I made some enquiries and then discovered that he had not even settled the original bill with your good self and thus it was not really his to sell. Of course, I refused. If someone is going to profit from the picture it must be you, Sir and I told him outright that he may be a speculator with the banks during the day, but he should not take his work home with him in the evening and certainly not bring his business out at night!"

At this Courbet let out a huge roar of approval, "He is a usurer, Khalil, my friend. For a man to be able to spend money usefully and without doing harm, he must have earned it himself. Every man must work. This stockbroker is going to cause me nothing but grief and I fear for my two beautiful angels. However, this is not your issue, Sir, kind as you are. You wanted a picture of those two beauties next to each other, but I will do you an even more beautiful picture. Imagine two women in bed together, one on top of the other, two luscious nudes asleep, worn out by their passion for one another. Imagine a picture in which you can smell the sex, Khalil, it would be too scandalous for even *your* private chambers, Sir and there is no higher (or lower) bar than that! I will call it *The Sleepers*, Sir, I will paint you something you have never seen before. Forget *Venus*, forget *Psyche*, these myths are out of a man's reach. I will give you people you know. We will call upon Whistler's lady, Jo Hiffernan, while he is away. I know her well, Sir, you will love her. She has red hair that would make The Great Nadar himself blush! You will see, Sir, I will not let you down. How would you like it, Sir, Jo on top or below?" At this, both men almost collapsed laughing as Nadar came back across the room carrying a folio of paper.

"What's this, Gentlemen?" Nadar said with an affected tone of indignation. "Not a joke at my expense, I hope. Ah, Courbet, they say you are the king of the real, well I have here a reality that even you cannot conceive of." He laid out a set of photographs on the table and there, in front of my eyes, I saw a photograph of a woman who had both the genitalia of a woman and a man. "There, Gentleman," Nadar proudly proclaimed. "And what do you make of this? It is medical, Sirs, I assure you, strictly medical."

"As is my interest, Sirs, no matter what you have heard," Khalil slyly interjected and Courbet laughed like he was dying and slapped the little Egyptian so forcibly I thought he would snap.

"Flaubert told me that Napoléon III's brother keeps a naked photo of every woman he ever slept with in a casket by his bed. Every single one, from kitchen girls to the highest princesses," said Jules de Goncourt, laughing. "He said this is your 'work', Nadar. Out of interest, do you get paid per photograph or are you held on an annual retainer?"

Nadar smiled out of the side of his face with the look of a man comfortable in any conversation. "I have no idea what you mean, Sir, I surely don't. However, I can tell you about these oddities: a woman with a penis! Something, eh? They were done for Monsieur Armand Trousseau himself, yes, Sirs. A man, I am happy to say, I saw just the other week and whose fame is only growing as he approaches his seventieth year. This lady he had me photograph is called a hermaphrodite. Look at these pictures, Sir, are these not *artistic*? Look, Gustave, look, you whose life is dedicated to the representation of real life. How do you compare with the great Nadar? How do you get more real than this, Sir, with your paints and brushes? Will you admit that you are no match for the camera? Take this one here, Sir. We had her lay on that chair over there, in this very room, Sir. Look how we positioned the camera right between the legs, do you know how hard it is to get the light right for this. You can see the penis and vulva with perfection, this is art, Sirs, would you not agree? This is art."

Having been released from my pose by the camera operator I passed the table as Nadar spoke and glanced over his shoulder. The lady had her legs split apart in the foreground. The camera had indeed been set up between her legs, which were spread open and hiked up on either side, bent at the knee. There were protruding veins bursting out of her shin. Taking the camera exposure into consideration, I couldn't help thinking that her legs must have been tired, the way she had been made to hold them up in the air like that for so long. Between them one sees a light sprouting of dark hair and underneath a small penis dangling over her female parts. She is sitting on a studded leather chair and wears white socks over her shins and white straps over her knees. Her upper half extended into the background of the photograph and was slightly out of focus, but I made out that she was wearing a long nightshirt, open at the chest with her right arm resting over her stomach. I noticed that she had chosen to raise her left arm up which must have ached after a few minutes of stillness. It rested over her face covering as much of it as she could manage. Unlike the men who I am sure were ogling over the middle I couldn't help focusing on the fact that she was trying so hard to cover her face, this poor creature. I remember feeling deeply sorry for her. She had been wheeled around Paris by Trousseau and his famous doctor friends as a circus spectacle to be poked and examined and catalogued. She had to lie there in front of Nadar's satanic machine for fifteen minutes without moving a muscle. How much were they paying her for this? Not enough. She probably wished the ground would swallow her up, probably wished she didn't even have a face or even upper body at all, if only to reduce herself to what she was for these illustrious men and how she would be recorded for posterity: just a bizarre pair of sexes, one above another, no name, no face and no life of her own. Little did I imagine how similar a fate I would end up having.

*

And me? How would one describe me? Well, it is impolite to describe oneself, hardly the thing to do, especially were one to describe oneself positively. Fortunately, I am able to fall back on the description of others. I was never that famous as a ballet dancer. However, I was contracted from the age of fourteen to the Opéra in Paris in whose service I remained for over a decade. I am proud to say I received enough write-ups to be able to furnish you with a general idea. Where to start? Well, with a part of my anatomy I guess, although not that part that you would assume. I was noted for my eyebrows. Why, one could ask, would a ballerina have her eyebrows singled out for specific praise. Alas, the reasons for fame are a mystery to me. Always have been and always will be.

Like all of us not born into fame and fortune I, of course, started somewhere, yes, but never at the very lowest of the low. Never, I say with all my honour, did I perform at the likes of the Théâtre Délassements where the girls were paid fifty francs a month for the show and had to scour the audience in the intervals for a man to fuck in the wings for five sous a go between acts. I am proud to have skipped that part of the career of an actress of my time.

I made my debut as a dancer, straight off with no funny business, in a starring role in 1854. I played the title role of Mysis in *Aelia et Mysis* for which I was applauded. I would pick out, if you will excuse my immodesty, the adjectives 'gracious' and 'distinguished' from *Le Constitutionnel's* review. That was me: tall, thin and graceful. I can still hear the sounds of applause. All performers will, I am sure, agree with me that this adulation stays with one after the words of praise have dispersed into the atmosphere of time. All those hands that clapped for me! How sad to think of them now as fleshless bones; metacarpals and phalanges buried underground, all falling away from each other. But my eyebrows, my eyebrows! Théophile Gautier himself remarked on me. Now they talk of him, when they talk of him, as the great critic of the day, admirer of Flaubert, critic of Courbet. I remember him at Nadar's wearing a ridiculous furry jacket, his hair flowing around his hat and that massive beard. He looked like Robinson Crusoe, some animalistic being of the forest. Maybe he had a thing for hair, I don't know, but he noticed mine just as I noticed his: "Mlle Quéniaux played the part of the evil

147

Countess and the wrinkling of her beautiful, black eyebrows... excited the Bravos! of the crowd."

Prince Napoléon himself came with Queen Christine to see me dance and applauded my art. They gazed at my thin, elegant face, remarking upon my eyes, those doorways to the soul as they are called, about which poems were written:

"Mademoiselle Quéniaux

Aux yeux si Beax!

Que disons-nous, des yeux!

Plutôt disons des cieux."

That was written by Janin, the little fat man. All wispy whisker chops. He was a man chairs feared when he entered the room. I remember him all too well. His complimentary words came cheap to us dancers, I hope they paid him more per word at the *Journal des débats*. And yet he too was lost for words, perhaps just a little bit, when he stared into my eyes: "Oh, such beautiful eyes! The heavens!"

How cruel is life, they speak of me still, more than they ever did when I was alive and danced, but sadly it is not the eyes that they speak of now, nor the beautiful black eyebrows, so admired, nor the knee, the patella ligament of my right leg that collapsed in a crunch before I had even reached my twenty eighth birthday, only a few weeks after they wrote of my talent: "full of freshness". Damn that ballet, *Sacountala*, I am glad it is not performed any more these days. I hope that silly piece is forgotten for all of time for what it did to my knee.

With that knee injury my dancing career was suddenly over but life goes on, one has no choice but to continue living even when all the plans for your life have fallen apart and your dreams are like the bunch of flowers that freshen one's dressing room one day and collapse into a wilted mess the next. That is where the freshness of my talent went, cut down to die like a bunch of blooms. I wonder if Courbet somehow guessed that it would turn out this way for me. Did he know this was how I felt when he gave me the only thing of value I ever received from that odious boar? He painted me a bouquet: tulips, irises, primroses and, yes, of course, the red downcast camellias, those suggestive whores of plants, that gazed at me every day for the rest of my life, that thing of pure beauty. And where are they now, those flowers of my youth, the camellias of my past? In St Petersburg, of course, where else? That dreadfully cold city that Khalil hated so, so much. All he ever talked about was how he despised that particularly Russian type of cold. You can find my flowers there; in the museum they call The Hermitage. If you go, wrap up warm and if you choose to pass through the lifeless walls in the lifeless rooms where they hang picture after picture, rows of masterpieces out of context, please go and see my flowers, my Courbet painting that once hung in my house, for my eyes only. If you do go there, please pause for a moment and give a little clap or two for me, one soft and one loud and listen to the echo in the high-ceilinged room.

What does a ballerina do when they can no longer dance? What a question! It was Paris, *la ville d'amour*! One did not *do* anything. The occupation of the day was simply to *be* and make sure you were seen. One would get up late, throw on a dressing gown of white satin (twelve hundred francs at least!) and matching gold-embroidered slippers, in case a gentleman should call unexpectedly, and call one's maid to help with one's toilet. One's skin needed polishing, one's hair needed tending; hours in front of the mirror getting the colour of one's complexion just right; a little red, but not too much, a puff of powder: the balance between sensuality and danger. And the eyes! Don't forget the eyes, always looking, mirrors looking into the mirrors of the soul. On the way out, one would check the book to see who had dropped in, calling cards would be left from gentlemen friends, acquaintances, forgotten faces who may have brought a pound of sugared raisins to one's box the night before and yes, enemies too. Invariably we all ended up in the same place; dressed in pink or blue in a carriage drawn by two fine black horses (the essential outlay of the day, ten thousand francs paid for in full – but not by you!) driving up the Champs-Élysées or in the Bois de Boulogne, wheels turning to go nowhere in particular, just to be seen.

I was particularly noted for my elegant fashion: muslin dresses with full panels from Worth, Indian shawls embroidered with gold thread, a Gagelin coat, satin slippers, thick gold chains, diamonds (as many as you can get), a new pair of gloves every day, bracelets and the most fashionable hats, so many hats that some never even made it out of their boxes. In the evening one must have boxes in all the theatres: Opéra, Théâtre-Italien, Variétés, Comédie Française. This was my world. This was where I loved to be. And then supper at La Maison d'Or, where I would watch with satisfaction as tables of leering men had tarts sent over from La Farcy's brothel to enliven their nights and give them disease. If we wanted something more sedate then maybe a quiet bite at home with a special friend at one or two in the morning; champagne and a little chicken, a glass of punch, hopefully someone who could play the piano passably well and company that wouldn't be totally boring: Counts, Dukes, Marquises, Old Generals and young Monsieurs from the country, first time in the big bad city, with allowances in their pockets and voids between their ears.

This was my world: the city of Camellias. Ever since young Dumas' book, everyone was wearing them; some for fun, some ironically, some in hope. At three francs a piece it was boom time for the florists. Flowers worth more than most people's daily wage were sent for in armfuls, fresh every day.

Into this world blew Khalil, like a hurricane, notable even amongst big spenders. He had come with money to spend and little else to do. He was a prize catch for a dancer earning at most four thousand francs a year whilst racking up expenses of over a hundred thousand. In 1865 he left Russia for Paris and his arrival was heralded by *La Presse*. Three years later he was bankrupt and had gone back into the service of the Ottoman Empire. But what a three years, what a three years! All of a sudden, he was everywhere, the Café de Paris, the Café Anglais and especially la Maison d'Or. He brought horses all the way from Arabia and seemed to have bottomless pockets of money. Admission to the Jockey Club was no issue for him as it was for so many who baulked at their excesses. After one night of dropping over a million at cards it was the club that was reeling from Khalil. No one could keep up with him. He rented Lord Hertford's apartments, stripped the walls bare and re-clothed them with every artist he could find: Delacroix, Ingres, Gérôme and of course, Courbet. Khalil wanted everything raised to a factor of ten: he wanted to be a bigger cad than Hertford (no mean feat) with a bigger art collection, he wanted Napoléon's mistress in his bed, he wanted the fastest horses and every rosette going. He never stuck, only twisted. And also, I humbly add, he wanted me, the least remembered of all his treasures and also, in some ways, the most famous.

What was I to him, he who had it all? Well, like all heavy gamblers Khalil was a superstitious man. After that day at Nadar's where we passed without speaking (although I later heard he did enquire after me) we met at the Baron de Nivière's. It was in the early hours of the morning. He had just lost a hundred thousand francs on two successive hands of baccara when he leapt up, like a man possessed, demanding the window blinds be hermetically sealed so that daybreak could not come until he had been revenged. I remember crossing the room and taking his hand; me tall and thin, towering over him as he bubbled over like a cauldron of energy. He looked into my deep, beautiful eyes and seemed to simmer down into my hands. He muttered that I was an angel, that I had come to save him, that Allah had sent me to redeem him. With that and still holding my hand, he retook his seat, calmly, as if nothing had happened and, with complete control, he started to win. I became his lucky charm and from that night onwards I was indispensable to him.

Chapter 2

To get to Courbet's, Khalil and I had to go south of the river. Ostensibly the trip was to see Khalil's new painting, *The Sleepers*. It was the talk of the town. Courbet had brought Jo Hiffernan back from Normandy and the word was that James Whistler had entrusted her to him whilst he was out of town. Whistler then disappeared to Chile, of all places, leaving his beloved Jo behind; that fire-haired Goddess of the Emerald Isle left in the hands of the most untrustworthy man in Paris. Inevitably, Courbet had his way with her and she had taken to posing for him in all manner of disgusting arrangements to suit the delectation of Courbet's clients. When that client was Khalil there would be no depth of indecency those debauched animals would not descend to. An artistic relationship that started with a fairly benign portrait of Jo brushing her hair in front of a mirror, fully dressed of course, with a lace collar buttoned right up to her throat, would end in *The Sleepers*; two naked women interlaced: lips hovering over breasts, legs over legs, crumpled sheets, broken strings of pearls, openings all over the place.

Khalil was practically licking his lips in anticipation as we passed the new theatre on our right, the Châtelet, and approached another of Haussman's project's, the Pont du Change. Those were the years when Haussman was manically ripping up the whole city as if it were his plaything. It was almost impossible to travel five minutes without some new avenue, bridge or building being erected in one's path. The wind that morning was the dreaded North-Easterly and as we mounted onto the bridge, we caught it full in the face; the stench of death coming down from the abattoirs of Montfaucon. We both had to cover our noses to prevent ourselves retching and Khalil coughed worryingly into the silk of his handkerchief.

"I'll give Haussman some credit," he said through the silk. "He did at least sort the sewers out, which was all well and good. But he then turned the bloody things into a tourist attraction, even Nadar is running around underground with his damned camera and mannequins, photographing skulls all day long! That being so, my question is: can the Baron not take a break from digging up every street around Rue de Luxembourg and sort out that God awful smell?"

"I was at the Odéon last night," I said, "and they were shouting 'Down with Haussmann', with the Emperor right there in the royal box. He must had heard it. I've never seen the like. Who do you think will win that one: the people or Haussman? People are saying that Paris has had it with his endless reforms and one day someone will throw him off one of his own bridges! He can look for Jean Valjean on his way down." Khalil coughed throatily and shot me a mischievous glance over the top of his handkerchief.

"So, you were at the Odéon last night, were you?" Khalil asked with a hint of jealousy in his tone. "And in whose box, I would like to know?"

"Well, yours of course, Monsieur, no one else's," I replied as innocently as I could.

"And with whom, if I may ask?"

"With *ladies* of the highest calibre, I assure you, the finest Ladies of the theatre; Caroline and, of course, Pauline."

"And no gentlemen there to buy you your famous sugared raisins from that little confectioner in the Passage de L'Opéra at the intervals?"

"Tragically not, I must say we were all famished and bored by the end of the ballet and the thought of sitting through a drama *and* a burlesque after the second interval was too much even for us! I even sent a note up to you to order in supper, but apparently you were *tired!* You weren't fiddling around in a box of your own were you, my dear?" I asked slyly. Khalil gave a short laugh and even though there was a handkerchief in the way I knew there was a smile spreading over his face.

"No one's box but yours, my love," he joked.

"Wait till you see Jo's! Apparently, Courbet went through a *louis* worth of red paint on her pubic hair alone! He was trowelling it on with a palette knife, they say."

"Ha! You naughty girl you." And here he dropped his handkerchief as the wind died down. Notre Dame towered over us on the left and there was a look of childish joy in his eyes mixed with a worrying tint of devilry. "But you are misinformed, my dear. Not a sous of paint was used for that aspect. As far as I have heard there is nothing to paint, not even with a sable-haired brush."

"Heard, Khalil? Or know?"

"Heard...heard, just heard." And he smiled to himself as we moved onto the Pont Saint-Michel on the other side of the Ile de Cité and I stared down the river at Notre-Dame's two stumpy towers and the spire thrusting up into the blue sky. "How ironic that you should enquire," he muttered.

Courbet was not at his studio. We waited for him on the corner of rue Hautefeuille and Boulevard Saint Germain. From there you could hear the singing coming from Brasserie Andler, the so-called Cathedral of the Realists where Courbet had, until a few years previously, been the High Priest. A man staggered onto the street spilling the dregs of a keg of beer on the cobbles and projected his vomit against a nearby tree.

"Andler is suing him for 3000 francs of unpaid bills apparently," Khalil nodded towards the tavern. "He tried to fob her off with a portrait but couldn't even be bothered to extend it to a half-length! Lazy bastard. Thought he would get away with a head portrait for 3000 francs of beer, that's socialism for you, always on the side of the working man!" Khalil snorted as he pulled out his pocket watch. "Bloody hell!" he continued, "I wish he would pay his fucking bar bill and stop traipsing all the way up to de Matrys, I'll be damned if I am going to chase him all around Paris just because he has been thrown out of every brasserie on the left bank. He wanted us to come down here and so we are here. The least he can do is show up. Bloody man has a stipend from his father and Austrian bonds that are roaring on the stock market. Bloody hypocrite socialist. I heard that in Ghent the Prince rode him around the streets in his own carriage, Gustave was over the moon. So much for his much-heralded class-less utopia? He gets drunk and shouts for realism: *Banish the mysterious,* HIC, *the marvellous,* BELCH, s*how me an angel and I'll paint you an angel!* Fucking hypocrite." He started laughing at his own joke and I joined in politely. Like all men, Khalil didn't like laughing on his own. It irked him.

"Shh, here he comes," I said.

Courbet rounded the corner preceded by his beard and then his belly, what a mass of flesh, you couldn't mistake it. Behind him trailed a mostly drunk line of disciples.

"Pasha, my Lord, my Sultan!" he boomed, "Come up, come up. I will show you something that will make you sweat, I swear to you. These gentlemen have seen it just this morning. One almost fainted." Murmurs of genius from the gaggle following him, "No! Messieurs," Courbet's face went an operatic red, "Not a genius. I am Courbet! Not a traditionalist, not a realist, I am the first Courbetist! There will be many more, I assure you, the whole world will try to follow me, but my painting is the only true one. I am the first and the only unique artist of the century, yes Monsieur, even on the street I will say it out loud. It can be no other way. I do what I have to do. I am accused of vanity. I am indeed the proudest man on earth."

"And I am cold, Gustave," Khalil shot back frostily. "Can you pause your self-congratulations for just a moment and open the door?" Courbet exploded in laughter and grabbed the small Egyptian in a bear hug that would have crushed most men.

"Of course, my friend, of course. Come see what I have done for you and," he glanced through his crumb-filled beard and winked at me, "what I will do."

155

Khalil cheered up as we stood in the studio looking at the picture that to my eyes was nothing more than two naked women in bed. The men may have used high words, 'the truth of the real', but to me it was the filth of the street. I recognised the gutter for what it was because, unlike those two men, I was born in it. Not like Gustave with his prosperous farming father in Doubs, or Khalil, born in Muhammad Ali's mansion in Cairo, although in fairness to the latter, at least he was proud of his wealth. I was the real thing, those two were just playing, making representations and images. Beautiful painting, maybe, but pale shadows in my opinion.

Khalil was smoking a Turkish cigarette and Courbet was draped over a chair, filling his pipe. I was standing by the window, next to the crumpled bed that still smelled of Jo, a bed I promised myself I would not get into.

"Excellent, Gustave, excellent. And so, to the next one, eh, the next step. As we discussed?" With these mysterious words Khalil suddenly turned on his heals and walked straight past me towards the door. He paused at the doorway and glanced towards me reassuringly. Then without a word he left.

Courbet was staring at me intently. It didn't worry me. I knew him, he wouldn't try anything with me, he wasn't that type. He would expect me to sleep with him but not because he would force me. He expected me to love him, for Gustave was a man who thought every woman alive would immediately fall for him the moment they saw him, fall for his genius, whatever that is. I knew I would do no such thing and also that he wasn't the type to get violent. He was too much of an egotist. He didn't want to own women, he merely expected women to want to submit to him. When they didn't, he didn't rationalise it by looking in the mirror at his bloated body or ugly face, he was merely stupefied, like a little boy. I knew he could offer me nothing, no status, no money, no position. Khalil knew it too. Courbet didn't know it yet, but that wasn't my problem. He could look, he could look as much and as long as he liked. Khalil was paying for it. Take a good look.

"Did he tell you want he wants me to do," he said in a gruff voice.

"No."

"Can I be frank with you."

"Might as well."

"He wants a picture of you naked." He said it straight. "He wants it to look like that photograph we saw in Nadar's. He wants a pair of legs and what's in between. He wants to see everything. He wants to own every bit of you. His *lucky charm*." He raised his eyebrows ironically, snorted and coughed at the same time. Puffs of pipe smoke blew out of his mouth and hung by the ceiling in a mist and then *poof* just vanished.

"Very well," I said. Not much I could say to that.

"I will do as he asks," Courbet said. "I want you to know that."

"Of course you will Gustave, you are being paid. Just like me." He shot up to his feet with anger in his eyes and his pipe fell out of his mouth to the ground. To me he just looked bloated and ridiculous.

"This has nothing to do with money," he shouted at me, spraying spit across the room. "How dare you mention that word in this place. This is the temple of art! Fuck you and fuck money, fuck all of you, you public! What do you know? In the arts a man must make no concession to the public mind against his own ideas. If he does, his originality doesn't exist. One isn't born a Genius, Constance, one is born with particular propensities and faculties; it's through will and work that one arrives at being a man!"

"Oh, give it a break, Gustave." I stifled a yawn, "Man man man, you know nothing. How do you think one *arrives* at being a woman?"

"Through your cunt!"

"Exactly, the only genius I am allowed. So, you shut *your* hole and get on with it. All your high talk is boring me and I want to get to the theatre this evening."

Courbet slumped back into his chair and leaned over his massive belly to pick up his pipe with an old-man's groan of effort. When he looked up, he had that sad look of juvenile confusion in his eyes. It was the look he wore when he came up against the reality of other peoples' negative

157

perception of him. I was having too much fun, so I faked another yawn, one of my specialities on the stage. I used to be able to do it so convincingly that I would send the whole dance troupe off with contagious yawning.

"Yes, well," he cleared his throat and relit his pipe. "So, you can model if you wish, or Khalil says we can go to Nadar and I can paint it from a photograph. It makes no difference to me," he said sulkily.

"No photographs. One painting, only one, for Khalil and Khalil alone." And with that boundary set, he immediately cheered up, rubbed his hands together and suddenly sparked into life with tangible energy.

"Ok, very good, very good. You take your clothes off and I will prep the canvas." I gazed wearily at the crumpled bed, so boring.

*

Gustave might have been a stuck-up pain in the ass but at least he worked quickly. From start to finish he knocked the whole thing out in around five weeks. Those were some of the most boring weeks of my life. Having got Khalil to promise he would never show the painting to anyone I resigned myself to it. I went to the studio each day, got undressed and lay on the bed with my left leg straight out and my right leg off to the side. Before long an indentation of my body had imprinted itself on the bed and each morning when I arrived it was there, as if a ghostly version of myself had morphed into the bed, awaiting my return. They say he bedded hundreds of women on that bed, which is something I can neither attest to nor deny, but I can categorically state that he never touched either me or the bed when I was there.

Nobody else was allowed near the bed while he worked on my painting. I recall one evening Champfleury thoughtlessly went to sit on it and Courbet turned on him with wild eyes popping from his fat face and screamed at him with a ferocity that I never thought him capable of: "NOT THERE!!!!" It was the only time I was ever truly frightened of him and I think the only time the studio fell totally silent.

I posed with a thin stretch of white sheet draped over the top of my body from my right nipple to my left shoulder. Every evening I carefully lifted it off like a leaf being peeled away from a cauliflower and every morning I carefully repositioned it exactly as it had been; with my left breast visible but my right one covered. Due to the diligence with which I returned each day to the exact same position he had no need to touch either me or the bed on any day except the first. Every morning when I was in position, he would hover over me murmuring: "Yes, that's exactly right, yes, perfect. Exactly as you were. Perfect." Out loud he would say, "Well, I must say you really are the most professional model I have ever come across. Yes, indeed, excellent. Very good."

Gustave would then position himself at his easel which was at the foot of the bed directly between my legs and stare intently at my genitles as if his real aim was to see past it and paint my colon. I noticed that rather than paint with defined brushstrokes, Gustave apply layers of paint, working up the image in degrees from shadow to light. Often, he would work for hours without even using a brush but instead smear the paint on with his pallet knife as if he was building a wall, not painting a picture. He would sometimes mumble to himself when we were alone, as if teaching a non-existent pupil:

"You see, it is not painting, not even drawing, really. It is colour application, shades, shadows, lights and tints and then as if by magic. Bauf! Voilà! You see, you see. You have to mix the paint so it is thick, see, like this, viscous and then mix and mix. Keep going, keep going. It has to be so thick that it reflects the light, see, that is the trick, like a mirror to the colour around it. And then: ha-ha! The shadow layer goes on top, layer after translucent layer so that the different layers shine through each other, see, look at Rubens, look at Titian, look at Rembrandt, dark to light, layer on layer, you see? Just like magic, see, just like magic." These were the moments I enjoyed the best, the brief, blissful ones when he forgot that I was there.

Sadly, these quiet moments when we were alone and he was lost in his work, when I felt somehow less real to him than the painting he was executing, were rare. Mostly, people milled around all day: painters, writers, philosophers, critics, poets and pimps. Most were taken aback when they first walked into the studio to be greeted by the sight of a female vulva gaping at them, but once the shock passed, they feasted their eyes and enjoyed a really thorough look at me. After that initial gorging I became just another object in the room: like the bed, the chair, the vase of flowers, the bowl of fruit. Mostly they were there to flatter Courbet and impress each other by coming up with witty aphorisms or rhyming couplets. But when push came to shove Courbet was the master of all the hot air, forever pontificating loudly to his audience.

"In our so very civilised society it is necessary for me to live as a savage, my friends. I must be free even of government. The people have my sympathies, I must address myself to them directly."

The people, indeed! From where I sat, Courbet was a fairly well-off artist, being paid a small fortune by one of the wealthiest men in Paris to paint the private parts of a thirty-four year old ex-ballet dancer who grew up in poverty with a mother that made gauze, and no father to speak of. Sympathy for the people! What a joke. Courbet did indeed live as a savage, but not in the way he meant. All these men were savages. They looked and they painted, they made up crap verses, they theorised and they owned.

It was made worse by the fact that the beer flowed constantly as he painted. He sang loudly when there were people about; gruff Norman songs, beer songs of hunting and killing and men and fucking. It was a stark contrast to the quiet murmurings of his solitude. He was performing for the crowd. I AM COURBET. I respected that, we performers recognise one another, we know each other. He painted, he drank, he laughed, he drank and everyone talked and talked and talked. So many words. If there had been a tax on words Napoléon would have had enough money to knock the whole city down and Haussmann could have rebuilt it from scratch.

I guess I should say something redeeming about Gustave, my mother always told me to be kind-in-spirit to my fellow man. So, I will say this about him: he worked fast, he never laid a finger on me (out of fear, rather than altruism, but nevertheless) and I think that deep down he was the saddest person I had ever come across. He just couldn't show it. So, he drank.

Chapter 3

Apart from the time I spent at his studio I never saw Courbet. We moved largely in different circles. His spare time, as far as I could tell, was spent touring the brasseries of Montmartre, those few that would still extend him credit, with a small following of acolytes whose main function seemed to be drinking with him, agreeing with him and generally praising him to the skies. When he was not painting, drinking, or speechifying he was generally out of town, visiting his father's lands where, I presume, he was sponging off daddy (a quintessentially left-wing pastime), drinking, hunting and socialising. In those days off, Khalil and I often visited other artists' studios and literary salons, but I never saw Courbet there. He simply did not seem at all interested in the cultural life of Paris other than what he himself was painting.

Only once did I meet him at anything vaguely cultural. I once saw him at the Opéra, at a performance of Berlioz's *Benvenuto Cellini*. I noticed him during the first act. I was sitting in Khalil's box and he was down below me in the stalls, crammed uncomfortably into his seat. I couldn't see his face, but I recognised his squirming posture and slumped shoulders. The poor gentleman next to him was being crushed into the left-hand side of his chair to avoid Gustave's expansive body and foul mood. I took pleasure in Gustave's obvious physical and psychological discomfort in this arena of coiffured culture and class (my domain) which clearly did not suit him. I had been cursed to spend so much of my time in his studio with his vile friends; I distinctly remember my disdain for the fact that, unlike me, he was entirely unadaptable. He always boasted of the Dukes and Marquises among his acquaintances in the low countries and yet I could never imagine him mingling in that sort of company. Here was my proof. He was, at his core, everything he hated most: a middle-class son of a landowning farmer done good. He was caught in between, neither properly ascended nor genuinely working class. Poor Gustave. There is a saying in French: to be "bien dans sa peau", to feel comfortable in one's skin – it was a comfort he never found.

Jo Hiffernan was sitting on the other side of him trying to enjoy the opera but was being visibly put off by Gustave's (probably audible) consternation. During the first break I caught Jo's eye as she scanned the boxes with her opera-glasses – I motioned her to come up and we met them in the corridor along with Gautier who Khalil had invited to our box.

"You are to be admired, my dear," Gautier quipped as he kissed Jo on each cheek, "for persuading your paysan to come to the opera. I can't remember anyone else succeeding in this task." Gustave just grunted.

"Well," Jo said in her gorgeous Irish-inflected French, "I think this is as much as I can manage, unfortunately. I thought I could tempt him with an opera about the famous sculptor Cellini, a man I know he admires as much for his life as for his art."

Gustave sighed, "I only agreed to come here because she told me Cellini was on the barricades during the sack of Rome, that he was stationed on the Castel Saint-Angelo, protecting the pope and picking off Germans one by one with an arquebuse. That's what I came to see." He mimicked holding a rifle with his hands and tut-tut-tut-tuted at each of us with his imaginary weapon.

Khalil smiled mischievously. "In the event of the sack of Paris, we all hope Gustave here is on the front line picking off the enemy but maybe, as well, he should be hotfooting it to the galleries. A lot of art was lost during that siege."

"I would do that too," Gustave solemnly proclaimed, a rather ironic interjection, as we would discover in time.

"Fine words! He says he won't stay after the interval. Too much singing for him, not enough fighting!" Jo said mournfully.

"If the music not to your liking, Gustave," said Gautier, "don't criticise it in front of me, I implore you. Please remember that Berlioz and I are very good friends, it is a tragedy that he stopped writing music. I blame the Théâtre Lyrique. They were brutal in their dealings with him over *Les Troyens*. They made the poor man cut the opera twice and even after that they only put it on for less than a fortnight before pulling it entirely. How can any artist accept that kind of treatment? Surely you agree, Gustave, that a piece of art, whether it be a picture, a novel or an opera should be preserved with the dimensions with which it was conceived as opposed to being constantly cut down. I have written to Berlioz many times underlining my support for him and imploring him to take up his pen but sadly to no avail. An artist can only take so much."

"Indeed, this is a tragic case." Gustave perked up at this turn of the conversation. "Art can only be as the artist intends. Sadly, for us real artists, us geniuses, the theatres, or in my case the Salon has too much influence over artistic production. It is for the artist to be free to express himself in any way he sees fit. I admit to being ignorant in this case of Berlioz but I fully support his right to create whatever music he sees fit without being in any way molested."

Khalil opened his mouth, presumably to assert the rights of the commissioner, but seemed to think better of it and kept quiet. Once a diplomat, always a diplomat.

"As we are on this subject," resumed Gautier, "I wonder if I could amuse you with the story of Pierre Ducré. It was some time ago now, a good ten years, more even, when Berlioz was at his lowest. Everyone was out to get him, you should appreciate that feeling, Gustave. The worst was that bloody Italian Scudo, the imbecile! What did he say about Hector: that his compositions were nothing but noise? It was too much! And yet, everyone was with Scudo."

"I heard Scudo died recently in an insane asylum," Gustave cut in. "Where all you critics belong if you ask me."

"An outlier to our fine profession," Gautier shot back with a grin. "Anyway, Berlioz played such a trick on them all! I think you will like this one. One day he turned up to rehearsals claiming to have discovered a tattered score that had been hidden in a secret compartment at the Saint-Chapelle which was being renovated. He claimed to have laboured for hours interpreting and transcribing, eventually bringing forth what he said was a forgotten piece: *L'adieu des bergers* by Pierre Ducré, a long dead master chorister from the 1670s. And what do you think? Everyone was entranced by it! A work of genius, they said! Of course, no one wanted to admit that they had never heard of this Ducré.

"At every performance there was a queue outside Berlioz's door – everyone clamouring and hoping for more Ducré manuscripts to emerge and be deciphered. Messages came from Germany, London, even Rome – all of Europe was trembling with anticipation! In the end Berlioz couldn't take it any longer and he came clean – of course it had been him all along. It had all been a hoax. He himself had written the score that had gone down so well. There never had been anyone called Ducré, he had made it up. Suddenly the mood changed, I heard one critic say that he didn't like the music now he knew it was by Berlioz and not Ducré. How does one answer that?"

"There is no answer! An artist never needs to answer!" thundered Courbet. "Besides, the genius is the artist, not the art. It would have come out in the end."

"I disagree, Gustave," said Khalil. "The artist turns to dust – he is a mere shadow of the stories that survive him. All that is left is a name: Ducré, Berlioz, Courbet. In two hundred years these are just labels hanging on the art which perseveres. Let me tell you something: the Ottoman Empire thought that the Sistine Chapel ceiling was painted by Raphael, not Michelangelo! Why? Well, there were once great tapestries adorning the walls of the Chapel that were the work of Raphael. When news reached Istanbul that the ceiling had been painted and it was miraculous, the diplomat who wrote the missive just assumed that it was also by Raphael. It caused all sorts of confusion and was queried in every diplomatic missive shuttling back and forth between Istanbul and the Vatican. Everyone agreed the painting was amazing, they just couldn't agree on who held the paintbrush!

"In the end, what does it matter? The painting is still a wonder. What's in a name? In Istanbul, Jesus is a prophet, in Rome he is God. How to prove it? You can't! History is a slippery thing, untrustworthy as a dancing snake at the bazaar. But the painting itself, the music, this remains – and you are free to tell any stories you want to about it."

While he was talking the Prussian ambassador came up and joined us. He was heading back to his box and stopped to listen to Khalil. "Ah! My friend, Khalil Bey! I could not help but overhear your fine philosophical speech. I remember well when you were an ambassador in the service of the very Empire of which you speak. You would not have spoken like this back then."

"My friend," Khalil spun round with a smile and clasped the German's hand warmly, "but in those days my words were not my own. Now I am free to speak as I please."

The Prussian ambassador smiled. "Freedom too is an illusion, Khalil," he said. "You speak of the slipperiness of History but in Prussia, history is a more solid thing. Mark my words, gentlemen," and here he looked around and waived his hands towards the opulence of the opera goers, who were making their way back to their boxes, "the frivolities of France will not be enjoyed for much longer. I fear for you, my friends. My country is in the ascendency and when Prussia ascends it does so with the force of the German spirit behind it. We do not fail. There is no dancing snake, no sleight of hand here."

But Courbet had already turned his back on the ambassador and was dragging Jo away by the arm.

"But perhaps my truths have offended you, dear Sir," the ambassador shouted down the corridor after him.

"Oh dear," tutted Gautier shaking his head, "must you always be so unpleasant."

"Really," Khalil seconded.

"I mean not to offend," the Prussian said in a thick accent, "merely to predict what is to come. You know this as well as I do, Khalil. The Ottomans should have never aligned so closely with the French. They are two stars dying together."

"Must we talk politics now? I am not sure the break is long enough. Maybe you should get yourself some five-sous sport with one of those wenches down there and relieve a bit of nervous tension."

"Out of action to be honest, still recovering the last bout! But seriously, I am telling you as a friend," and here the Prussian ambassador drew close to Khalil and lowered his voice. "You have always been good to me Khalil, I don't forget. Please, hear me now. Get out, get out of this country or you will see things you don't want to. This decadence has run its course. All societies who get to this level collapse under their hubris. This country has lived life to the full and now the bill has come. It has to be paid. It is a fact of history."

"Even Prussia then, one day?" Khalil answered with a provocative smile.

"Not Prussia." The German said pulling himself up to his full height and twiddling his moustaches. He clenched a fist and beat his chest with it, "The only place I will see the downfall of Prussia, is seated on a golden chair in the throne room of heaven. Do you Muslims even have a heaven?"

"We do. But in ours we recline. We do not sit."

"Like I said! Decadence!"

Chapter 4

As we were finishing up, Courbet was already moving on to other projects. He was anxious about his Salon entries for the year. I had made Khalil tell him that the painting of me was never to be exhibited publicly, so he was forced to rework sketches of Jo for another nude that he could submit to the Académie instead. This time he painted her lying on a crumpled bed (the very same crumpled bed) with her legs open and a parrot alighting on her index finger. The viewer's angle was on the opposite side in order to tone down the shock value. He painted her with her hair in the foreground, splayed out like estuaries running to the sea and her legs extending across the canvas with the bed sheet partially covering her hairless privates. Just to annoy him I asked how he was going to get a parrot to pose in mid-air for him for four weeks without moving. He just humphed at me.

"The parrot will do as he is asked, like all of my models."

"Shall I get Khalil to drop in the details of his taxidermist for you. We can't have any movement get in the way of your realism."

"Very good, dear." And he muttered under his breath that he would be glad to finish and be done with me.

There were students milling around, patching up old, ripped canvases which they thickly overpainted to hide the rips.

"You see, it's totally fine," Courbet shouted at one of them. "No need to waste money at Lefranc and Cie buying a new canvas, this will be fine.

More primer, you! More undercoat, imbecile! Smooth, I said, smooth."
The bustle about him seemed to bring forth a nervous energy in him.

"He always gets like this near the deadline for the Salon," Thoré
whispered to me, as I was leaving one evening. The great critic, who
discovered Franz Hals and Vermeer, was swinging on the back two legs
of his chair, running his fingers through the luscious beard that
completely hid his neck. He was wearing a black suit, his favourite one,
the one in which Nadar had photographed him. His lucky suit. There
was a lot of superstition around the great rationalists of the day.

"I wouldn't have thought he cared what the Salon thinks," I said
mischievously, "what with his originality and genius and everything.
Surely only *'the people'* could judge his work." Thoré laughed and rolled
his eyes.

"I will put that phrase down to feminine naivety if you don't mind. If
not, I would have to take you as thoroughly cruel." He allowed the chair
to bang back onto all four legs and the sunlight flashed off his balding
head. He shot me a cheeky smile. "Evidently he cares. Why do you think
he went so crazy when the Goncourts described his pictures as: 'ugliness
and more ugliness, ugliness without the beauty of ugliness.' He was so
mad I thought he was going to challenge them both to a duel, at the
same time!" Here he paused, as if deciding whether to go on or not,
weighing up whether I was trustworthy. "In the end he is just like
everyone else; he says he doesn't care what anyone thinks but that only
holds as long as they are applauding. He wants the Salon Judges to love
him and reject him simultaneously, just like any child. That is what all
painters want these days, acceptance by the State for the money and
fame without damaging their rebellious outsider status. Artists are
nothing but neuroses and internally combusting egos, stay well clear of
them my dear."

"Nearly ready," Courbet called out from the next room.

"Hmmph, he doesn't care about the Académie des Beaux-Arts, does
he?" Thoré was staring at his nails, absentmindedly talking in a low
voice. His eyes had glazed over as if he were conducting an interior

monologue, one he had practiced over and over in his mind but had never had the courage to verbalise. This is how arrogant men often talk when they are with women, especially women they hold in contempt. They talk as if they are talking to the walls, as if we are not even there. "He hates it, does he? Rip it up, he says, this abomination: *the most conservative artistic institution in the world!* Don't make me laugh." Suddenly he looked straight at me and started as if I had appeared from nowhere, invading his space. He gave a soft, rather patronising smile, leant over and whispered to me like he was explaining something rudimentary to a small child, which is the other way men like to talk to women. "Why do you think I am here? So I can accompany him to dinner with Count Nieuwerkerke and try to sell this crap to the state." He nodded at the half-finished nude with sketched-in parrot. "Really! An Irish slut with a parrot, painted just so. Nothing refined about the picture at all, no beauty or history to it. No class. He is the mannerist of ugliness. Look at that flesh, nothing idealised in it at all. I have told him to smooth it off, think of Ingres. As you can see, I have had no luck. So, I told him, fine, just do a nice landscape for the Count and – *quelle surprise* – that is exactly what he is doing. Why do you think they are patching up that canvas over there? It will be a lovely clearing with trees and a stream, with a few roe deer thrown in. Courbet wants prizes like they all do – especially the Légion d'Honneur that he missed out on a few years back. So that is what he must do: porn for the Egyptian, landscapes for the Academié. It is the perfect balance, Gustave gets paid, he can stop sponging off his dad, or at least tone it down a bit. After that he can go off to the brasserie with all his friends and hold forth about his precious freedom as much as he likes!

"... Ah Gustave, ready to go? Mustn't keep the Count waiting."

*

"When is a painting finished, Gustave?" I could hear Thoré and Champfleury as I dressed behind the screen. I have an image of them at the table by the window, drinking wine, enjoying the warmth of the Parisian spring, sunshine streaming in through the open windows, filling the room with light and heat. They were discussing art, what else, while Courbet lightly layered the white fur on the deer in the left foreground of a picture, the one looking upwards as if God had just called out to him.

"Ah, that is an easy one, Gentlemen," Courbet said, standing back to look at the Count's landscape. "It is finished when the artist says it is finished, not before and not after. We are the masters of our canvases. We build them up layer upon layer until you get to the final touch, what your man Franz Hals called '*The Master's Touch*', eh, Theo? Yes, I have read your work, I know you think I am an unlearned paysan, but I am not so ignorant as you think. You forget I have travelled to the same cities as you, to the Low Countries and I have gone to these museums of which you speak. But when I went there, I was such a success they closed the museums just for me. I was accompanied by Counts and Princes, you know this well..."

"Ah, but you only followed where I led, Gustave," Thoré said with a smile, "you forget I discovered Vermeer; I discovered Hals. They were lost before me." Courbet looked up and snorted.

"When is a painting finished, you ask?" Courbet continued. "'*The Masters Touch*', yes. I call it: '*My Dominant.*' No one can copy this. It is the final stroke, a detail that brings the picture to perfection. Follow this comparison if you will: we are enveloped in the morning twilight, objects are only barely perceptible. Then the sun comes up and they are suddenly visible in the light, they are defined in all their fullness. I do in my pictures what the sun does in nature. What once was only in the power of the Gods is now the preserve of the great artist like me, I bring it all off, thus, by the force of the wrist." He leaned back and smiled at the roe-deer whose white arse winked at him.

"So, it is all down to the artist, eh?" said Champfleury.

"Of course."

I came out into the room and sat next to the table by the mirror. No one even acknowledged my presence. I knew Khalil would arrive soon and that would all change. In his company I was someone, something, made so by his proximity, his wealth and their greed. Alone, I was barely an inanimate object.

I took out my muslin bag of powder and began to make up my face. I always used a light dusting of a powder that I learnt to mix myself: white starch, a drachm of rose pink, essence of jasmine and otto of roses. Although I was never one for deep rouge, like those harlots from the théâtre des Délassements-Comiques, I did apply a hint of colour to my cheeks as I felt that it made me look a bit more natural. Needless to say, I was not one of those who painted her lips, however I did dab them a little with some damp red crepe paper that gave a natural, but rosy glint, whilst still keeping them looking moist. In front of me the painting sat on an easel behind a cover. I knew I would need all my composure to hold my face, not to react to it, no matter how sickening it made me feel. I had to paint my mask on and suck in my soul, push it deep down into the pit of my stomach and think of the money.

Thoré dragged at his cigarette and blew out rounds of smoke through the open window. "Let me tell you a story of one of your favourites, Gustave, the great Rembrandt's portrait of Jan Six.

"Rembrandt was a cad, a shyster," Thoré continued, "he was basically a little shit. I know you make your models sit for a few weeks, Gustave, and I am sure you make them uncomfortable after the sessions! Yes, you know what I mean! But Rembrandt wanted to torture his sitters. He hated them, he wanted to destroy them, humiliate them, you just want to shag them all. He had a chip on his shoulder. Yes, he had become successful and rich, but he did it by kowtowing to the Burgemeesters and he knew it. His only revenge was when they sat for him. He would make them suffer, then he would try to rip them off.

"It was a scam. Rembrandt would leave the portrait rough, barely finished and then send it over to the client. When it came back with complaints that it was unacceptable, he would charge a touch-up fee over and above the agreed price. The man spent more time embroiled in legal disputes than you, Gustave! When he was on the up and everyone wanted paintings from him it was fine; they would put up with the rudeness, the lateness, the long hours of sitting and he would gloat: 'Those bastards want a picture from me, the great Rembrandt? So fuck them! To get a picture from me one must beg and beg and then add money!'

"But what goes up, Gentlemen, must come down and soon he was ruined. Bankruptcy was inevitable. Rembrandt was a busted flush, a bitter, washed-up has been, with the creditors knocking down his door. No one wanted to be seen with him or commission work from him, it was as if he had leprosy. Of his old acquaintances, only the Six family still gave work to him and that was out of sheer charity, hence the famous Portrait of Jan Six.

"Rembrandt has painted him in a liminal space, as if he is in the corridor – but is he going out or coming in? His coat is draped over his shoulder and his bare right hand grasps the mustard glove on his left. But is he pulling it on or about to take it off? The paint is so thin it is almost not there, translucent, you can see the ground base on the canvas coming through in places. The yellow ochre brushstrokes that make up the fastenings of the coat are so faint they are almost an optical illusion, as if solidity is being hinted at rather than rendered.

"It is regarded as a great painting, yes, but is it finished? The blur of the brushstrokes makes one think not, I wonder what you would make of it, Gustave. It is now seen as a masterpiece, one of the greatest portraits ever painted. But this is not Rembrandt's masterpiece. It is Jan Six's masterpiece!

"Even though Rembrandt owed Jan more than he could ever repay, even though Jan was the only one still commissioning from him, Rembrandt was up to his old shit again. He was dragging his heels. He wrote a letter to Jan demanding a higher fee because the portrait was so perfect that he simply could not let it go. He said it was breaking his heart to part with it, that he would keep it. He said that he needed at least ten sittings of ten hours each to get the light right.

"Jan got more and more annoyed at these tricks that eventually he went over and demanded to see it in whatever state it was in. This was

173

how he found it, just as it is now, what we see as a masterpiece of art: all smudges and flashes, the paint thinned to such an extent that Six wondered if Rembrandt had mixed any new paint at all for the portrait. The artist demanded more sittings. He told him not to move for at least seven hours. Then he could do the left eyebrow. He was moaning that paint was so expensive, the vermillion for the red coat was exorbitant. That he needed to up the fee. Jan lost his temper:

"'How do you know? You have hardly used any paint! And I am not a fucking idiot. I know you well enough. That isn't even vermillion there, it is red ochre – one normally only uses ochre for the lower base layer!' He turned to one of Rembrandt's few remaining apprentices, hiding behind his partition pretending to paint the top ground layer onto an old canvas that he was priming for his master to reuse and said, 'You there, yes, you. Box it up and send it round. I will take it as it is. My man will be up to help you.'

"Rembrandt realised he had overplayed his hand. He tried to grab Jan by the arm and apologise. He fell on his knees:

"'It's ok,' he said, 'You're right, don't take it. It isn't finished. Please, I can make a masterpiece for you. Please. You can't have it. It's mine! I am the artist, I am Rembrandt. You can't! I will finish it. I promise. By next week. Please. No cost. It will be my gift to you, please. By next week. Not a problem. After all you have done for me, it is the least I can do. Your eminence. My friend. Please. You can't, it is mine, it is mine. The glove is barely painted, please, let me at least touch up the glove. It is not finished.'

"'It is to me.'

"That was that. Jan Six took it with him and that is how it still is to this day. The painting was finished when Jan Six said it was finished, not Rembrandt, eh, Gustave. What do you make of that?"

*

They fell silent when Khalil entered the room. There was a lot of male back slapping and hand shaking. In the end the message got through and the assorted acolytes filed out and down the stairs until only Khalil,

Courbet and I were left in the room. It was a horrid moment when he pulled the cover off. I could hardly make myself look. The worst was that he had got my eyes just right, my eyebrows were perfectly rendered. It broke my heart. I felt a little bit of vomit rise up my throat, but I managed to swallow it down. I tensed the back of my jaw imperceptibly and tried to stare just past the painting to a spot of the wall. If I just focus on that, I thought, nothing will show on my face.

Khalil and Courbet talked around each other as they always did, nothing but empty words; flattery and falsity. There is only so much of it one can take. I looked in the general direction of the painting without bringing it into focus for as long as I could but, in the end, I had to turn away. I walked over to the window and allowed the warmth of the sun to fall on me. Behind it all, I thought, was this, the sun and sky and water and air. These were real, I thought, things that make the flowers grow and allow nature to flourish. More and more I felt the need to be away from this disgusting city, peopled by these horrible men. I closed my eyes and, in my mind, I went to my calm place. This was my dream; a little cottage on the coast. From the window on the second floor there were no buildings to be seen, just the cliff edge that fell away to the sea that rolled back and forth over the beach, imperceptibly wearing the stones and rocks down from solidity to nothingness. It was the house my mother had always told me stories about. We would go there when we had enough money to leave Paris, she had promised, but we never did, it only ever existed in our minds. In front of the house there would be a garden with a mature cherry tree on one side. In my dream it was always springtime and the white blossoms would be out, fluffy, round and high up like clouds. On the other side of the garden there would be a patch of tulips with lines of colours; white, pink, deep purple and the two-tone ones with vertical lines of yellow and red. The Triumph tulip, always were my favourite. If I just closed my eyes and breathed deeply I could smell the fresh scent with its slightly citrus notes. In my mind I could walk through that garden whenever I wanted; admiring the puffy little pink balls of azaleas that looked solid enough to pick up and throw into the air. When the sun got too much, I could lounge under the shade of the violet wisteria archway whose cascading cluster of fragrant flowers would seem to protect me from the world as if its pendulous racemes were a giant suit of armour. This imaginary garden always seemed more real and tangible to me than the hazy city with its smell of shit, its incessant building work and its countless idiots, useless men whose constant chatter brought me back to this reality I hated.

"For crying out loud, Khalil!" I heard myself say. It was as if the words were coming from deep inside my subconscious.

They were arguing about Courbet cutting the canvas down to remove the head. This went on for a bit longer with no resolution until finally we left. I remember that first step I took on the street outside, when I paused for just a moment as Khalil descended the last few stairs behind me and I swore to myself I would never set foot in that accursed studio ever again.

Chapter 5

Khalil kept it hidden away behind a green curtain in his dressing room as some kind of perverse after-dinner amusement for his friends, he probably jerked off to it as well. So be it. Boys will be boys. Not much can be expected of them. I made him swear never to reveal to anyone that I was the model and as far as I know he never did. It would obviously have been impossible with the face on it, but I just cut the canvas down myself which solved the issue.

The rest of the year went by smoothly. I had two or three income sources other than Khalil at that time but with the rest of them it was like getting blood out of a stone. Every request for payment was a delicate and complicated affair involving cajoling, promises and ritual humiliation. Very often these negotiations were conducted by Collette, who ran the flower shop below my apartments and helped me out, for a fee of course.

Everyone took their cut, that was the way Paris worked. Best friends, even those as close as Pauline Dameron was to me, would offer to collect three hundred francs for you from a Count to spare a scene and when you check the envelope you find two hundred and seventy. Ten new hats came from the milliner paid for by the Grand Duc de Whoever but most of them didn't even make it out of their boxes, they went back and forth as currency. Three weeks later you'd call on Collette to send up a bouquet of violets and, what do you know, she would be wearing one of them. That would be the last you would see of that. There was no point making a scene. Just shrug it off, the famous Gallic shrug of the shoulders, flick your hands and Bouf! Who cares?

With Khalil it was different. The other men knew how to use their money to get what they wanted; they realised their ability to pay your expenses was their leverage. Khalil didn't care about any of that. He coasted through life with the ease of someone born into money, someone who has never had to think about it. He never used it against me. It was there for the taking. The trick was to get as much as you could and spirit it away before the whole thing came crashing down. How many lighters and cigarette boxes must that man have got through? Every time I borrowed a lighter it went in my purse. The next day Collette took it to the pawnshop. It was not much in itself but it all added up. Then there were the big things. He never asked the price of anything, he never checked accounts. He just paid and paid, so when you went to the jewellers you would always get three pairs of earrings instead of one. Monday morning, Collette would take two back for cash. The shop made a cut, Collette made a cut and my nest-egg grew.

However, by 1867 you could see it was all falling down around his ears, poor man. My golden goose. Every time he went to Nice or Cannes for the sun or for a horse-race it would be a scramble to clear out as much as we could from his apartment. He would come back and all the furniture would be different. He never once mentioned it, I don't think he even noticed.

When it all collapsed and it came to the auction I organised the whole thing. We had all the pictures crated up and shipped out to the Hôtel Drouot. Khalil didn't want anything to do with it, fine by me. Did he think I was being loyal to him? Did he think I was his friend? Who cares? He probably thought I loved him. Men always think everyone loves them. It is a juvenile, tiresome but profitable trait. The only thing he cared about was *her*, that Courbet painting. The atrocity.

Khalil was back from Nice and getting all worked up about her. It happens to them all in the end. When the game is finally up, they all sink into a useless emotional mess and start bleating on about how ashamed their mothers will be and crying over their fathers' disappointment. Same old same old. I have seen my fill of bankruptcy; always the same play. Khalil was all over the place, running around like a mad dervish, but he still thought of *her*.

"The picture behind the green cloth, Constance. Don't forget it. It is my lucky charm. I need it. There is no value to it. Who will buy this thing anyway, it's impossible! And *The Sleepers* too, I spent thousands of francs on that, didn't I? I did, didn't I? Who will buy them? It's impossible. They can't go to the auction, Constance, surely you see that, you of all people. You must separate them out from the rest and send them onto Vienna. Do it quietly. Spirit them away when no one sees and send them on. Surely you can see that these cannot go into auction, can't you? Here is the address in Vienna. Wait until April and then send them. Quietly."

I had '*her*' crated up separately from the rest and marked with a circle of red lipstick, so it didn't get mixed up with the ones going to auction. I kept *The Sleepers* back too. I suppose it would have been easier to just destroy them and be done with it once and for all. I seriously considered it, I did, but in the end, why bother? Courbet had had a fairly good Salon in 1867 and his name was on the up.

The Drouot auction was the talk of Paris. Gautier had written the preface for the catalogue and it was being distributed all over town. Khalil, Courbet, Delacroix, Ingres. It was all everyone was talking about. Drouot had been worried about attendance numbers. I distinctly remember that it was a bitterly cold January and the snow was lying thick on the ground. Despite the weather, the queues were ridiculous. People froze to get in, their breath creating a mist that ran around the block. It was the *only* social event going. You just *had* to go. So, I thought to myself, why not get a little more for these two if I could shift them on the quiet? What was the harm in it? I was hitting thirty-six and I knew I was playing a young person's game. I needed to scrape together every franc I could and get out or I would end up destitute, coughing up blood into a two-day old handkerchief.

I spent the week touting the canvases around my friends at the ballet. The vagina was tough to shift, unsurprisingly. I told Rosa Didier, she of the stupid giggle, that it was a nude picture of Jo Hiffernan and not to spread it about. She inevitably spread it so widely that someone even told me *in the strictest confidence*! It was the only game of Chinese whispers where the sentence did not change, not even by one syllable. It went all over Paris and beyond.

I heard that Whistler was back from his gun-running trip to Chile and was staying in London. I wrote to him and offered it for a good price along with *The Sleepers*. I wrote that I had heard Jo had modelled for them both.

In the end that dreamy baritone Jean-Baptiste Faure bought *The Sleepers* and paid me what I asked for it. I hadn't even considered he would buy it. Shows how things go. The only reason I spoke with him was to ask him to give the letter to Whistler as he was going to London to sing at the Royal Opera House. When he came back, he said he had delivered the letter, but I never heard a reply. I guess Jo and Whistler weren't a thing anymore. My letter probably went straight in the bin. However, all's well that ends well. Jean-Baptiste said he was starting an art collection and would take *The Sleepers*. I tried to throw in the vagina for a cut-down price, but he wouldn't have it. He said it was obscene porn. I couldn't exactly argue with that. Although an image of two naked women in bed didn't seem to fuss him much. *Chacun à son goût?*

In the end I just had to get rid of the thing, the crate was taking up too much space in the apartment. All I could do was take the picture around the antique dealers but even they turned up their noses at it. It was unsigned and undated, which was an issue and I couldn't very well take it back to Gustave and ask him to autograph it for me. Finally, de Narde took it for a tiny down payment and that was the end of the story for me. He said he would contact me if he got something decent for it, but I never expected to hear back from him. And I didn't.

Who cares? I put on a new black dress with pristine white gloves and went to the first night of the theatre; I can't even remember what the show was, I went to so many. Was it *The First Day Of Happiness* by Auber or *Petit Pouce* at the Athénée? I lived at the theatre. I could go every day of my life and not get bored of it. I had just enough money to enjoy it without worrying.

Around that time, my best friend Pauline Dameron and I became close to Auber. In my opinion he was the greatest composer of the time. He was in his mid-eighties when we got to know him, but he still had a *joie de vivre* about him that I always admired. We looked after him, Dameron and I along with Riquer and Rosine Bloch. We brightened his final years. He simply loved being around pretty girls; we didn't have to do much more. It's not like he was able to indulge any more rapacious desires at that age. He was harmless, although he talked a good game; he said we made him feel like he was twenty-four. We were called his protective girls; we guarded the Emperor. There was a bit of social chatter about the relationship but nothing serious, nothing that stuck. It became a little Paris joke for the balls and parties. A joke that fluttered by when no one had anything better to talk about or when *Le Figaro* had nothing to write about. He was my last good payday. A combination of him and Khalil set me up. All we had to do was to get through the 1870s and we could enjoy the fruits of our wise choices.

Chapter 6

The 1870s were hard years, hard for me and especially for Courbet. The Prussian ambassador was right, in 1870 that idiot Napoléon took Bismark's bait and declared war on Prussia. God alone knows what he was thinking. The man was all ego from the tips of his boots to the ends of his curly moustaches. What a fool. All men want to be greater than their dead fathers, this one had Uncle Napoléon Bonaparte to contend with. What a waste of life, what a waste of a country. In the end war is a simple thing: the men tend to die and the women tend to starve. That was the nub of it. In July everyone gathered in Place de Bastille to watch him off, singing *la Marseillaise* and chanting: "To Berlin! To Berlin!" By September the French army was basically done for. The third and fourth Prussian armies were camped outside Paris ready to besiege. The city was cut off. It was lockdown.

Paris was so quiet that first week. There was some gunfire and a bit of shelling but very little. I remember it more as a period of stillness, like a hibernation. It may sound like a strange description, but it felt like the whole city was locked in a crate and someone had thrown away the key. My beloved theatres had closed and were being converted into hospitals. They packed up all the pictures from the Louvre and the crates were stacked up in piles on the side the road, stamped *Fragile*. We went down the (aptly named) Rue D'Enfer to see them off at the station. That's the way it is when the world goes to the dogs; the rich, the politicians and the priceless art flees first.

Soon all the shops closed down and barricaded themselves up. There was no point to being open. Everyone who had any wealth or goods had got it out of Paris before the Prussian army encircled. Nothing got through, not even the post. You had nowhere to go so you hid your valuables, locked the door and prayed. The worst thing about it was that I had worked my whole life to free myself from poverty and now anyone could just come and take it all away. There was nothing I could do: French National Guard, Prussian Infantry, just a little shit from the street, anyone. A quick robbery and probably a rape for good measure and that would have been me. Back in the shit and pushing forty. It was a nightmare.

On the whole, women didn't go outside. I sent Collette down to the bakehouse to get our rations and she stood with the rest of them for three or four hours in the ice-cold mud, soaked to the skin. At the beginning you could still get boiled mutton but soon it was all gone. The wheat ran out quickly and the bread was made of oat and rice. What came out was black and slimy, almost inedible. Kids ran up and down the line selling rats. At the beginning they were shooed away as if it were a sick joke but by the end it was a serious proposition. Prices for rat started to shoot up, forty cents apiece. The chefs who used to work in the best restaurants in Paris were making it into rat paté. It was a tough sell. We went through everything else first. We ate my horses, we ate the dogs, the cats, anything. Then it was the choice between rat or starvation.

Gautier came to visit and told me Victor Hugo was back. That was all we needed. He had been sitting around in Guernsey for the last twenty years writing *Les Miserables* and now he turns up just in time to save Gautier's horse from being turned into a steak sandwich. The Lord be praised! What a guy! Just what Paris needed. We were starving to death and facing national annihilation, only for another poet with a Messiah complex the size of their expanding waistline to arrive. It was the only time I went out for dinner. I went with Nadar and we ate with Hugo and his son in their luxury apartment on Avenue Frochot. Edmond de Goncourt was there, dressed in black, mourning the death of his beloved brother from syphilis. I think it was the first time I had ever seen one without the other. Hugo talked solid shit about how he preferred Paris as he found it. "I wouldn't have liked to see the Bois de Boulogne in the days when it was crowded with carriages, barouches and landaus. But now it's a quagmire, a ruin, it appeals to me." Hugo was rich and famous; it was a treat. That was the only reason I went. We ate antelope and bear which they had slaughtered at the Zoo in the Jardin Des Plantes and were selling to the highest bidder. The next day I passed Roos' butchers on Boulevard Haussmann and they were selling bits of an elephant from the zoo. He was right there in the window: "Exclusive: the world-famous Pollux the elephant. While stocks last." Roos was touting it out for forty francs for a pound of fillet and part of the trunk. I wouldn't have been surprised if it ended up on Hugo's table that very evening. As far as I could see all Hugo did was sit around and eat the zoo. Hardly the work of a saviour.

I already knew the story of Castor and Pollux from the Rameau opera, but women are always assumed to be more ignorant than we actually are, so I allowed Goncourt to educate me. I felt sorry for him, he was obviously dying to tell it, it was my way of being charitable. With a tear in his eye, he told me that in Greek myth Castor and Pollux were brothers. Castor was born mortal and Pollux was immortal. The way the story goes, Castor was wounded in a fight and on the verge of death. There was no way to save him, so Pollux sacrificed himself. It was the only way they could stay together. The Gods sent them up into the night's sky as the star constellation Gemini. Goncourt told me that it made him think of his own brother and started sobbing uncontrollably in the street. I couldn't help wondering for whom the elephant Pollux sacrificed himself. For Victor Hugo? What a waste. I wonder if Goncourt would have sacrificed himself for his brother and taken the syphilis in his place. When the chips are down it is impossible to say what one would do. We had too much time to think in those long, starving days. I think we all went a little crazy.

*

As an example, who would have thought that of all the people in Paris it would be Nadar who would step up. He, at least tried to make a difference. Although, like all these men, he was doing it more for himself than any sense of altruism. He had always been a nut about hot air balloons but with the city cut off Nadar took advantage of the chaos to set up the French Army's No.1 Balloon Regiment, which consisted of him and two others. I am sure it had the Prussians quaking in their boots. He installed himself and his balloon in Montmartre, loaded it up with instruments, lunch and wine and up they went; four hundred feet in the sky to note the position of the Prussian regiments. He invited me up the hill to admire him. I must admit it was a sight to behold! They went up and down about six times a day, like a yo-yo. Later in the year I heard that they even flew out to Tours to smuggle post out past the barricade and send intelligence reports to the Government of National Defence. Hugo joked that Nadar dropped hundreds of business cards complimenting the King of Prussia and Bismarck as he passed over the Prussian positions. There was a voucher on the back offering money off photography portraits for when they finally made it into the city. Nadar angrily denied it, menacingly waving his antelope leg at the writer. It wouldn't have surprised me if he had, though. The man had a business to run after all and times were tough.

Nadar also set up a pigeon division to fly messages back and forward from Tours to Paris. You had to admire the man's craziness. I liked him. He flew the Interior Minister out in October. Guess who it was, none other than one-eyed Leon Gambetta, that young lawyer I had met a few years back at Khalil's. That young man seemed so nice, if a little eager to please, I wouldn't have clocked him as the saviour of France. I saw him hanging out of a balloon basket disappearing over the top of Montmartre waving a tricolour flag in one hand and his fur hat in the other, shouting out *Vive la République!* while the Prussians tried to shoot

185

him down. He made it out with only a gunshot wound to the hand. Sadly, it was not the hand he wrote all his interminable speeches with. In those days there was no food but a surplus of great, white men trying to change the world on their own with words. The story never changes.

None of it made any difference, of course. Just after New Year 1871 the Prussian decided they had had enough of the siege and started the bombardment. It was a bit ironic really, Napoléon and Haussman had pulled down so much of Paris and rebuilt it all so beautifully only for the Prussians to bomb it all to hell anyway. A double waste of time. The Prussians efficiently finished the whole thing in just over three weeks and the city was a wreck of dead bodies, starving skeletons, roofless buildings and smashed up roads. It was carnage. There was no food, horsemeat was a distant memory, a turnip cost eight sous and you could forget about butter or cheese. Paris was just about pulling through on cheap diluted wine, coffee and almost inedibly hard bread. So the entire male population was pissed, starving and armed. The women and children were simply starving. I didn't see Nadar anymore, I guess he went to ground or fled when the bombs started to fall; I wonder if he ate the pigeons. The French National Guard had no chance of saving us, so after the Prussians had marched victoriously through what was left of the city, we were left to finish ourselves off.

Poor Auber, it was by some miracle that he made it through the war, but he couldn't take what followed. This was the nightmare of the Commune. It was crazy, we were all ruined but clinging on in a mode of survival as our beloved city lay destroyed around us. There was an attempt to hold an election in the midst of it all, but this was doomed; most people turned a blind eye to politics as they were struggling to find any means to get by. Gambetta and his Government came back from Tours, took one look around and then cleared out pronto, leaving the city to the ultra-radicals to govern. It was the first attempt at running what was touted as a society of the people, governed by the people for the people: 'a Commune of our peers'. It was pure mayhem, Paris in one corner and the rest of France in another, just like so many civil wars before it.

The Communards barricaded the streets. They stacked bricks on top of the decaying carcases of the men and horses who lay all over the city centre. Not even the dead were allowed to rest. They bombed out the remains of buildings across Haussman's new wide boulevards and turned the rubble into a war zone. Most of Paris, already depleted and dilapidated, now became No-Man's Land. Volatile, hot-blooded young men walked around with guns. They got drunk and attempted to discuss socialist utopic theories on the organisation of the people. We ladies stayed inside waiting for everyone to kill each other so we could safely emerge. There were meetings all over the place, in churches converted into political club-rooms, in the abandoned mansions of the rich, in the Louvre. It turned out the Communards hated a lot of people; they shot a lot of Catholics.

They organised a public display of Communard power and legitimacy. The message was passed around that everyone had to go to the Place de Vendôme to see them tearing down Napoléon Bonaparte's Column. Imagine my shock at seeing Gustave Courbet at the centre of that mess in a position of authority. Somehow, he managed to get himself on the Central Council with responsibility for the arts. The moment I realised that fat mess of neuroses, alcohol and ego was at the top table I knew they were done for. I thought back to the opera all those years past when we had discussed Cellini defending Rome. And the world turns! Here he was, trying to rip Paris to pieces.

Courbet had wheeled a band out to play *La Marseillaise*, out of tune. There were rumours in the crowd that Karl Marx was there, but no one actually saw him, he was probably tucked up by the fire in London. The crowd was pushed back to a safe distance as they triumphantly pushed and pulled at the Column to topple it as a symbol of their victory, but it did not budge. Typical! The Prussians could raze an entire city to the ground before lunch, but Courbet couldn't even pull down a single column. It was embarrassing, like watching a comedy where every joke falls flat. By the end everyone feels so sorry for the actor that the whole audience is willing him to be funny, just to break the tension. One disaster follows another. It always ends the same way, nervous laughter in all the wrong places, curtains down, no encore, show's over.

Finally, some tart called Magnier pushed through demanding to speak with Courbet. She was well known to the theatre crowd. Before the war she had caused a bit of a stir because she had a good thing going with some minor Duke but had been roughly dumped when he found out she was also seeing some young engineer with whom she had fallen in love, silly cow. After that she disappeared from society and we all forgot about her. Well, out of nowhere, there she was, looking shabby and moaning about her poverty and bad fortune. She dragged her engineer lover out with her and said he could bring the column down without issue, but she wanted six thousand francs for the job. Courbet ummed and ahhed while the crowd laughed at him, flailing like the fat moron he was. He finally gave in. The engineer explained how to bezel cut the bottom of the column and lo and behold the bloody thing fell down with an almighty crash. Magnier and her engineer got their money and the crowd all went off to loot the President's house. The rest of us went home and waited it out. Courbet just ended up looking like a bloody idiot; I am pretty sure no one will ever write an opera about him.

Gambetta and the rest of the French Government in Versailles let the chaos run for a bit and then got their act together. They sent the army into the city in May. The air was thick with fear. Despite their claim of governing for the common good, the Communards had been executing people on a massive scale. There were bodies all over the place; hangings and shootings without provocation. You could have someone killed for nothing more than a whisper of an accusation, a personal slight or simply a grudge. It was a good time to kill people. There were lots of guns and no repercussions.

The French army turned up and this time there was some real fighting. The Communards versus the army. Cousins, brothers and friends who just a few months previously had stood side by side against the Prussians now lined up on opposite sides of the freshly constructed barricades: blue on blue, French against French.. This time they could properly tear each other to shreds. It was hell. The city was on fire. It was May and it was hot, the air was gummed up with smoke from the fires and gunshots echoed from morning to night. All you could do was hide indoors and hope your building didn't get set alight or that a stray bullet didn't come through the window. After that you could pray that you didn't get robbed. And for God's sake, don't pray out loud, if someone heard you praying, you'd be ratted out and shot as a Catholic.

They called it 'The Bloody Week'. The fighting was street to street, there were summary executions on both sides. The Communard burnt down the Tuileries and the town hall. Ambulance carts were blown up as they ran through the streets. There was no air left, nothing could live or grow, only the smell of gunpowder lingered and then death. Blood and body parts were everywhere, bundles of them, lying like messy off-cuts of meat over each other. Anyone alive was crying or screaming or rocking compulsively waiting for it all to end. One side called it victory and the other defeat. It was over. There were more executions: this time it was the Communards who hung from the lamp posts.

They captured Courbet but didn't hang him. Maybe they couldn't find a lamp post strong enough to take the weight. Instead, he was held responsible for the Column and put in prison. They made him pay to put it back up again. That was the end of him. He should have just left the thing alone: Magnier did him no favours. Instead, he disappeared off to Switzerland to die, poor man. I did feel a bit sorry for him, to be honest. For a socialist, he loved money and attention, it must have hurt to lose it all. On second thoughts, maybe that's why they didn't just shoot him. They knew taking his money would be much more painful for him. After that his name was shit, his reputation was shit. It was open season on the man.

Back in the '60s he had sent me a painting of a bunch of flowers, Camelias at the centre. I think it was his idea of a joke, him and Khalil; men can't let you forget who you are or what you have done. I presume

Khalil paid for it. I was thinking of burning it in 1871, it would have been worth more as firewood, but in the end, I kept it. I don't know why, what good is a painting in the middle of a war when you are starving and freezing. I admit it doesn't make any sense, but as it turned out, it was another good move on my part, if I may say so myself. What was it that Goncourt used to say, 'A book is never a masterpiece: it becomes one. Genius is the talent of a dead man.' So there, Gustave could rest in peace, sleep softly and time could get on with the job of genius-making, not that he would ever know anything about it.

Chapter 7

It was in 1877, the year Courbet died in La Tour de Peilz on the shores of Lake Léman in Switzerland, that I last saw Khalil. I ran into him at the Palais Garnier. It was spring, the time of year where Paris looks most beautiful. The sun was bright and the café tables were venturing out tentatively, like hibernating animals waking from their winter sleep, the pink chestnut blossoms filling the streets with colour and scent.

The streets started to fill up between the showers and weather-beaten posters announced the first premiere of the season. On the ground the puddles of rainwater glistened as the sun peeped out from behind the drifting clouds. In 1877 the first show was Massenet's *King of Lahore*. It was like serendipity in a way. As I listened to Auguste Bourdouresque's beautiful baritone encouraging the people of Lahore to pray to God for deliverance from the evil Muslim invaders, my mind floated back over the years of the Commune, back to Khalil and Courbet. Those were the years in the middle of my life where things could have gone either way for me, but which ended up being the foundation of my good fortune and the scaffolding on which my honourable life was built. Imagine my surprise therefore, when I ran into him in the corridor on my way out, the arias of de Reszke's soaring vocals still ringing in my ears.

He called down the corridor to me and I was surprised to hear my name being called in that foreign accent of his, like a voice from the past echoing down the years. He had aged badly. I could see his eyes straining as he hurried in my direction and remembered what he used to say about his early life in Cairo: 'There are ocular problems caused by the dust of Cairo, my dear, sands from which I must escape.' I remember thinking that he obviously had not escaped them, the sands had seeped into his soul through his eyes, just as the years had passed through his body and weathered his skin.

"Constance, my dear."

"If you please, Sir." My blood froze in terror. I quickly answered him using the most insulted tone I could muster. I knew we were in public. It was vital above all to keep up appearances. "I am not sure we are acquainted, Sir. Please, do forgive me if I am mistaken. Sadly, age has not been kind to my eyes."

Standing by his side was a beautiful woman with thick dark eyebrows and a long handsome face; she shot him a scandalised look. At the time, he would have been in his mid-forties but by the look of her she couldn't have even been twenty yet, a mere child, walking around permanently shocked by public life, like an animal caught in the glare of a light.

Khalil stopped suddenly and looked me up and down with a quizzical look. It took him a moment to take in my comportment and finally his scrunched face relaxed and a smile broke around the edge of his mouth.

"Madame, you must forgive me. A thousand apologies. I must have mistaken you for the famed ballet star Constance Quinéaux, whom I had the pleasure of knowing many years ago before this fair land so brutally tore itself apart."

"Ah, but it is I, Sir." I squinted my eyes in theatrical fashion. "Yes, now it is starting to come back to me, Monsieur, ...Monsieur..."

"Halil Şerif Pasha, Madame. Currently serving the wondrous Ottoman Empire as her ambassador to France. To my friends I am known as Khalil Bey."

"I don't remember us as friends, Monsieur, but now I cast my mind back I do recall our paths having crossed. And this must be your,..."

"My wife, Madame." He turned and opened his palm towards the woman next to him, "Princess Zainab Nazlı Khanum Effendi."

"Enchanté, Madame." I curtsied as I spoke. 'A princess!' I thought. 'Khalil has done well.'

"How did you know my husband, Madame Quinéaux?" The Princess asked in a soft, heavily accented voice.

"An excellent question, Princess. I must admit that I have a faint recollection of his being in a group of gentlemen with whom I was acquainted at the time of his previous sojourn in Paris, but the precise details escape me." I spoke sternly in the hope he would let it drop.

"Come, Madame Quinéaux," said Khalil smiling mischievously, "I am sure you can recall our mutual friends: the writers Maxime Du Camp and Gustave Flaubert."

"Ah, Khalil," the Princess's eyes lit up, "I didn't know you knew Flaubert. I am such an admirer of his."

"Of course, I do, my darling. I will be sure to arrange a meeting if you wish. Maybe Madame Quinéaux could accompany us. Do you see much of those people from the old days?"

I laughed and tried to look as bored as possible. "If you remember anything about me, you well know I was never one for society, Monsieur. The theatre is my only vice in that respect."

"Hmm, quite...." There was a pause before Khalil spoke again. Finally, he looked me directly in the eye as if having come to a decision. "Now that I recall, I remember a dinner that was very amusing at the time, I wonder if I should tell the story. My wife may be offended by it... Damn it all, I will tell it anyway!"

The Princess glanced nervously at her husband with a wariness that tacitly admonished his penchant for telling risqué stories in public. He ignored this, almost rudely staring at me with that unstable look that I knew so well, that of a gambler who should fold but can't resist the risk of the game. Then he started to speak; "Flaubert and Du Camp had just come back from Egypt, the birthplace of my wife, and were regaling us with stories of their travels. The Countess de Loynes, she was the elegant Lady we met at dinner last night my dear, was there as well. In those days she was not yet a Countess and not yet a millionaire. She was called

Jeanne de Tourbey and rumour had it that Alexandre Dumas fils had found her in a brothel and raised her up to become the companion of Prince Napoléon, no less." Khalil paused as his wife inhaled deeply with shock at the scandal. Her husband lightly placed a comforting hand on her arm before continuing. "One would not guess it to see her today in all her splendour and social success, but back then she was making her way through the world from the basest of places. I guess it just shows that one can never tell with elegant looking women in Paris nowadays. Anyone can *look* respectable." He paused slightly to look for a reaction, but I had steadied my face into a stone-like expression, so he continued.

"Anyway, she had become a firm friend of Flaubert, amongst others and I imagine he was vexed with her in some way because all through dinner he did nothing but tell scandalous stories of his trip to the Nile. It came to a head with the story of Kuchuk-Hanem. You must remember this Madame Quineaux? No? Really? I will relate it then.

"It was 1849 and they arrived just after the death of Mohammed Ali, the Ottoman Governor of Egypt and defacto ruler of that great country. My father was a loyal servant of the great man, I myself was born in his palace. Little did I know that a young writer called Flaubert was in the same city as me at the same time. Since the 1830s Mohammed Ali had banned all prostitutes from Cairo so young men who came to the city looking for these kinds of base pursuits were forced to take a boat down river towards Luxor.

"Just past a bend in the river after Luxor was a town called Esna, which had transformed itself into a Babylonian city of vice, may Allah protect us. It was there, in a small house at the top of a steep staircase that led to a roof terrace, that one could see the dance of the legendary Kuchuk-Hanem, *The Lady of The Dance*. She wore a light blue veil under which shone the blackest of eyes, painted with Kohl like the female Pharaohs of old: Cleopatra, Nefertiti. Her sleeves were transparent and through it one could see the Koran was tattooed onto her arms in blue ink. By her side lay a lamb whose back was covered in yellow henna patterns. Du Camp said it was like an apparition.

"She danced a frenzied dance called *The Bee*, where the dancer writhes about the room like a crazed dervish as if being attacked by a ferocious, stinging bee. As the dance progressed, sweat and clothing flew manically over the terrace until the sun had gone down and she and all her spectators were naked and dripping with perspiration.

"A far-fetched tale, from a master storyteller. Flaubert swore that it was true, but was it? Did this woman ever really exist or was it all just a frivolous dinner time fantasy? Well, let me tell you that I never heard anything about this when I was growing up in Cairo, not that I am the kind of man who would be interested in this type of smutty diversion." At this I could not resist a slight raise of my eyebrow, which I am sure he noticed. "However," he went on, "I suspect she was real. I once read a book, by the American writer George William Curtis, which tells a similar story. He relates the mode of her dancing in great detail, covering two feverish chapters, that no self-respecting lady should read.

"We therefore know she was a real person, we know about this dance *The Bee*, which has never been seen since as far as I am aware. We have a sordid description of her body in the most intimate terms. Apart from this..." Here he paused and stared at me, straight in my eye, "she is totally forgotten to history, disappeared. A naked body and a dirty story. Nothing else, nothing."

The air hung heavy as he stopped speaking, abruptly, brutally. The Princess vainly attempted a polite laugh, but it was clear to us all there was nothing to laugh about. The poor thing was caught in the undercurrent of a conversation she could never understand. I let it hang a little longer so as to destroy any sense of camaraderie between us. I cleared my throat and smiled.

"You must excuse my age, Monsieur," I said dryly, playing the game. "The story rings no bells and I struggle to understand its relevance." I turned to look as sweetly as I could into the deep, dark eyes of his poor, young wife and smiled, "Perhaps you Gentlemen had retired to the drawing room to smoke and we ladies had been left behind. That is the way in these dinners. There are some conversations that are not for the ears of ladies, do you not agree, Princess? Now, I am afraid it is getting late. I really must go."

"Before you leave Madame. Could I detain you for one more moment?" Khalil burst in, "I remember at the time you were collecting some pieces of art and furniture. I have restarted lately my passion for the arts and wondered if you had any pieces, maybe some pictures, from the old days. Perhaps I could call on you and make an offer on some of them if I could be so bold."

"I have but one piece," I replied, "but I am ashamed to say it is by that disgraced painter Gustave Courbet, that butcher of the Commune who as we speak is exiled in Switzerland." Khalil's eyes lit up as if he had won a hand of cards. I paused to string him out, I'm afraid I couldn't resist it. After indulging in a fake cough or two I let him down brutally. "Yes, Monsieur, it is a most lovely still life depicting a bunch of flowers. I keep it in my reception room and it really livens up the space. I am sure I could not part with it for any amount. I do so love flowers, my wish for my final years is to cultivate a nice garden somewhere by the sea and dedicate myself to the care of plants. I am sure you would think this a most silly way to spend time, but it would suit my personality down to the ground. I am afraid that I am a frightfully dull person. Always have been."

"Not at all," the Princess had visibly cheered up at the change of subject, "I, for one, love my garden in Cairo. The weather and environment are very different to France of course, but beauty can be cultivated there none the less." Realising that he had lost control of the conversation, Khalil slumped back into himself like a deflating balloon.

"Absolutely, Princess," I said. "Flowers do not last for ever, but somehow their beauty does. Coming out of this fine Opera, set in India, reminds me of a story I was once told. It concerns the sages of old that once lived in the north of that country. It was said that there were tribes of wise people there who made the most fantastic art. I think they were called *rangoli* pictures, although please don't ask me what the word means. These artists would make the most beautiful pictures ever seen by man on earth. They would spend hours, days even, on each picture bringing them to a point of perfection never witnessed outside Heaven itself."

"And do you own one of these pictures, Madame?" Khalil shot in greedily.

But I just smiled and tilted my head at him patronisingly, as one would do at a child. "Oh no Monsieur. No one does. The pictures were made by mixing and blending different coloured sands. Then the trees would shift as the winds blew and poof, and just like that they were gone. Gone without a trace."

*

That was the only time I ever met the Princess. I heard their baby died in Paris during the heat of the summer. The Princess was heartbroken. By September they were gone. The wind blew them back to Istanbul carrying their grief with them. Khalil died there a few years later. They say he died sitting on his horse in the middle of a Royal parade.

The sun shone and he dropped down dead right there, by the feet of *The Bloody Sultan*, Abdul Hamid II, the man responsible for the horrors of the Armenian Holocaust. It was not a very diplomatic, or even dignified end for poor Khalil, but, in reality, he was never much of a diplomat and the Sultan, as history was to show, was not one to be squeamish about death.

I wonder what Khalil's last thoughts were, as he fell from that horse, vainly clutching at his chest. I wonder if the last image he saw in his mind's eye was my brown vulva and a white breast hovering above it. What am I saying? These are silly thoughts and unworthy of me. Everyone's last thoughts are the same. They think of their pain and then they die.

Chapter 9

Did I ever look for the painting? To be honest I did. It was the end of the 1880s and I was approaching my sixtieth year. The eighties had been a good decade for me. That nice boy Gambetta had been Prime Minister for a few years and he helped me a little with some investments I made. I was a respectable lady with independent means. I had no husband to ruin my life and, frankly, no problems.

Most of my time was taken up with my charity work. I had been involved with Marie Laurent's Orphanage of the Arts almost from its inception. It was a school for the children of artists, composers, dancers, painters, engravers and sculptors. We took in and cared for orphans aged between four and eighteen. In 1882 we were recognised publicly by the State and from then on funding became easier. It is not mentioned in any documents, and I didn't tell anyone at the time, but I can tell you that I take credit for that. Gambetta signed the form, but I was pulling the strings. All the children we got off the streets, we got them out of those destructive households and helped educate them. They were my children. I am proud of each and every one of them.

I was mainly involved in fundraising and being fortunate enough to have good contacts throughout Paris, especially amongst the artists, I was able to get some pictures donated to the orphanage, which we then put up for auction. In addition to these we sold manuscripts, trinkets, anything that we could get our hands on and that would fetch a price.

We worked mainly with Salon artists like Lami, Duez and even Vibert, whose wife I became quite friendly with. I was the one who persuaded her to join the committee herself.

This was not the only charitable work I was involved with, although far be it for me to highlight my meagre deeds for posterity. Throughout those years I actively made myself available to assist any artist who had fallen on hard times, a fate from which God mercifully spared me. I stepped in to raise funds for the actress Alice Lavigne, for instance, when the poor dear was struck blind. I have consistently found, throughout my life, that women and children are often the primary victims of life's hardships and I dedicated myself to helping my fellow humans wherever I could. I was a *Friend of the Louvre* and supported societies that helped unknown artists financially. I would hope that someone would have stepped in to help me, had I fallen into a state of dire need. Alas, I remember well the burial of my dear friend Pauline Dameron, whose financial circumstances were much more strained than my own. Despite my advice, the poor dear bet too heavily on Auber and that miser left her nothing when he passed away. For me, Auber was only the final top up, the icing on the cake. I wouldn't have relied on him to secure my fortune. She did and it cost her. At that time, I was not in a position to help her, something I do regret.

I remember bumping into Edmond de Goncourt at a charity event one last time. It must have been 1889 or 1890. He was unchanged, scribbling in his notebook and gossiping. We spoke a few polite words. He told me that he wanted to set up an artistic society to help struggling French authors with a literature prize attached, which he immodestly called the Prix Goncourt. Ostensibly he was speaking to me to get some advice on the matter but in reality, he talked about himself for ten minutes and asked me nothing. He was the type of man who wrote drivel like: 'There are no women of genius; the women of genius are men.' Given this was his view, I am sure you can imagine that he was not the kind of man who frequently asked for someone else's opinion, especially not a woman's, more is the pity for him. After a while the one-sided conversation fell flat and I was just about to move away when a thought struck him and he grabbed my arm.

"Well, you will never guess what I came across the other day," he said as I was looking around the room for someone else to talk to. "I was in one of those antique shops in the 7th and the chap there said he had something I would not believe. Anyway, I was curious and had nothing better to do so I waited. He brought out a dusty cabinet on the front of which was a landscape of a snow-bound chateau. To call it mediocre was to be kind. The man in the shop insisted it was by Courbet. I understand his reputation is on the rise now among these modern painters. Some even say he is the father of Impressionism, although whether that is a good thing remains to be seen in my view. Pissarro swears by him and apparently carries a photograph of *Woman With A Parrot* in his wallet. A painting I consider pure ugliness, but that is by the by."

"I am sure it is a painting I have never seen," I said tersely.

"No of course," Goncourt broke into a sly smile, "not for a lady of your sensibilities I'm sure, but still, a totem of realism none the less. Anyway, I was far from impressed with his box and was on the verge of leaving when the man in the shop grabbed me by the coat. 'Look, Sir', he said, 'a secret for your eyes only.' He unlocked the box and I looked inside. Nothing to see. I wondered if the cur was playing some sort of trick on me, but he released a catch and the bottom of the cabinet slid across. It had a false bottom, this thing. Well, on the base, of all things I see the picture that your old friend Khalil Bey had commissioned. The one of, well, Jo Hiffernan's bits, which he kept hidden behind that green curtain. I had seen it in his dressing room after a dinner once and can't say I was amused by it but there you are. It had ended up there, in a smelly antique shop of all places. I must say I do find it an objectionable thing, so I bade the gentleman farewell and left. However, as I was walking home, I couldn't help wondering, what do you think it would fetch these days? Curious story, huh?"

I acted uninterested and casually asked the name of the shop, but by the time I got around to enquiring about it, the owner said it had gone, offloaded onto another dealer. He told me that he had sat on it for years, and that it was a strange thing that had elicited a bit of curiosity but which no one wanted to buy. He seemed very surprised that a lady should be asking after it. I told a fib, pretending to have no idea what was in the box and claimed that my cousin from Switzerland lived near the Chateau and was fond of it. I was therefore asking after it solely for the purpose of acquiring the landscape. The shop owner accepted this and promised to follow it up, but he never did.

Quickly I forgot all about it. I moved out of Paris to the coast. There I bought a comfortable little villa overlooking the sea and dedicated myself to my garden. It was here that I set about fulfilling a dream which brought me much joy in my final years, as well as, I humbly add, the award of a Horticultural Gold Medal for the most beautiful garden in Cabourg. I cannot, of course, in all honesty claim full credit for this success myself. I was ably assisted by my gardeners in this work and of course God, who tends to all living things.

The picture only once more came to my mind, in one of the last years of my life, 1906, my seventy-fourth year. I enjoyed spending time in Cabourg, of course, but I still kept my rooms in Paris where my Courbet flowers hung. I had spent so many hours staring at that painting, however curiously I never felt that it reminded me of my youth, of Gustave or of Khalil. I had always thought of those days as finished with, packed away somewhere, in a cabinet, under lock and key. I would gaze at the painting and had somehow trained myself to think only of my lovely garden by the sea; of my tulips and azaleas, nothing else. However, if I were to be wholly honest, there was a shadow there, I must admit, like a *déja-vu*. Perhaps it was more like that in-between time when you are not fully awake but also not asleep and you're not sure whether you are still dreaming.

All the talk amongst the artists I knew was of new forms of art. I went to see some of those pictures during my trips to Paris: this Cézanne chap with his blocks and cubes of colour, like crates stacked one on top of another.

People talked of the Catalan group up in Montmartre. I heard stories of them in the strangest of places, like in the old pharmacy in Rue Lafitte where they sold the cream that eased the pains in my joints. When the old pharmacist, who I had known for decades, died, God rest his soul, Clovis Sagot took over the pharmacy and turned it into a picture gallery.

He was a strange man, Sagot, a huge grinning thing who told me that he used to work as a clown with the circus. Thankfully he still had the left-over stock from the pharmacy that he used to sell off cheaply as the store filled up with more and more pictures. This was fine for me. I was pretty certain I would be dead before he ran out of stock of my cream.

The pictures he sold were awful to my eye, flat and ugly without charm or class, but this was just my opinion, I was no expert. This was where all this experimentation had led, to a schism between what was in the world and what was shown on the canvas. Sagot showed me a painting of a teenage girl holding a basket of flowers.

"Here, take a look at this painting before it is collected this afternoon. This is the future of art: Pablo Picasso, Madame, remember the name."

"The old have no need for the future," I replied curtly, "for people of my age there is only the pain of the present and what memories we are still able to retain of the past, Monsieur. I fear that this artistic future you herald is not for old eyes like mine. To me this is ugly." I was worried he may have taken offence at this but instead be leaned back and let off a clownish laugh of immense proportions.

"Quite right, Madame, quite right. Even the young agree with you, I think, they just don't have the confidence to say so, or the courage. This picture is sold to some Americans, a brother and sister; Leo and Gertrude Stein. They go all over Paris asking to see what is new, everything new, they say, anything new, so I show them Picasso. The sister, Gertrude, says that the head and body are good enough, but the feet are ugly, 'monkey's feet' she calls them. But this is what is new I say to them. They are Americans, they have a lot of money and no sense, they will buy everything, anything, as long as it is new. I know I could not sell this to you, Madame, to the cultured French eye this is garbage, but to the Americans, *pas de problèmes.*

"So I tell this Madame Stein, 'It is ok, Madame, we will cut off the feet and the picture will be less ugly.' The brother refuses and so it is left as it is. Later the brother sent me word that he will buy it as it is, feet and all and that he will come this very afternoon. So, in the end it all works out well and I don't have to cut the feet off after all or change the size of the frame. This is why it is the future, Madame, not because it is beautiful, but because the Americans buy it and they buy it as it is. *Comme ça.*"

As I left, I must confess my mind flashed back to the picture. Is she still out there, that picture of a decapitated me? I had done the opposite of what the clown suggested to this American, Gertrude Stein; I had cut off the beautiful bit and left the ugly, had I done more harm than good, was there something to repent in this act, long since forgotten? It sent a chill down my spine when the image of that painting came back to me. It was the representation of the least of me, the most base. Looking back, maybe I did regret not just burning it when I had the chance. What difference would one less smutty picture have made to the world, one less piece of proof of the lechery of man over woman?

Chapter 10

I organised myself well. By the end I knew it, we all have a feeling of when we will be taken. I put my affairs in order, left instruction and funds to look after my Godson and my Goddaughter. I made sure to leave enough for Élisa, my maid. She had been so loyal to me. She would never need to work again. Everyone from the doorman to the footman was listed and would receive their share. I thought of them all, just as God thinks of all of us, his children. Much of my estate will go to the charities I supported; children suffering from tuberculosis, aged artists, the blind. Hôtel Drouot sent a man around to value my paintings and the furniture. I must admit that I am happy for the final auction to be held there, of all places, especially after all that happened, all those years ago, in a life so long past that it does not feel like it could have been mine. I am proud to look back on where I came from and where I ended up. I will die on my own two feet, owing nothing to anyone as a proud, single woman who fought hard for her freedom in a world that instinctually sought to deny and oppress her.

I will be buried like my mother; no flowers, no wreaths, a simple funeral. She didn't have anything at her funeral because she was poor. I was blessed in that I had the means to choose. I chose humility. We will be buried together, her and I, in the vault I bought for us in the Cimetière du Nord.

In the end we both ended up in the same place. In the end we all end up in the same place.

Epilogue: The Painting

After the cameras went away, after the chairs had been cleared, after the museum had been closed and the doors locked, we paintings have time to relax, to think. Constance's story reverberated through the corridors and bounced around those high-ceilinged rooms. Who was she? Finally, shifting through the years of resentment, she started to come into focus for me, not as an assassin but as a hero. In her own way she had stood up in her society and established herself as an independent woman on her own terms. She had done something that Lucie with all her wealth and Sylvia with all her fame didn't even come close to. She had rid herself of society, of men, and she had done it despite poverty, despite injury, despite failure, despite war, despite famine and despite deprivation. She had done all this and died with honour and with enough money to pay her way at the end. Considering the times through which she had lived, this was no mean feat. She had given to charity and she had made a difference. The only price she had to pay for this life of resounding success was me. She had to reject me. Maybe that is why she had helped all those lost children, all those orphans. Maybe that was her penitence for orphaning me.

Constance was my mum, the female role model I had been searching for all my life. She had been there with me all along. For the first time in my life, I felt proud and I wanted nothing more than to continue to live.

For a long time, nothing much happened and then all of a sudden in 2020 the electric lights went out one night and they did not come on the next morning. The winter sunshine streamed through the window onto the main hall as it did every day, but that morning was different. There were no people. The next day was the same and the next. Where had the people gone? After a few days the paintings started to relax, they eased out, the hall was filled the sounds (inaudible to the human ear) of paint stretching and flaking, of marble brushing with air, of wood expanding and contracting. There was peace and quiet. The odd human came round but now they were wearing coverings over their faces. Their eyes were bloodshot with a terror that looked existential. What was going on?

As I said before, it is assumed that art as a whole is static. More art is always being created but you humans believe that what exists at any given moment will always be there. Even the most cursory glance through history shows this confidence is misplaced. You humans think we must feel secure, locked in our museum prisons, but we do not, we have longer memories than you. We know that man is the great destroyer. When push comes to shove, human beings destroy, that is what they do. How many bronze statues over time have been melted down to be made into cannonballs. They are converted into weapons when war is prioritised over culture. How many religious art works have been defaced, burned, cut to shreds. They are destroyed when religious debate is prioritised over culture. How many paintings have been burned for fuel. They are burned when the survival of the human is threatened by the cold. It is a question of resources. When resources become scarce, we cease to be depictions of ideas and revert to being what we are to you: just objects. We are objects that can be burned for warmth or bartered for money and that is what will happen to all of us, eventually, if we don't succumb to the slow decay of time. In those first few weeks of silence these thoughts of endings, destruction and death reverberated through the museum. Was this the end? When would the humans come and end it all? What had happened to all the people?

But that *end* did not happen. The people came back. They walked around in groups of two, keeping as far away from each other as they could. They made plans and jotted in notepads. They came with their cameras and they made videos of us so that we could be 'accessed remotely.' They hired orchestras to play in the main hall, they filled the air with heavenly music and then filmed it so that they could share it with all the rest of those humans who were locked up just like us, alone and afraid, staring at their screens. A woman with a flute played in front me in room 20, just her playing alone, such beautiful music and a film crew wearing masks stood by the door, a few meters away from her.

When we realised the humans would not destroy us, that they were not threatened enough this time to blame us, we relaxed into the silence to recharge ourselves and, for the first time in many years, to enjoy the peaceful passing of time.

But only momentarily. Every debt needs paying. Every single one. Somehow.

They will be back soon.

Other novels, novellas and short story collections available from Stairwell Books

A Fistful of Ashes	Katy Turton
The Department of Certainty	S. C. Paterson
Widdershins	L.A.Robbins
100 Summers	Ali Sparkes
Skull Days	PJ Quinn
The Broke Hotel	Clayton Lister
Equinox	Ruth Aylett, Greg Michaelson
Not the Work of an Ordinary Boy	Victoria L. Humphreys
Black Harry	Mark P. Henderson
Eboracvm: Carved in Stone	Graham Clews
Down to Earth	Andrew Crowther
The Iron Brooch	Yvonne Hendrie
The Electric	Tim Murgatroyd
The Pirate Queen	Charlie Hill
Djoser and the Gods	Michael J. Lowis
Needleham	Terry Simpson
The Keepers	Pauline Kirk
Shadows of Fathers	Simon Cullerton
Blackbird's Song	Katy Turton
Eboracvm the Fortress	Graham Clews
The Warder	Susie Williamson
Life Lessons by Libby	Libby and Laura Engel-Sahr
Waters of Time	Pauline Kirk
The Water Bailiff's Daughter	Yvonne Hendrie
O Man of Clay	Eliza Mood
Eboracvm: the Village	Graham Clews
Sammy Blue Eyes	Frank Beill
Virginia	Alan Smith
Poetic Justice	PJ Quinn
The Go-To Guy	Neal Hardin
Abernathy	Claire Patel-Campbell
Tyrants Rex	Clint Wastling
How to be a Man	Alan Smith
Border 7	Pauline Kirk
Homelands	Shaunna Harper
The Geology of Desire	Clint Wastling
When the Crow Cries	Maxine Ridge

For further information please contact rose@stairwellbooks.com

www.stairwellbooks.co.uk
@stairwellbooks

Milton Keynes UK
Ingram Content Group UK Ltd.
UKHW041829081024
449420UK00004B/111